Love on a Winter's Tide

Linen and Lace - Book Three

Rosie Chapel

First printing 2017
ISBN 978-0-9954303-6-5

Ulfire Pty. Ltd.
P.O. Box 1481
South Perth
WA 6951
Australia

www.rosiechapel.com

Cover Images Courtesy:
Period Images and Deposit Photos

Cover Artwork: JF Holland

Other Books by Rosie Chapel

The Hannah's Heirloom Sequence
The Pomegranate Tree - Hannah's Heirloom - Book One
Echoes of Stone and Fire - Hannah's Heirloom - Book Two
Embers of Destiny - Hannah's Heirloom - Book Three
Etched in Starlight - Hannah's Heirloom - Prequel
Hannah's Heirloom Trilogy - Compilation - Kindle only

Prelude to Fate

Regency Romances
Once Upon An Earl - Linen and Lace - Book One
To Unlock Her Heart - Linen and Lace - Book Two
Love on a Winter's Tide - Linen and Lace - Book Three
A Love Unquenchable - Linen and Lace - Book Four
A Hidden Rose - Linen and Lace - Book Five

His Fiery Hoyden - A Regency Novella

Contemporary Romance
Of Ruins and Romance
All At Once It's You

Anthologies
The Highway Man's Kiss - Once Upon A Love Anthology
Heart Rescued - Tales for the Season Anthology
Luck be a Pirate - Kiss My Luck Anthology
Finally Home - Tempting Fate Anthology
Love Kindled - Building Love Anthology - TBR Dec 2018

Dedication

For Mum, for everything with all my love

Acknowledgements

To Julie, for her tireless efforts in creating this and my other
beautiful covers (to be honest, I am surprised she is still
speaking to me) thank you so much!
My heartfelt gratitude to Janet and Jess, for being gracious
enough to proofread this book.
Huge thanks to Graham at *A Fading Street Publishers,*
for his awesome editing skills.

Although I recently updated the covers on my Regency series,
I remain forever grateful to my sister, Helen,
who created the gorgeous originals.

The Linen and Lace Clan

An exclusive club, only accessible to the fortuitous few. Those who - no matter their differences in money, title, background or position - marry for love. In an era when status, influence and wealth are bolstered under the guise of marriage, you are like rare gemstones - admired and envied. May your mutual respect, and true affection for one another, be the beacons by which you navigate the rough and the smooth of life's journey. Therefore, whether your clothing be of the cheapest linen or the finest lace, may the blend of either or both bring the richest and happiest union.

Love on a Winter's Tide

Linen and Lace - Book Three

Chapter One

Lady Helena Trevallier, sister of the fifth Earl of Winchester, gazed around the sumptuous ballroom. It was a wonderful riot of light, laughter, and music. Couples moved across the dance floor, ribbons of colour flowing back and forth, their cadence hypnotic, yet although seemingly fascinated by so elegant a display, Helena's mind was elsewhere. On the face of it, Helena was a typical young woman of the elite. At nearly two and twenty, she was enjoying, apparently, her second season, slightly delayed owing to the death of her father nearly two years previously and a mourning period that Helena, by choice extended. Not ready to face the glamour and glitter of the city, she stayed an extra year at Whiteoaks, their country estate, the tranquil atmosphere assuaging her grief.

Persuaded by her mother to return to London, Helena attended balls, soirees, musical evenings, picnics, and dinner parties. She wandered the museums and art galleries, took long horse rides and enjoyed brisk constitutionals — weather permitting — around Hyde Park. She flitted here and there, rather like an exotic butterfly, and had several men trailing in her wake, in the hope she might favour them with a dance or better still allow them to escort her to one of the many social gatherings.

Helena however, had a secret; one which, had her social set known anything about might have seen them throwing up their hands in horror. She spent her days helping the poor, the downtrodden and the abused.

The only people who did know, were her family, Lord Beaumont's family, her closest friend Tabitha and, latterly,

Stephen Caswell. The last one had surprised her. Stephen was the older brother of Billie Trevallier, now Helena's sister-in-law, and she had not imagined such a man would care for the underbelly of society. However, Stephen worked for the government in an undisclosed capacity and often mixed with those less fortunate, his sympathy for them, sincere.

Further, Stephen was courting Tabitha. In fact, Helena had a sneaking suspicion he would approach Tabitha's father for her hand sooner rather than later; it was obvious the pair were smitten with each other — quite sickeningly so. An affable gentleman, Stephen accompanied both women to most of the Season's events and had proven himself quite adept at keeping some of Helena's more enthusiastic suitors at bay.

By chance, one evening he overheard Helena and Tabitha talking and, worried for Tabitha's safety, coaxed the truth out of Helena. From then on, when he was able, Stephen insisted on escorting both ladies to the old building that had been turned into a shelter for those in desperate need. Despite Helena having her own, thoroughly reliable driver, should Stephen not be able to accompany his two charges, he sent Havers, the Caswell family groom as added protection.

Both Helena and Tabitha had sworn him to secrecy and in fairness, of late Tabitha rarely attended, other matters filling her days. The women they helped were not there to be gawked at by inquisitive society misses who had nothing better to do, nor did any at the shelter need that kind of attention. Sanctuary House, as it was called, was a haven; somewhere women could recover from whatever they had fled and, if they chose, learn a craft or a trade.

Lady Sophia Beaumont, a family friend — and a force to be reckoned with — was a patroness of the shelter, thus, its existence was not unknown among Society. This allowed Helena to cajole her friends into donating anything they no longer needed. Cloaks, wraps and shoes were always gratefully received, but most especially dresses — which, in reality for many of Helena's friends, meant gowns probably only worn twice and discarded; for it was not done to be seen in the same attire more than occasionally. Any garments were quickly altered to make the most of the materials and soon the shelter had a whole room dedicated to storing any amount of clothes, for those who might require them.

Up until recently Helena delighted in these social gatherings, she loved being asked to dance, relishing the attention heaped on her by handsome men seemingly interested in her. Then it began to pall. She found herself indifferent and, to be honest, rather bored. Moreover, she realised it was her generous dowry that captivated many of these young bucks not her at all, and none seemed able to chat about anything more controversial than the weather.

Helena was busy every day at the shelter, so by evening she was exhausted. It took all her will power to allow Nancy, her maid, to help her dress and primp her hair and, given the choice, she would prefer to stay at home. She needed stimulating company, someone to challenge her mind, or she would likely doze off in the middle of a conversation. Her mother, however, wanted a good match for her daughter. Many of Helena's friends were already either married or at least betrothed and, because Helena had missed nearly two seasons, her mother worried that she was no longer of interest to eligible bachelors.

Augusta Trevallier — Helena's mother and Dowager Countess of Winchester — had been most concerned when her youngest daughter demanded to be allowed to assist at Lady Beaumont's shelter. Although not in an area of the city considered dangerous, it was still in a relatively seedy district, and nowhere near the homes of the nobility. Thus, while Lady Winchester believed those with means should always help those without, when it came to her own child she was less than enthusiastic. Nonetheless, after visiting the shelter with Helena and Lady Beaumont, Lady Winchester admitted, grudgingly, that it was well organised. Moreover, there were always trusted men, usually ex-soldiers, protecting both those who sought refuge within its walls and those who cared for them.

Lady Winchester also knew that if she forbade her rather wilful daughter to help at the shelter, Helena would find a way to go anyway. Bowing to the inevitable, she insisted her daughter be escorted by a groom, and was pleased when Stephen offered his services. The Caswell family had become close friends with the Trevalliers, and Lady Winchester knew Helena would be safe under Stephen's watchful eye.

Helena dragged her attention back to the present moment, and slowly the dazzling ambience of the room pushed away scenes of women struggling to get through each day in a creaky old building in one of the more questionable areas of London. Thankful that the Season was drawing to a close, she pinned a bright smile on her face and tried to enjoy herself. Stephen and Tabitha were walking towards her, having just enjoyed at least three dances together, to the delight of Tabitha's mother. Tabitha grasped Helena's hands.

"Helena, my dear, you simply must have a dance, the music is quite divine. Stephen…" she said, gazing at her suitor, her huge blue eyes beseeching, "…please…" Tabitha needed to say no more, Stephen was unable to think straight when she did that; she knew how to get her own way. He grinned and held out his hand.

"Lady Helena, please do me the honour of the next dance," he pleaded, his eyes twinkling mischievously. Helena chuckled, and placed her gloved hand in his, allowing him to lead her onto the floor. The pair chatted, as they danced, about nothing of particular importance, catching up on what they had been doing since last they met.

"I do believe you have declared your hand rather openly, Stephen," Helena commented as the music faded and they made their way back to where Tabitha was sitting. "Three dances in one set…" She left the sentence dangling and Stephen smiled sheepishly.

"I haven't yet spoken to her father, so this was the next best thing. I want her family to know I'm serious before I make my approach. After everything that happened last year they may not think me a suitable match." Stephen's family had been caught up in a scandal less than twelve months previously. His sister, the aforementioned Billie, accused of murdering their father and burning down their home.

At the time these rumours were circulating, Billie was found wandering near the Winchester country estate, injured, drenched and with no recall as to who she was or how she got there. Eventually the truth — which involved sensitive government documents and French spies — came out, the family was cleared of any wrongdoing and Lord Ashbourne — Stephen and Billie's father — was thankfully also discovered to be alive and well. Despite this, there were always those who loved to cling to scurrilous gossip, and whose 'well-intentioned' asides could thwart a budding romance.

"I think you will find Lord Bridgewater is more than amenable to your suit." Helena smiled as they reached Tabitha, who beamed up at them from her comfortable chair. A tall gentleman was standing nearby, seemingly lost in contemplation, but as Stephen glanced at him, his face split into a wide grin at the same moment as Stephen recognised his long-time friend.

"Drummond! My good man, what a surprise. When did you arrive? How long have you been back in London? How are your family?" The tall gentleman laughed at the barrage of questions as he shook hands with Stephen. Helena and Tabitha, who rose as Stephen greeted his friend, waited quietly at one side.

"I arrived here maybe fifteen minutes past. I have been in London for a sennight, and my family are as well as can be expected, thank you for asking." He bowed as he said this, acknowledging the ladies, who both dropped curtsies.

"Lady Helena Trevallier and Lady Tabitha Daubery, may I present Mr Hugh Drummond? He is something quite important in shipping." The two ladies said it was their pleasure. Helena murmured that they were just going to get some refreshments and would be back shortly. Turning on her heel she dragged Tabitha with her. As they walked away, and for no reason she could think of, Helena glanced over her shoulder, surprised to meet the coolly remote gaze of Mr Drummond who raised an eyebrow and smirked a little at her scrutiny. Helena snapped her head back as a low chuckle reached her, but although she refused to turn again, she could feel his eyes boring into her back all the way across the room, and it was all she could do not to shiver.

Puzzled, Helena could not think what had prompted such a reaction from a man she didn't know, nor her own response. Determined not to think on it anymore, she and Tabitha made a beeline for the fruit punch and were soon caught up in a crowd of their friends, immediately forgetting Mr Drummond. Sometime later, after several more dances and a lot more gossiping, Helena decided she needed to go home. It was late, she was so tired she could barely stand upright and had no desire to fall asleep on the dance floor. She made her way to where Tabitha and Stephen were sitting, noticing Mr Drummond had gone.

"I am so sorry, but I must go home." Stephen made to rise. "No, please stay, I know neither of you are quite ready to depart," she urged, winking at Tabitha who sent her a relieved grin. "I will make my own way home, 'tis only around the corner and I shall not be alone," she said, referring to the fact that Nancy, acting as chaperone, was waiting close by.

"I do not like you walking the streets at night Helena, it is not safe." Stephen's tones were anxious, and he stood, in readiness to leave.

"Oh tosh! 'Tis quite safe, Nancy will be with me and the Watch is about. There are enough people coming and going that no one would dare accost me. Stephen, trust me, we will be fi—"

"Would you allow me to accompany you home, Lady Helena?" Helena was interrupted by a deep voice behind her and, mildly astonished, she whirled around to see Mr Drummond leaning casually against one of the marble pillars surrounding the ballroom. How had she not seen him? "I too find myself tired of proceedings and would be pleased to ensure your safe return home." Helena stared at him, ruminating over whether this was appropriate, twisting a lock of hair around her finger as she did so, a nervous habit she found impossible to curb. Mr Drummond raised his hands. "I have no desire to mar your reputation Lady Helena, 'twas merely a gesture." Helena relaxed and smiled, albeit rather tentatively, for the man in front of her looked quite stern.

"Thank you, Sir, I would be most appreciative. I did not wish to cut short the night for these two," — waving her hand at Stephen and Tabitha, the latter of whom blushed becomingly — "but I have had a long day and am wearied."

Mr Drummond nodded absently at her explanation, adding he would wait at the front door while she retrieved her wrap.

Chapter Two

Helena bade goodnight to her friends and, not wanting to delay Mr Drummond any longer than necessary, rushed to the retiring room. She retrieved her wrap, slinging it around her shoulders with more haste than care and, after collecting Nancy, was at the front door in less than five minutes — somewhat breathlessly it must be admitted. Mr Drummond made no comment, although he did raise an eyebrow at her rather precipitous arrival.

"I did not wish to keep you," Helena gasped, clarifying her breathless state.

"Thank you. 'Tis unusual to meet a woman who concerns herself with such things."

Helena stared at him, his tone was light but his countenance closed. He offered her his arm and, after dithering a moment, she took it — Nancy was right there to act as chaperone after all — what could be the harm? They strolled along the path without speaking, but strangely, it was not an uncomfortable silence. It was late June, the night was balmy and although nearly midnight, it was not quite dark. The long summer evenings meant the sun had only just set, the sky slowly turning from soft purple to inky blue. Carriages rumbled by and sounds of partygoers marred the quiet. Helena sighed heavily, suddenly wishing she was at Whiteoaks, admiring the sunset over the Great Park, and counting the stars as they twinkled into existence; they always seemed much more abundant there.

"Does something ail you, Lady Helena? That was a mighty sigh." Mr Drummond's tones were solicitous in his enquiry.

"I do beg your pardon. No, I am fine. I was just imagining an evening such as this at our estate. I love watching the moonrise, when everything is still." She coloured, glad that the dusk would hide her hot cheeks. "I must sound addled," she muttered, "'tis just I miss the countryside. Make no mistake,, I find the vibrancy of the city most congenial, but sometimes I would give anything to be on my own, away from it all without worrying about … well anything really."

There was a pause.

"I understand, Lady Helena. I too appreciate peace and quiet. Often, when on board ship, I go up on deck and take a few moments to appreciate the night sky. It is so vast and makes me realise how insignificant we are. 'Tis a good leveller." He looked down at her and didn't smile as much as there was a softening of his expression, and patted her hand in much the same way he would a child. Helena could think of no reply and so, without thinking, squeezed his arm.

Too soon or so it seemed to Helena who, unexpectedly, was enjoying their walk, they were in front of Winchester House.

"Thank you, Sir. It was most kind of you to do this and I am grateful. Maybe we will meet again."

"For my part, I think that would be quite agreeable," he replied.

Then, Mr Drummond untucked her arm from around his and, staring into her eyes, lifted her hand to his mouth and kissed it, his lips warm through her delicate glove. As he did so, Helena felt a curious frisson snake up her wrist, but it was gone so quickly, she thought it her imagination. Ignoring it, she extracted her fingers, dipped a curtsy, and climbed the steps to her front door, which opened as though by magic when she reached the top step; soft light spilling out, silhouetting Helena's slenderness. At the last minute, she turned to see her escort watching her; an unreadable expression on his face, and that same frisson ran all the way down her back. Inclining her head, ever so slightly, in final acknowledgement, she slipped inside and the door closed.

Hugh Drummond stood motionless for several minutes after Helena had gone. He surprised himself this evening. Not one for socialising and, as he was not a member of the *ton*, Hugh rarely received invitations to such extravagant occasions, attending even fewer. Obligation prompted him to make an appearance at this ball, as his family had close connections with the Earl and Countess of Faversham, the hosts. Hugh's father,

Arthur Drummond, and Lord Faversham had known each other for decades. The earl had invested in Trentams, the Drummond family's shipping company, which was now — having repaid the investment in full — wholly owned by Hugh, following the untimely death of his father seven years previously.

He also avoided such functions because they seemed to be stalked by mamas looking to marry off their daughters and, a state of wedded bliss was something in which Hugh had no interest. He was too busy managing the shipping line and had no need of a wife whose only joy was dancing and frivolity. If — and it was a huge if — he ever married, it would be to a woman as capable as he, not some giddy society miss.

Intending to stay only for as long as deemed acceptable, Hugh had been glad to come across Stephen Caswell. The two became great friends during their university days and still kept in touch. In fact, it was Hugh with whom Stephen had been staying the night of the fire that destroyed the Caswell's home. The pair had fallen into easy conversation, updating each other on their news and the evening had flown by.

Hugh had been about to take his leave, when he overheard Lady Helena say she was going to walk home alone, adamant Stephen not curtail Tabitha's evening to escort her. The mere idea of such an innocent young woman risking goodness knows what on the dark streets of London did peculiar things to Hugh's head and he shocked himself by offering to take her home. He could not explain it; he had spent scant minutes in her company, yet her face teased his thoughts. Her glossy black hair, piled up in the most ornate style, a single lock escaping its confines to be twirled in an abstracted manner that should have annoyed but instead fascinated him. Her eyes — a kind of violet grey — seemed to see right inside of him and her smile, oh that smile…

"Enough!" he ground out, uncaring that he was talking to himself. "You know nothing of her, she is doubtless some air-headed chit only happy when attending balls or shopping." He turned on his heel and strode down the quiet street into the night.

In the meantime, Helena said goodnight to her mother, who was entertaining guests, and fled upstairs before she could be questioned about her evening. Her bedchamber was at the front of the house and she chanced a peek through the window, noticing that Mr Drummond, still standing where she left him. Odd! She admired his upright bearing, the tilt of his head and the line of his clothes. He was taller than Stephen but not heavily built; his physique seemed athletic. Studying his shadowed features she wondered what it would be like to kiss him. Appalled at her train of thought, Helena shook her head, dismissing it of such nonsense and ringing for a maid to help her undress, was soon fast asleep.

The following days continued in their usual pattern. Helena, always the first up would, after a hearty breakfast, hop into the Caswell carriage — leaving the Trevallier coach for her mother's use — and disappear into another world for most of the day. Currently, Stephen was busy with government work, so Havers — his groom — was Helena's regular escort. Growing up in a household where every member of staff was valued, Helena was never anything other than respectful with their own or anyone else's, understanding that without them, she would be stranded and helpless. Moreover, Havers was an affable young man, and the two had known each other for long enough that they spent the drive from and to her home chattering away as though the best of friends.

Three weeks after first meeting Mr Drummond, Helena was at another ball, in almost exactly the same state of boredom as she had been at the Faversham's. Although now the Season was officially over, there always seemed to be some excuse for a celebration and her mother liked that she attend as many as possible. Helena felt she had danced, talked, and been pestered or, as polite society liked to call it, wooed, quite enough and was trying to come up with a reasonable excuse to leave, when a familiar voice startled her.

"Good evening Lady Helena, you look particularly lovely this evening." Helena jumped and pivoted around, almost colliding with a tall figure standing in the shadows.

Peering into his face, she exclaimed "Mr Drummond! You gave me a fright. It is not done to sneak up on people you know." She wagged her fan at him, her warm smile removing the edge from her words. Hugh bowed.

"I beg your pardon, my lady. My intent was not to unsettle you. I did not expect to see anyone I know and suddenly, here you are." He spread his hands as though her appearance was more important to him than his words implied.

Knowing she was being fanciful, Helena simply dropped a curtsy and replied. "It is of no matter. I was just trying to decide whether I could take my leave without anyone noticing. I am beginning the most fearful headache."

Hugh started to apologise for intruding when Helena gave him a sly wink, causing a bark of laughter. "Maybe a stroll in the garden might alleviate the ache somewhat?" he suggested in amusement. Helena hesitated, unsure whether he wanted to, deciding he was a man who rarely said anything he didn't mean.

"That would be lovely." Nodding to Nancy who followed behind unobtrusively, Helena accepted Hugh's arm, the couple walking out onto the terrace and down among the beautifully manicured lawns. There were plenty of others doing the same, the subdued evening light giving the garden a dreamlike quality; even conversations seemed muted.

"I think, here in this garden, you might find some of the peace you crave, Lady Helena," said Hugh. Helena glanced up at him, expecting mockery but seeing only genuine concern.

"I do not believe London will ever offer me the peace I crave, Sir but thank you for proposing that it could." Her voice sounded melancholy, which seemed at odds with the woman Hugh assumed her to be. He imagined she would thrive on the adulation received from the crowds of young men who were always following her around like lost puppies. Earlier in the evening, he had watched her; impressed with the way she handled their attentions, talking to all in equal measure without giving any of them hope she wanted more than one dance or a brief chat. As they strolled along the pathways, he was starting to surmise Lady Helena was a bit of an enigma.

"Tell me, Mr Drummond, what of your shipping lines? To where do you ply trade? Do you transport goods around England, or further afield? The Americas maybe or the Indies?

Are you specific in the items that you transport or are they varied? Coal? Tea? Spices? Silks?" Helena chattered on for several minutes, her knowledge of maritime trade astounding Hugh, who gaped at her, making Helena giggle.

"My father taught us in all manner of things; not just reading and writing. He wanted us to understand history and geography, trade and politics. I have to be honest and admit much of it went right over my head, but Papa took us to the opening of the East India Docks. I was only ten, but it was so exciting. My brother Giles and I were riveted. Charlotte, my sister, didn't care for it at all, she didn't like the smell, but we loved it. The thing I remember most was the salute by the guns, goodness I thought I would be deafened, oh and the parade of vessels. So majestic." She paused, smiling in recollection of that day; the blustery wind whipping through her hair, the salty air, the noise of the enormous crowd and the wonderfully tall ships — adventure bound.

"I am stunned your father would allow you, a child, to go to such an event." Consternation clear in Hugh's tones.

"Oh, it was fine, Mr Drummond. Do not take on so. It was all very genteel and proper. Everyone who was anyone was there, men, women and children. It was the place to be seen and no one talked of anything else for weeks." She tried to sound haughty but failed dismally, dissolving into laughter at his pained expression. "To return to my point, I am interested in what you do, I should not have asked otherwise."

By this time, they had reached one of the ornate wooden benches scattered throughout the gardens and by tacit consent sat down. Hugh leaned back, stretched out his legs and linking his fingers over his stomach, began to talk about his company. He was proud of what they had achieved, handling both domestic and international trade. Coal and tea were their mainstays but recently, they had begun to include spice. Helena was fascinated and asked what she hoped were insightful questions, feeling she was gaining a good grasp of his business, but why she should want to, was a whole other matter.

In the guise of concentrating on his words, Helena took the opportunity to study Hugh while he spoke. His dark blonde hair was rather unruly, a lock falling over his forehead, a shadow of stubble darkened his jawline and his eyes were brown with gold flecks, almost tawny. These things along with the fact he had obviously been pulling at his cravat — loosening it to the point of it coming undone — gave him a rather piratical appearance. Helena itched to straighten his collar; at least that was what she told herself. Engrossed in their discussion, they lost track of how long they had been sitting when, without warning and almost in the middle of a sentence, Hugh shot up off the bench.

"Lady Helena, please forgive me. I have monopolised the whole of your evening, how appallingly rude of me." Helena dragged her attention back, smiled and stood slowly, brushing down her skirts.

"Well, for my part, I have enjoyed listening to you. It is most engaging to hear a man talk about something that does not revolve around the vagaries of the English weather or how I feel about horse racing. I am not a simpleton. I consider myself quite well educated and love to read all manner of books. I am not like a child's doll dressed up to look pretty and say nothing, in the hopes of snaring a suitable husband — something I have little interest in anyway. I have a mind, and would like to put my knowledge to a worthwhile cause, otherwise I cannot see any point in my existence." Helena's colour heightened as she spoke, realising she sounded less than genteel, but wasn't about to retract anything. So, she just stood, hands on hips, and waited for the derisive laughter she usually got from her bevy of suitors.

Chapter Three

Nothing happened. No howls of mirth, no questions regarding her sanity, nothing. Hugh simply regarded her with a mixture of humour and something that might have been pride.

"I am glad to hear it, Lady Helena. It is most refreshing to talk with a lady who is partial to lively debate on a variety of topics." His tone cooled, "However, I believe we should return to the ballroom, we have been gone for quite some time, and I do not wish anyone to think this is more than it is."

Helena frowned, aware of a subtle shift in his demeanour. Had he not listened to what she said? Did he think her on the marriage hunt? That she purposely kept him talking so questions might be asked? Charming! Helena turned to Nancy who had found a seat out of earshot, a little way behind them, and was waiting patiently until needed.

"Come Nancy, I think it is time we left. I certainly do not wish anyone to think this is more than it is. Good evening to you, Sir." She tossed her head, lustrous black hair bouncing over her shoulders as she marched back up to the terrace and in through the open French doors, annoyance bristling out of her.

Chagrined, Hugh followed slowly. It had not been his intent to upset her; it was more he was concerned about her reputation. To spend any length of time, virtually alone, with an unmarried gentleman inferred an interest he didn't think either of them was quite ready for. Even as he thought this, however, an image of Helena, curled up on one of the huge leather chairs in front of the fire in his study, popped into his head and, curiously, he could not imagine a more fitting place for her to be.

Helena was furious — with herself for over-reacting and with Hugh for thinking her so shallow. She thanked her hosts for a delightful party and rushed down the steps to her carriage without a backward glance. Which was a shame really, for had she done so, she might have noticed a tall, and somewhat unconventionally handsome gentleman, standing at one of the windows, observing her departure.

The warm sunny weather broke the next day. A wild storm ripped through the city and in its wake a torrent of rain continued to fall. The roads became like churned fields and the paths did not fare much better. Helena was frustrated because getting to the shelter was nigh impossible in such inclement conditions. Carriages would get bogged or a wheel would likely snap, and to walk was folly.

Finally, by the third day after the storm, it improved enough for Helena to risk the walk. Her mother was unimpressed, but refrained from commenting, knowing to suggest Helena not go out was tantamount to ensuring she would. To be fair, her daughter did wait until after luncheon before she ventured over the doorstep, both she and Nancy well wrapped up against the damp day. After a lengthy walk, which cleared the cobwebs, the two arrived at the shelter and Helena was soon absorbed in her work.

Although she had learned how to sew, Helena was hopeless at it, thus had taken it upon herself to teach the women to read and write, as well as some basic arithmetic. There were always several women eager for their next lesson and the minute Helena appeared, a gaggle of them dragged her off to what was laughingly referred to as the schoolroom, chattering nineteen to the dozen. By chance, Nancy knew one of the women who frequented the refuge and she joined her friend who was busy making children clothes out of ball gowns. The incongruity of it would have been funny had it not been so poignant.

The afternoon slipped away. Helena suddenly realised she had been at the shelter far longer than expected, and it was beginning to look quite murky outside. Had the day been sunny, it would have been light enough to walk home without worrying, but the rain had returned, and there was nothing to lift the gloom. Seeking out Nancy, Helena suggested they take their leave and, knowing trying to hail a carriage in this district would be fruitless, experienced a twinge of anxiety at the thought of their long trek home. Nevertheless, she squared her shoulders and the two women, huddled into their voluminous cloaks, stepped out.

Conscious of her status within society, Helena never drew attention to herself when she visited Sanctuary House. She had appropriated several drab and dowdy dresses from goodness knows where and always scraped her black tresses into a tight bun. Unfortunately, there was little she could do about the glossiness of her hair, her soft hands and flawless complexion, but she had worked out that she could detract from them somewhat by dint of rubbing dark powder over her face so she looked a bit grubby and hoped that this, along with the large hood of her faded cloak and scruffy gloves, would be enough to avoid any unwanted attention, especially today.

They trudged through the wet streets, hurrying to reach the less perilous areas of the city where the roads might have dried enough for the hackneys to be running. It wasn't pouring down, more a heavy mist, but it was obscuring everything, and Helena was starting to feel uneasy.

Chivvying Nancy along, the two were almost running, heads bent against the weather, when Helena ran slap bang into a solid object — one that grunted on impact. Helena slipped, her feet going from under her and she landed hard on the muddy path, the breath knocked out of her.

"The devil! Are you beetle headed? Watch where you are going!" An angry voice and one, which sounded vaguely familiar, remonstrated, but Helena had no wish to find out whose it was. Ignoring the proffered hand, she scrambled back to her feet, brushing mud and filth from her cloak, bowing her head as she muttered an apology. There was a strained silence then —

"Nancy?" shock laced the tones as Nancy replied,

"It is, Sir, so sorry, Sir we didn't mean t'run into ye. 'Twas that we was tryin' to get 'ome afore her ladyship worries."

Helena, her head bent, ostensibly righting her clothes and hoping whoever it was would leave them alone, felt a hand grip her arm before being spun to face the speaker. Biting down on a panicked yelp, she glared up into a pair of tawny eyes, their gold flecks seeming to spit with anger. It was Hugh. He gawked, taking in her shabby clothing and smudged face.

"Lady Helena? Good God, Lady Helena! What the deuce are you doing here?" He sucked in a sharp breath. "Please forgive my language."

Helena gulped at Hugh's expression — currently a cross between incensed and astonished — but determined not to look completely helpless, forced her fright aside and drew herself up to her full height, which meant she was facing his chest. She had to angle her head see him properly.

"Walking home, what does it look like?" she replied as tartly as she could manage, given she was still trying to catch her breath.

"It is not safe, my lady. Why did you not hail a hackney?"

"Surely you jest, Sir? All the way down here? It is probably more prudent to walk." Helena shrugged off his hand, which was still holding her arm, aware again of that curious tingling.

Hugh was horrified she thought it safe to walk these pathways. What was it with this woman and lonely streets? Never mind that, what on earth brought her to such a district? It was only by chance he had come upon them. He was taking a short cut home from his office down on the docks, and although not the worst area of London to be taking a constitutional, neither was it a place for a gentlewoman to be, even with a chaperone. He swallowed his anger, borne of concern for Helena, and spoke in more measured tones.

"Permit me to escort you home. I cannot in all conscience let you continue alone." His entreaty worked and in truth Helena was glad of his company. His height and bearing would deter any with hostile intent.

"Thank you, Mr Drummond, I would appreciate it." She sounded weary and Hugh searched her face, seeing the pale cast to her cheeks and the fear lurking in the smoky depths of her eyes.

Determined to distract her, he grinned engagingly and tucking her hand through his arm, declared. "I am glad. Let us sally forth, three intrepid explorers forging their way through the dank forest of stone in the hope of discovering a warm and bright parlour. Preferably one which has brandy, or at the very least hot chocolate." It did the trick and Helena chuckled at his banter. Hugh set a brisk pace, a little concerned the two women would get chilled and it did not seem long at all before they were back in more genteel surroundings. Moments later, they rounded the corner into Portman Square. Hugh escorted them all the way to the front door, but declined Helena's invitation to join her for a hot drink.

"Thank you, Lady Helena, but I have pressing matters to which I must attend before this day is out. Maybe another time?"

"I do believe I will hold you to that, Mr Drummond," she replied. "Thank you for your kindness today, I will not forget it." Hugh bowed over her hand, squeezing her fingers gently, and suddenly Helena didn't want him to let go. Her hand felt so right engulfed in his large one, secure somehow. She raised her eyes to his and for a split second it was as though he could read her mind. He smiled, inclining his head and abruptly, was gone, disappearing into the damp twilight before she had chance to say goodbye.

Helena stared after him, lost in thought; wondering what it was about this man that made her feel so peculiar. One minute she was full of cheer, the next almost melancholy. He frustrated and intrigued her; it was baffling. A subtle cough brought her back to the present and she saw Hudson, their butler, waiting for her to come inside.

"Goodness me, Hudson! I am so sorry, making you linger in the cold." She grinned an apology at the elderly man who had been with the family since a boy, and had watched the Winchester children grow into fine, well-rounded young people. He knew what Helena did during the day and was as proud of her as though her grandfather. He chuckled at her expression and took her cloak, noticing the large splat of mud down the back. "I slipped." She explained, rather sheepishly.

"No matter my lady, we'll sort it out. You weren't hurt when you fell were you?"

"No, well except my pride," she giggled and, patting him on the arm in thanks, sped up the stairs to change before her mother saw what a scarecrow her daughter had turned into.

None the worse for her damp walk home, Helena was back at the shelter the next day. It would take more than one little fall, embarrassing though it was, to interrupt her routine. The weather returned to that more typical of English summers, long sunny days, and balmy nights. Unfortunately, the heat had a tendency to become stifling in the middle of a large city. For those able to spend an afternoon in one of the parks, a pleasant breeze could often be found, but Sanctuary House was nowhere near a park and although the docks were not far, they were no place to seek out fresh air. A huge old building with high ceilings meant that the shelter itself did not get too hot, but the streets round it were cramped and overcrowded. Tensions simmered beneath the surface and after several days without so much as a puff of wind, people were getting crotchety.

Those who ran the shelter were worried. One or two of the men, whose wives had fled to the charitable institution, had started to threaten them and the staff, determined their spouses return home. To be fair, once married, the husbands owned their wives, regardless of how brutal a relationship they might share and the charity managing the shelter had no legal right to prevent the men from reclaiming their 'property.' Thankfully, the implacable guardians discouraged most attempts. A dozen or so ex-soldiers standing sentry around the property was usually enough to intimidate even the most bullish of men.

Hot weather, belligerence and lack of sleep is a volatile mix however, and one afternoon, perhaps a fortnight after her last encounter with Mr Drummond, Helena's lesson was disturbed by a loud crash and the sound of raised voices. Bidding her group stay where they were, Helena peered through the door. Nothing untoward in the corridor, but the sounds continued. They seemed to be coming from the refectory. At the end of the hallway stood a burly man; it was Mr Barnes one of their protectors. Helena motioned to him and he came quickly to where she waited.

"Mr Barnes, do you know, who or what is causing such a racket?"

"I think 'tis mebbe Archie Miller, my lady. Be 'im or Seth Collins, both have been comin' around lately, pesterin' thu'rn wives. I didn't think they'd risk a beating though." He smiled grimly, bunching his shoulders.

"Well, as neither Sybil nor Lynette are in my class, I think we can leave them here unguarded. Come, Mr Barnes, let us see what's afoot." The two hurried along the hallways, following the sounds, which became louder the closer they got to the refectory. Mr Barnes, asked Helena to let him go in first and upon entering, she was met with a vision of utter chaos.

Chapter Four

Crockery and cooking implements were scattered across the floor, there was food everywhere and in the midst of it all a goliath of a man was bellowing orders to a tiny, bird-like woman who was screeching back at him like a fishwife. It went along the lines of:

"Please come home my dear, I miss you terribly," to which the response was,

"Oh, I am so sorry, my sweet, I cannot do so quite yet. I am busy trying to recover from the last beating you gave me," or words to that effect. Of course, the language was rather more raucous, even Mr Barnes was shocked at the expletives streaming from their mouths, but to each other, their reasoning appeared sound. Helena tried to make herself heard over the cacophony, hoping that if they would listen to her, she might talk some sense into either or both of them, but it was a losing battle.

Eventually, when it appeared as though this was going to last the remainder of the afternoon, Helena — tiring of the racket and feeling a headache starting to niggle — picked up a large pan. She walloped it hard against the table, causing a gong-like boom to reverberate around the refectory. In its aftermath, there was a sudden silence and both Sybil and Archie turned to Helena, their mouths dropping open in shock.

"Thank you, now would you two please sit down." Calmly indicating the end of the table closest to her, currently the only clean space in the room. Sybil did so immediately. Archie hesitated, shuffling from foot to foot but, unable to think of a way to tell this refined lady to go to the devil, did the same. Without raising her voice, Helena continued, "Please explain your behaviour." They both started speaking at once, clamouring to be the first to get their tale across and when it seemed that the same old argument was about to start all over again, Helena held up her hand and waited for quiet.

"As you were obviously not an invited guest, Mr Miller, I believe Sybil should speak first. Sybil…" Helena opened her palm encouraging Sybil to talk. Sybil took a breath and it all spilled out. Archie liked to drink, in fact he regularly drank away all their coin, then expected her to go out to earn extra so he could drink more. She refused; he got mad and used her for boxing practise. It was a tale Helena had heard more times than she cared to count. Many of the women at the shelter had similar complaints. The sad thing was, for the most part, these men loved their wives, it was just they loved the grog more, and felt they deserved to imbibe a limitless amount as recompense for the backbreaking labour they did day in and day out.

"I love you Archie, truly I do, but you scared me. I thought you was gonna kill me. Here I'm safe. There's no drinking — save tea or hot chocolate — and I can sleep without worrying that yer gonna come home completely jug-bitten an' 'it me for no reason."

Helena didn't think there was ever a reason a man should hit his wife, but she let that go for now.

"Now you, Archie."

"Sybil, please come home I can't cook, I haven't eaten a decent meal in days. How'm I supposed to work wivvout enough food? What abaht me clothes? I'm sorry I 'it yer, but you drive a man to despair, with yer naggin'." Archie honestly thought this was the way to win back his wife. Helena was dumbfounded. The man was a fool.

"Archie, love. You can get a meal from yer mother, she'd be 'appy to feed yer. I ain't comin' home 'til you give up some o' yer drinking. I'm fed up of all me 'ard earned money disappearing down yer gullet. I want us ter 'ave summat saved, summat set aside so we could 'ave an 'oliday. Mebbe when I've been away a bit longer you might appreciate me and what I earns." Sybil squared her fragile frame and stared Archie down. The huge man crumpled under her gimlet-like gaze and for a brief moment Helena almost felt sorry for him. Underneath all his bluster he was rather pathetic.

"But I love yer, Sybs," he whined.

"I know yer do, Archie and I love you, but yer near bust me arm and me jaw. Yer don't realise 'ow strong y'are. I'll come 'ome when I'm good and ready and not a minute before." She folded her arms and tapped her foot. Archie vacillated for a moment, debating whether further argument would persuade Sybil, but her expression was enough to dissuade him and he slunk out of the room, glancing back once, desperation on his face. Wanting to reassure Archie that his wife just needed time, Helena walked with him to the front door.

"Just give her a few more days, Archie," she pleaded. "I know she wants to go home, but you really frightened her." She pressed his forearm in her desire to make him understand, but Archie jerked her hand off, turning on her and snarling —

"'Tis all your fault, you and them other blummin do-gooders. You made my wife fink abaht fings and it aint good for 'er. If she's not 'ome by end o'the week, you'll be sorry." He jabbed his finger at Helena, the threat clear and stomped down the steps. Helena watched him leave, determined not to let his words bother her, but suddenly she shivered; he was a big man and could easily hurt her. Then she remembered all the guards at the shelter, she was in no danger from Archie.

Spinning on her heel, Helena went back into the refectory where Sybil was sobbing noisily into her apron. Dragging a chair across, Helena sat next to the pitiful woman and drew her into a warm hug.

"There, there, Sybil. Let it all out, you poor dear," rocking her charge and patting her shoulders gently as she would a distraught child. "You were so brave. I am very proud of you."

Sybil spluttered a less than coherent explanation about what just occurred, apologising over and over for the damage her husband caused. It seemed quite clear to Helena anyway, it was the same story variously repeated by the majority of women whose fear led them to Sanctuary House.

Wives fleeing husbands who turned violent when soused. Husbands not prepared to change their ways. Eventually, the wives, under increasing pressure from said spouses, gave up and returned home, the cycle starting all over again. The shelter tried to act as a go-between, somewhere these couples could attempt to sort out their problems. It rarely worked, but it did give the battered women a place away from the drudgery and the beatings, and also to be assured it wasn't their fault.

None who ran the shelter tried to persuade wives to leave their husbands — that was not their purview. More, they offered a shoulder to cry on, activities to distract and a place to heal if required. They had a doctor who treated the injured and sick, and many willing helpers.

"Think nothing of it, 'tis soon sorted. You sit here and gather yourself while I make a start." Helena gave the thin shoulders one last squeeze, and began to tidy up the mess. Several other women arrived to assist and as Helena promised, it was quickly cleared up. Sybil did make an effort, but she was too distressed and in the end one of the other women, deciding that sleep might be more beneficial, took Sybil off to her bedroom, insisting she rest until the evening meal.

Helena made sure everything was back in order then, collecting Nancy, the two went to find the Caswell coach awaiting them in the laneway at the rear of the building. Helena had to be home in time to prepare for the evening — another ball her mother wanted her to attend and the following afternoon, a picnic. Helena's head was aching badly now and she wished she had some of Billie's herbs; her sister-in-law had a knack of knowing what should help. Unfortunately, her brother and his wife had returned to Whiteoaks several weeks previously and it was unlikely they would be back until the following year, both preferring the serenity of the country to the bustle of London.

As Havers helped them both down from the carriage, Helena thanked him, confirming that she would be returning to Sanctuary House three days hence. Once inside the cool of her home, she requested a bath be drawn, asking Nancy to find out whether they still had any of Billie's headache curatives. As luck would have it, Nancy discovered bottles of lavender, peppermint, and feverfew. Sighing in relief, Helena read the instructions and after relaxing in a warm bath — to which she added a few drops of lavender — dabbed a small amount of the peppermint under her hairline and took a pinch of the feverfew for good measure, praying the combination of all three would work.

A couple of hours later, she was talking quietly with Tabitha in a dimly lit corner of a ballroom. Helena's headache had not abated; everything seemed to be exacerbating it and she was starting to feel queasy. The light from the multitude of candles hurt her eyes; the music grated on her ears, the chatter and even the rhythmic tattoo of shoes on the dance floor seemed overly loud.

Stephen, carrying iced drinks for the two women, noticed how ill Helena looked. She was pale and her eyes were dark with pain.

"Should you be here, Helena?" he asked. "You look quite indisposed."

"'Tis just a headache," she replied smiling wanly, "today was…not the best. I am too warm though. I think I may take a stroll outside." The two moved to join her, "No, please stay, I shall be fine, I just need some fresh air." She slipped through the open doors, walking to the far end of the terrace and, uncaring whether it was decorous, sank down onto the top step leading down to the garden, leaning her hot head against the cool stone of a pillar.

She had been sitting for maybe half an hour, the evening breeze, and relative peace of her makeshift seat in no way alleviating the pain and Helena wondered, absently, whether she would be able to find her way back into the ballroom. The pain was so bad now she could scarcely see. The sound of footsteps disturbed the quiet and, realising she should probably rise, started to do so. A voice forestalled her.

"No need to get up, Lady Helena. I understand you are feeling less than sprightly and I came to check on you." Mr Drummond smiled down at her seeing, even in the waning light, her ashen face, dark shadows under her eyes and a jaw clenched in pain. Helena attempted to smile back but the effort was too much.

"Good evening, Mr Drummond, thank you for your concern. I am afraid I find myself in the rather awkward position of being unable to stand." She took a breath and tried to focus, her mouth suddenly unable to connect to her brain. "Be might you so to Nancy as ask kind to come?" Her words made no sense and were beginning to slur. She knew she sounded drunk, but she was losing concentration. Flashing lights marred her vision and the ground was sliding away from her. "Not tispy...oh dear..." she heard her muddled words and, desperate to clarify, made a valiant attempt to get up, using the pillar as a support. Helena's legs refused to hold her, however and she began to fall. Her head felt as though it was about to explode and she heard a strangled cry. Before she could work out who it was, oblivion claimed her.

Chapter Five

Helena had no idea Hugh darted forward, catching her before she toppled down the steps. He lifted her easily, carrying her indoors and, familiar with the layout of the residence, along to the library. The ever-watchful Nancy seeing her mistress collapse, hurried after Hugh. Shoving open the door, Hugh was pleased to see the room was dim, quiet and empty.

Carefully laying Helena down on one of the sofas, he stood aside allowing Nancy to tend to her. The young maid was used to her mistress' headaches but Helena was normally at home when they struck, where everything was to hand. She needed cool cloths and lavender and perhaps even laudanum, but knew it was unlikely she would get them here. Hugh noticed her agitation and asked whether he could be of assistance. Nancy explained her quandary.

"Leave it with me Nancy. I shall go and talk to Stephen and Tabitha, we will work something out." he paused. "Is Lady Helena afflicted with severe headaches often?" Curious.

Nancy shook her head. "Not any more, Sir. She used to get them more often, terribly bad, the pain made her ever so ill so it did, but the doctor said she would grow out of them. She gets them only rarely now, mostly when she's overtired. Bless her; she had a hard day today." Nancy's motherly comments tugged an amused smile from Hugh's lips, the maid being at least three years younger than Helena. He slipped out of the room, and found Stephen and Tabitha, deep in conversation in one of the quiet alcoves surrounding the ballroom. Sorry that he had to spoil their time together, Hugh nevertheless knew Helena's need was greater than theirs. He coughed as he approached, immediately attracting their attention, and they both turned expectantly.

"I do beg your pardon for interrupting, but Lady Helena is quite unwell. I think we must get her home." He went onto explain what happened.

Tabitha tutted. "She takes on too much. This was inevitable," she said, and with that cryptic comment, flew to help her friend. Hugh turned to Stephen questions in his eyes. Stephen shrugged his shoulders.

"Not my tale to tell, Drummond. You'll have to ask Helena. Suffice it to say that what you see and what you think, are not all you get with Lady Helena Trevallier."

Something Hugh was beginning to understand. Slowly, the two men followed Tabitha, Stephen asking Hugh about his latest ship, a schooner not far from completion — bringing Trentams fleet to twenty. During the construction of this vessel, there were several unexplained accidents; the resulting injuries were minor but had raised questions in Hugh's mind as to the cause. As the two men chatted, Stephen enquired whether things had settled down. Hugh mentioned one or two more strange incidents, but he was hoping they were the result of carelessness rather than anything malicious.

"Keep a close eye on things, Hugh," warned Stephen. "You know how competitive the shipping industry is now. Are you sure you can trust your men?"

"Wholeheartedly, but I will increase the guard and my own vigilance." Hugh assured him. Their conversation dwindled as they entered the library. Helena hadn't roused, her face waxen and her breathing erratic. Tabitha had persuaded one of the staff to bring her a bowl of tepid water and some cloths, and was currently pressing the damp material to Helena's wrists and forehead trying to lessen the pain.

"Stephen, we have to get her home. Nancy says they have treatments there for her, we can do nothing here."

"Should we wait not until she has come around?" interjected Hugh. Tabitha shook her head.

"She could be like this for hours, home is the best place for her. Please can you help me?" She looked at Stephen as she spoke, but before he could do anything Hugh scooped Helena into his arms, saying as he did so.

"'Tis your carriage, Caswell. You go and get Havers to come to the garden entrance, I'll carry Lady Helena, she weighs no more than a feather pillow. Lady Tabitha and Nancy can come with me, that way propriety is observed." Seeing the sense in Hugh's argument, Stephen rushed off and while Tabitha went to explain their sudden departure to their hosts and that they would leave through the side gate so as not to disturb the other guests, Hugh and Nancy made their way back along the terrace and to the garden gate.

A member of staff was there to let them out and within seconds the Caswell coach pulled alongside. Tabitha appeared through the dusk while Nancy, after ensuring her mistress was settled inside, hopped up beside Havers leaving more space within for the remaining four. Hugh still refused to relinquish his hold of Helena, although had anyone asked why he could not have told them. Even though Stephen was Helena's friend and no one would question his carrying her, Hugh was reluctant to let her go. To his growing consternation, Helena hadn't stirred, and her face had regained none of its normal colour, although her breathing did seem steadier.

The carriage rattled through the empty streets, the evening drawing to a close and the sky beginning to darken, the muted mauves of twilight dimming to midnight blue. They were soon outside Winchester House, and Nancy ran in to inform Lady Winchester of Helena's collapse. The dowager countess waited at the door and although she raised a quizzical eyebrow at the strange man carrying her daughter, seeing Stephen and Tabitha following them up the steps, didn't waste time fretting over it. Directing Hudson to escort Hugh up to Helena's bedchamber, Lady Winchester gave out a list of instructions and staff hurried to do her bidding.

"She said her head ached, I thought she was feigning," the countess murmured. "'Tis years since she had such a bad attack. I wonder what caused it?" Unfortunately, neither Stephen nor Tabitha could shed any light on the matter, and ever the hostess, Lady Winchester ushered them into the parlour ringing for hot drinks and a whisky each for Stephen and Hugh.

"I am going to check on my daughter. I am leaving you unchaperoned, please do not abuse my trust." She smiled as she walked out, knowing a kiss or two would no doubt be stolen, but also knowing Stephen would never open Tabitha to even a hint of a whisper of scandal.

Upstairs, Hugh laid Helena on her bed, the action wringing a moan from her pallid lips and, as he stepped away, he had the oddest notion of loss. Shaking his head, he turned to leave the room and was confronted by Lady Winchester. She eyed him up and down.

"You are?" she demanded imperiously.

Hugh bowed, "Mr Hugh Drummond at your service, Lady Winchester. I…err…caught your daughter when she fainted."

"And it seems you could not let her go," she countered archly.

Hugh replied sheepishly, "It was the most logical idea. Stephen needed to call their carriage. Tabitha could not carry her, so that left me. Please believe me when I say at no time was your daughter compromised."

Lady Winchester studied the tall man appraisingly and was reminded it was he who had protected Stephen after the fire at Ashbourne House. He was something in shipping if she recalled correctly. He seemed polite and amenable and Stephen obviously trusted him. That was enough for her. She relaxed and a grateful smiled hovered around her mouth.

"Thank you for your kindness, Mr Drummond. I am glad 'twas you who found her, not some rake who would think nothing of risking her good name."

Hugh affirmed he was pleased to have been of assistance and, after bowing again, left the room in search of Stephen and Tabitha. Hudson escorted him to the parlour adding that a hot chocolate and a whisky awaited him there.

The three enjoyed their drinks in companionable silence, unwilling to leave until they knew Helena was at least awake, but accepting she would probably sleep out the night. Sometime later, Lady Winchester appeared in the doorway. The two men stood as she entered, but she waved them back to their seats.

"Helena has woken briefly. She tried to tell me she was not drunk and please would I apologise to Mr Drummond on her behalf for being unconscionably rude." The countess' lips twitched as she delivered Helena's message. Her daughter hadn't woken enough to tell the whole story and her words were still garbled, but Lady Winchester was used to these bouts and worked out what probably happened.

Hugh said it was nothing and Helena was not to worry, assuring her mother Helena had not done anything she need be embarrassed about. Then he stood again and, after thanking his hostess for the drinks, took his leave. Lady Winchester watched as he walked to the front door, where he turned and bowed, disappearing into the night.

"Now, I wonder," she murmured tapping her lips in thought. Filing it away for now, she returned to the parlour and suggested Tabitha stay the night as she had no chaperone. Stephen could leave a message at the Bridgewater residence informing them of what transpired so no one worried when Tabitha was not in her bed on the morrow. Everything settled, Stephen departed and Nancy took Tabitha upstairs to the chamber she always used. Lady Winchester made a last check on Helena and soon the house fell silent.

The next morning, Helena woke much later than usual. She felt a bit odd, sort of light-headed and couldn't think why. As she lay, memories of the previous evening filtered through and she had the vaguest recollection of being drunk. That couldn't be right, she rarely touched wine and certainly not spirits. Then she remembered her headache and talking to Hugh — Mr Drummond, she corrected herself — then nothing. A flush ran up her cheeks, had she done something stupid? She searched her mind, but there was only a blank. Frustrated, she realised she was going to have to ask someone. Nancy would know; she had been with her.

Ringing for her maid, Helena threw back the covers and started to get up. She felt sticky and wrung out, rather like one of the sheets at the shelter when it had gone through the mangle. The image that popped into her head made her chuckle and she was still grinning when Nancy knocked. While

Nancy prepared a bath, she told Helena everything, which only added to her mortification, but her maid informed her that Mr Drummond was the complete gentleman ensuring Helena's well-being at all times. After a refreshing soak, Helena felt a little more human and hurried downstairs to see whether there was any breakfast left. Hudson affirmed her mother and Tabitha were in the dining room, and that breakfast was still being served.

At Helena's entrance the two women turned and smiled, glad to see her looking none the worse for her collapse.

"Helena my dear, how are you feeling?" her mother enquired, as Helena piled a plate with all manner of tasty food.

"Much better, Mama thank you. I am sorry I worried you, and you Tabitha. I apologise for cutting short your evening."

"Do not fret about it. I knew you were unwell, you should have gone home when I first suggested it."

"Maybe, but I did not think it would become as bad. 'Tis years since I had so severe an attack."

"You have been working too hard, Helena," chided her mother gently. "I know you love helping at the shelter but you need to take a break occasionally. You will be no good to those women if you fall ill." Helena knew her mother was right and there were enough people to help if she was unable to go, but she didn't want to be considered superficial, only helping with the easy things, and giving up when she was tired.

"They are always fatigued, Mama. Most work long into the night just to put bread on their tables. I merely teach a little and help with preparing the meals. I can come and go as I please. I have a warm bed and a loving family. I am safe and protected, they don't have that. I do not want them to think I will abandon them when it seems too hard."

Lady Winchester regarded her daughter steadily. Helena could feel hectic colour staining her face, and she shifted uncomfortably on her chair. "Helena, you have been working at the shelter for over a year, day in and day out. There have been very few days when you have not attended, and that has been owing to the weather. Except for Giles' wedding, you have not taken a holiday. My dear, you are not, and should never think you are, indispensable, for that smacks of pride."

Her mother's tones were kind, taking the sting out of her reproof, but Helena was cut to the quick. Was that what she was doing? No surely not. If so, it was entirely unintentional.

"M-mama, I n-never intend to b-behave so," she stuttered in her agitation, appalled her mother would think this. Her mother patted her knee.

"I know my darling and I know you want to help these poor women, but look at what it is doing to you. You are exhausted from trying to burn the candle at both ends and down the middle. You collapsed at a ball. You must see you cannot continue like this. I do not wish to forbid you and, as you are past your majority, I know that in truth I cannot stop you, but I would like you take a little more care of yourself. Would you promise to do so…for me?"

Lady Winchester cupped her daughter's face as she beseeched her, cool hands calming fiery cheeks. Helen nodded, not trusting herself to speak, and her mother smiled.

"Good, I am glad and now we'll say no more about it." With a deftness gained from years of practise, Lady Winchester turned the conversation to lighter matters and soon the room was filled with laughter and chatter and the shelter was, for a little while, forgotten.

Chapter Six

Helena decided not to attend the picnic, she was not in any mood to fend off admirers and the day was hot. It would not take much for her headache to return and she preferred to relax in the quiet of her home. Typically, after such an attack, she felt peculiar and rather disconnected. This normally lasted a day or so, but she struggled to concentrate until it had cleared. Thus, sitting with a book in their modest garden under the shade of a leafy plane tree, was a far more attractive prospect than a picnic in the scorching sun. Tabitha went home shortly after breakfast, the two having made plans to meet again the following day.

The afternoon was nearly over and Helena was dozing, when a cough woke her and she opened her eyes to see Hudson standing, rather diffidently, by her chair.

"Yes Hudson, what is it?" sleepily asked.

"There's a gentleman to see you my lady, he is most insistent." Hudson paused and whispered, "he is the one who carried you in last night." Helena shot out of her chair and patted her hair to make sure it was as tidy as could be hoped.

"Do I look presentable, Hudson?" she muttered, straightening her skirts.

"You look quite perfect, my lady," he said grinning genially. Helena beamed back and waited as Hudson escorted Mr Drummond through to the garden. Hugh bowed over her hand and asked how she was feeling, his eyes searching her still pale face for any signs her headache lingered.

"I am much better thank you, Mr Drummond and I hear I have you to thank for preventing me taking an unseemly tumble down the steps. I am afraid I have no recollection of anything other than you asking after my health." She smiled at him as she spoke and he felt the strangest prickle run up his spine. Ignoring it he replied —

"We were worried about you. I am glad to see you have suffered no ill effects."

Helena invited him to sit and, after a few moments of awkward silence, they began chatting as though well acquainted. Hudson brought them some refreshments and the time flew by without either of them noticing. Hugh did discern, however, that Helena was starting to look weary and did not wish either to outstay his welcome or call down on his head the wrath of her mother, for tiring her.

"I think I should take my leave. Might you permit me to call on you again?" Helena cocked her head to look at him. There was nothing she wanted more, but was concerned she might appear too eager. His eyes held hers until she was quite sure she was falling into his tawny gaze.

"I believe I would find that altogether acceptable, Mr Drummond," she whispered, suppressing an irrational urge to straighten his cravat. The man never seemed to be able to keep it in place.

"I look forward to it." He took her hand, lifting it to his lips and, at the last moment turned it upward, dropping a light kiss on her palm. Helena swallowed on a kind of hiccup, totally unladylike but she could not help it. Suddenly, she wanted him to hold her, to feel his arms around her and his lips on hers. Goodness, she wished she had her fan with her, as heat flared up her cheeks for what seemed like the hundredth time that day.

"I...errr...I...well...hmmm..." She gave up; her brain simply would not follow instructions. Instead of speaking, she dipped a curtsy, it was the best she could manage and stood rooted to the spot as Hugh inclined his head and walked away. She looked at her palm, expecting to see the imprint of his lips on the soft skin. Nothing, yet she could still feel it. Abruptly she sat down, waiting for her head to behave itself, her thoughts in turmoil.

What was going on? Why was she feeling these things? Where was Charlotte when she needed her? Referring to her older sister who had, inconsiderately, gone to the country with her husband and Noah, their newborn son, the city too stifling at this time of year. Charlotte once told Helena that when the right man came along she would know. Everything would suddenly become quiet; the distractions, nonsense and noise of life would fade away and you just knew. Helena thought this romantic taradiddle, but the emotions running through her were inexplicable. Well, there was nothing she could do about it now. She pushed it aside and went indoors. After an early dinner, she begged to be excused, claiming fatigue and treated herself to an early night,

Helena slept well, waking the following day feeling quite herself again. She spent the morning attending to some letters she had been neglecting, nothing vitally important, the majority were replies to invitations and a few thank you notes. By mid-afternoon she and Tabitha were enjoying a carriage ride along Rotten Row; the day was cooler than of late and the breeze, pleasant. They had been out for an hour or so, when two horses reined in at the side of their carriage.

"Well, what a surprise," cried Stephen. His tone suggesting this was entirely contrived in order for him to see Tabitha, who giggled, the two immediately falling into excited conversation. Helena smiled self-consciously at Hugh, who manoeuvred his horse around to her side of the carriage.

"Good afternoon, Lady Helena," He smiled while he greeted her, tipping his hat.

"Good afternoon, Mr Drummond. 'Tis a lovely afternoon for a ride is it not?" she said, holding his gaze for a moment longer than was acceptable. By now, Stephen and Tabitha were completely oblivious to all else around them, causing Helena to fidget on her seat and fuss with a wayward strand of hair, quite uncomfortable in the face of such intensity.

"Would you like to take a short walk, Lady Helena?" enquired Hugh, taking pity on her. She nodded, gratefully and tapped Tabitha on the shoulder, indicating she would be stepping down from the carriage. Tabitha nodded absently leaving Helena convinced she hadn't heard her. Peter, Tabitha's groom, jumped down to drop the step, assisting Helena from the carriage while Hugh dismounted. He also readily agreed to keep an eye on Xerxes — Hugh's stallion — who, after being presented with a tasty apple procured from one of Peter's pockets, was persuaded to wait. Hugh offered Helena his arm and the couple dawdled along the grass.

"It is fortuitous that Stephen suggested a ride this afternoon." Hugh commented after they had walked for some distance without talking, their silence congenial.

"It is?" Helena — rather puzzled, glanced at his face. He grinned at her.

"Of course! I did not expect to be as lucky as to see you again so soon, yet here we are."

"I do not think this was a last-minute suggestion on Stephen's behalf," she noted, angling her head in the general direction of the carriage.

Hugh sighed dramatically, "Ahh, young love," his attempt to sound old and jaded might have worked if not for the amusement tugging at his lips. Helena chuckled in agreement as they continued their walk and, as they always seemed to, eased into cheerful conversation. Presently, Helena asked about the new ship and Hugh looked at her in surprise.

She grinned and continued, "Stephen told me about it when I was asking…" — she faltered realising she was about to admit to gleaning information about Hugh from her friend — "…we were talking the other evening," she amended.

The awareness that Helena was interested in him sent an unfamiliar eddy of warmth all the way down Hugh's body, right to his toes. The bright young woman walking alongside him had begun to chip away at his shell. With no title and having spent years learning the shipping trade from his father, not to mention seeing the worst mankind could throw at each other on the battlefields of the Peninsula, Hugh had long eschewed the idea of marriage. He often travelled overseas, which was always risky and he recalled how his mother used to worry whenever his father was on a voyage; it was a fear Hugh could never inflict on someone he loved. He was shocked therefore to discover that Lady Helena Trevallier, in their scant few meetings, had somehow crept into his heart.

Hugh pretended not to notice her fumble and launched into an animated monologue about his new ship, when it would be complete, where it would journey and what it would transport. Helena, her equilibrium restored, asked several questions, her interest decidedly not insincere. As they were talking, an idea popped into her head.

"I wonder Mr Drummond, whether you might be agreeable to showing me this new ship and mayhap giving me a brief tour of your yard?"

Hugh goggled at her. "Shipyards are no place for a gentlewoman such as yourself, Lady Helena. They are dirty, dangerous places where one misstep could send you into the river or the bowels of a ship."

"Do you think me incapable of watching my step, Sir?" she demanded, conveniently forgetting how lacking she had been in that regard two evenings previously. Hugh spread his hands, hoping she would understand his disinclination.

"My lady, 'tis is not that at all, but the dockyards are covered in grime and oil. There are sharp tools and ropes and tar. It is not exactly a pretty place to view."

"You would be amazed at what I see that isn't pretty, Sir. Moreover, I used to visit the docks occasionally with Papa, especially if a particularly large ship was due in. Mr Drummond, I love the sea and to watch a ship on the water is as though we have tamed the waves, however briefly. I know what perils lie in a shipyard and should I visit, I imagine you would be there to ensure my safety. I expect Stephen would likely accompany me and I trust with two of you guarding my every move, I will make it out alive." She twinkled at him encouragingly, little realising how beguiling she looked.

Dammit, the woman was a siren. All Hugh's objections seemed to evaporate; he found he could not make his mouth form the words to stop this folly. Helena knew the minute he capitulated and squeezed his arm in delight.

"Thank you, Mr Drummond," she said equably, but gave a little skip as they walked, an indication of her pleasure at his concurrence. They continued with their constitutional, Helena chattering about when she might visit the docks, Hugh still trying to come up with ways to prevent her, until suddenly he realised they had walked a long way from the carriage and were quite alone.

"I think we should turn back, my lady," he urged. "I have no desire to place a blemish on your reputation. Your mother would not be pleased."

Helena turned to face him and for a moment it was as though everything around them had stilled. Hugh was staring at her, the afternoon sunlight highlighting the golden flecks in his eyes and she could see her reflection within them. Neither spoke, and Helena held her breath as imperceptibly, Hugh bent his head towards hers. Helena's heart was thudding in her chest — surely, he must hear it.

"I think my mother trusts you, Mr Drummond," she whispered.

"And I am trying desperately not to abuse that trust," he muttered. They were so close now; Hugh's lips a hair's breadth from Helena's forehead. She raised her chin the better to hold his gaze, half of her willing him to kiss her, the other half anxious she not seem utterly brazen. Hugh's heart missed a beat as he looked into her beautiful eyes and, conscious he was breaking every rule in his own, not to mention Society's, book, was unable to stop himself from brushing her lips with his.

Chapter Seven

It wasn't even a kiss, but as their lips touched, Hugh felt a force stronger than anything he had ever experienced in his life surge through him. It was stronger than the ropes holding fast the billowing sails, stronger than the tumultuous gales whipping across the oceans and for a split second he wondered whether some form of mania had struck him. He lifted his head, noticing Helena's eyes had darkened to damson grey, and hoped she was as moved as he.

"I do beg your pardon, Lady Helena, that was frightfully presumptuous of me and although I ask your forgiveness, I admit I desired quite desperately to kiss you." His deep voice wrapped itself around her and Helen sucked in her breath, tried to speak, failed, and tried again.

"Please, Mr Drummond there is no need to apologise. If it didn't make me sound shameless, I would admit to being excessively pleased you did…kiss me I mean." Her voice was husky and she could not tear her eyes from his. A sudden gust of wind made the trees around them creak, the noise bringing both back to their senses and Helena stepped away, Hugh's proximity causing the most extraordinary thrill to ripple through her. "Errr…perhaps we…errm…should we return?" she questioned, biting her lip hesitantly. She had no idea how to behave at this point. What did they do now? What was she supposed to think? Did they pretend it never happened? She felt a pink blush stain her cheeks and could not think of anything sensible to say.

"Much as I would be delighted to spend the rest of the afternoon here, talking with you, I do believe we had better make our way back to Stephen and Lady Tabitha. However, should you permit me, I would very much like to take a walk with you again and very soon."

Helena was so relieved she replied incautiously, "Surely it will be enough that we meet when I visit your shipyards, Mr Drummond? I do not wish to monopolise your time," in deliberate referral to his comments the evening in the garden; a wicked imp within her wanting him to know his observation had stung. Neither did she want to appear over-eager. Helena's words hit their mark and she caught a glimmer of something in his eyes as his face fell. Despite a cacophony of warning bells going off in her head, she couldn't bear it and, after a moment, pressed her gloved hand on his arm. "That said, I always find a walk most convivial." She smiled gently, and lightly squeezed the arm she was touching.

Hugh, who felt his heart tighten, as she seemed to rebuff him, relaxed and smiled back, his rather solemn countenance lighting up, making Helena's own heart trip.

Mindful they should delay no longer, the two sauntered back towards the carriage and Helena, with all the poise of a young lady used to putting people at their ease, broke the rather awkward silence by asking Hugh about his family. Without giving too much away, Hugh described his somewhat chaotic family life, which consisted of his mother, brother and sister — Hugh being the oldest. His brother Nick, three years younger than Hugh, had shown no great interest in the family business, but was at least helping out until he found something more preferable.

Helena thought she detected sadness in Hugh's tones as he talked. It was obvious he truly loved being in shipping and it must be hard to accept his brother lacked any real desire to be involved.

"Give him time, Mr Drummond. I know he is four and twenty, but that is still quite young and sometimes the harvest looks richer in another man's field. If you push him one way, he will turn hard in the opposite direction, as surely as night follows day. Pretend it does not bother you; offer to assist in his search for employment that pleases him. If he thinks he has your support in whatever his endeavours are he might just begin to appreciate what you do. I presume that a shipping office is quite a diverse environment with a variety of tasks that require managing. Encourage him to try different aspects of your trade, you never know he might suddenly realise shipping is the most fascinating business in the world and if he doesn't you know he's tried. What about your sister, has she shown any interest in helping you?"

The thought of Jessica, his exuberant sister, working at Trentams was so foreign to Hugh he could not help but gawk at Helena, who sought to clarify,

"Not in the yard itself Hugh, please give me some credit, but what about your office? Women tend to be very good at organising, keeping things tidy and up to date, making sure papers and important records don't go missing or get filed incorrectly. It would be something I would enjoy very much as might your sister, just an occasional hour here and there. Not only would it increase her knowledge of your business, which can only be beneficial, but also would give her the chance to earn some coin of her own, while helping you to keep things ship-shape, as it were." Aiming for levity, as Hugh's brow was furrowed and she worried she had upset him. "Pay me no mind, I am speaking out of turn. I merely hoped to be of some help…" Helena trailed off, not wanting Hugh to think she was interfering. Her mother constantly told her she jumped in where angels feared to tread.

Hugh was quiet, mulling over her words, she was right. He had never asked Nick what he wanted; everyone simply assumed he would join Hugh in the business. Similarly, no one had thought Jessica might like to help at the shipyard in any capacity, yet as a woman from a merchant class family, it would be acceptable for her to undertake paid work. Hugh considered, absently whether there was any chance she might be interested.

By now they were back at the carriage. Stephen and Tabitha were still gossiping away, so engrossed in each other they didn't notice the return of their friends. Helena extricated her arm from Hugh's and allowed Peter to assist her into the coach. Hugh had barely spoken since she shared her thoughts, leaving Helena convinced she had irritated him and, even though she could not understand why, the notion left her bereft.

She was sitting quietly, waiting for Tabitha to make her farewells with Stephen, when Hugh raised his head, conscious Helena was no longer at his side. He saw her in the coach and she looked quite alone, despite her friend's presence. Helena's face was closed and, as he gazed at her, he wondered what emotion she was holding in check, realising he had not responded after she made her suggestions about his siblings. Her words came back to him and he knew he needed to assure her she had not upset him.

"Lady Helena, forgive my distraction. Your point is well made and it has shed new light on my current dilemma, for which I am most grateful." Holding her gaze, as the groom handed him Xerxes' reins. "Nor do I feel you were speaking out of turn. I find your conversation wholly refreshing."

Helena felt her cheeks flush at his words and, although still dubious as to whether he meant it or was simply being kind, could not prevent a bright smile from curling her lips. Then the moment was lost, for Stephen and Tabitha finally said goodbye to each other, the coach lurching forward as Peter clicked the horses. Helena twisted in her seat to watch Hugh, and was gratified to see him raise his hand, which she acknowledged in kind.

"So, Lady Helena, do tell me all about your constitutional." Tabitha's tones were lightly teasing, and Helena giggled at her friend's expression.

"'Twas naught but a brief stroll, Tabitha Daubery and don't you go reading anything into it." Helena exclaimed in mock chastisement. "You should be more concerned about your own good name. You and Stephen really must make things official."

"He's going to ask Papa this weekend," Tabitha's face took on a dreamy expression. "I am so happy I can scarcely breathe."

Helena caught her friend's fingers and squeezed them gently. "Oh Tabitha, I cannot tell you how delighted I am. Stephen is quite perfect for you and he loves you to distraction which is exactly as it should be." Tabitha laughed, agreeing that this was indeed the case, the merry sound like a peal of golden bells and, for the briefest moment, Helena envied her.

Ignoring it, she plunged into excited gossip with Tabitha about her future.

Meanwhile, as Hugh and Stephen watched the carriage roll away, Hugh recalled he had forgotten to ask what caused her such a severe headache the night of her collapse. It warmed him that this would prove a good excuse to see her again, if only to ask the question.

It was several days before Helena saw Hugh again. Busy at Sanctuary House, she didn't have time to contemplate what may or may not be unfolding between Mr Drummond and her. Sybil still hadn't felt brave enough to leave the refuge and Archie had not forgotten his threat. Seth Collins was also making a nuisance of himself, determined to force his wife, Lynette, to return home. Lynette, whom he put in hospital during his most recent bout of drunken rage, had decided she wanted no more to do with her husband, and although Seth had been informed, he refused to accept it.

The guards were on alert however, and the women who managed the refuge were determined not to let two men, belligerent though they were, get in the way of their efforts. Helena took her mother's advice, reducing her hours a little, but she loved her days at the refuge, helping those whose lives were beneath the attention of many in Society, and knew that every bit of support, however small, made all the difference.

As promised, Stephen approached Tabitha's father to ask for her hand in marriage and that fine gentleman, who was not at all surprised by the request, approved the match wholeheartedly. Their betrothal was announced since when, Tabitha had been walking around with her head in the clouds and Stephen wasn't much better. Despite the Season being over, Tabitha's mother declared a ball befitting the occasion was essential, intimating, less than delicately, that the couple should consider getting married sooner rather than later. If not, everyone around them would be heartily fed up of their scatterbrained behaviour before too many months were out. Tabitha and Stephen readily agreed.

Thus, it was the evening of Tabitha and Stephen's betrothal celebrations when Helena finally saw Hugh again. She found she missed his company and hoped he hadn't forgotten his promise to show her around the shipyard. She had mentioned the possibility to Stephen who, although felt moved to question her sanity, agreed to accompany her and of course, if Stephen was going, Tabitha was not going to be left out.

The evening was in full swing; the ballroom was full of light and colour and music and laughter. Tabitha looked exquisite and Stephen could not take his eyes from her. Helena had been twirled off her feet by her usual flock of admirers, but took care to permit them only one dance each. For some reason, they seemed like little boys, and all she could think about when she was being pirouetted around the floor was how it would feel to be in Hugh's arms.

The music faded and thanking her latest partner, Helena walked over to the quiet corner where she had left her glass of ratafia and her fan. The room was stuffy and she glanced through the large glass doors, contemplating a stroll in the fresh air. She leaned back in the chair and fanned herself idly, letting the happiness of the evening wash over her.

"Good evening, Lady Helena." A deep voice jolted her out of her reverie. She jumped out of her chair too quickly, nearly bumping into the person who had spoken. "Take care, my lady, 'tis only me."

Only him, dear lord there was no 'only' about him, Helena thought distractedly, as she strove to calm her fluttering heart.

"Good evening Sir," she replied, quite steadily she thought, smiling up at him, seeing his lips curve in reply. He bowed over her hand and just touched his lips to her fingers as she dipped a neat curtsy. "How goes the shipping trade?" Admiring, as she spoke, his dark grey trousers and matching tailcoat, over a snowy white shirt, claret coloured waistcoat, and matching cravat, which — as seemed his habit — was askew.

"'Tis cruising along quite nicely thank you," he winked and she chuckled appreciatively at his word play. "Mayhap we can arrange a convenient time for you to inspect my new schooner." He looked out over the throng as he spoke, his attitude seemingly nonchalant, but was on tenterhooks awaiting her answer.

"That would be wonderful, Mr Drummond and I am happy to fall in with whatever time suits you. You know best your schedule. It would be most impolite for me to arrive when you are in the middle of something vital that cannot be set aside in order for you to show me around." Although her voice was warm, Helena knew she sounded precise, but it was that or throw her arms around him and she didn't think the latter was altogether appropriate. Hugh glanced at her, reading more in her expression than she realised, which prompted his next question.

"Would you do me the honour of the next dance, Lady Helena?" She stared at him. Here it was she would get her wish, yet unexpectedly she was shy. Suddenly the room felt airless and over-crowded. She dragged at the neckline of her gown as though it constricted her.

"I...errr...very much...oh...too hot" Good gracious what was it about this man, her words fell out all in a jumble — again. With as much grace as she could muster, Helena fled through the glass doors onto the terrace, hoping the gloom would hide her hot cheeks. Perplexed, Hugh followed her, spying her leaning against the cool stone of the balcony, mostly in shadow.

"Lady Helena, are you quite well?" He heard a soft sigh and made his way towards her.

"Yes, I am perfectly well, just a complete ninny." Her tones chagrined. He took a step closer, but ensured a suitable distance remained between them, sensible to Society's penchant for gossip; thankful to see Nancy hovering near the doors Helena just rushed through. Casually, he positioned himself on the stone balustrade half-sitting, half-standing.

"Please tell me what bothers you," his tones so gently persuasive that before she could stop herself Helena was telling him she had been hoping he would be at the ball and would ask her to dance.

"So why are we out here and not on the dance floor?" Mystified.

"Because my body and my head refuse to act in co-ordination when you are near," she revealed. "My body wants to dance with you but my head loses all sense." She gulped realising she sounded rather brazen. Her shoulders slumped "Oh, I do beg your pardon Sir, that was not how I intended to make my point. Now do you see? This is what you do to me and I find myself at a loss to explain it." She spread her hands beseeching him to understand.

Hugh stared at her, raking his eyes over her willowy frame, taking in her silky black hair slightly tousled from all the dancing, and her silk gown, in the most incredible shade of grey, which shimmered violet when she moved, the colour almost exactly matching her eyes. His heart was hammering in his chest and he wished they were alone — so completely alone that should he sweep her into his arms and kiss her and dance with her forever, there would be no one to stop him.

He dragged his attention back to Helena, who was still looking at him in entreaty.

"I believe I appreciate your predicament, Lady Helena. I find myself afflicted by the same peculiarity. My tongue ties itself up in knots preventing me from making any sense at all."

Helena gaped at him, "Truly?" she queried in astonishment, as he nodded. "So, it's not just me? Oh, thank goodness for that, I was beginning to wonder whether I was losing my mind. Well in that case, you won't mind if my words are garbled and I trip over myself when you are around. I suppose it's a compliment really. No one else has ever made me behave this way." Guilelessly spoken, little realising how much she was giving away.

Hugh grinned as she said this, a warm glow coiling around him. He was the only person to affect her thus. Yes, it was indeed a compliment. As Helena relaxed, chattering artlessly about the party, and coming to visit the shipyard, Hugh found himself falling deeper and deeper under her spell and for the first time in his life, could muster no desire to fight it.

Chapter Eight

The rest of the evening passed pleasantly. Champagne flowed to toast the newly affianced couple and there was more dancing. Hugh did manage to entice Helena onto the dance floor more than once, causing a murmured conversation between Lady Winchester and Lady Bridgewater — Tabitha's mother — about Mr Drummond and his apparent admiration of Helena. Their discussion covered how handsome he was and whether he was appropriate husband material, culminating in trying to remember which shipping company he was a part of and, whether he owned it or was merely an employee. A conversation neither Helena nor Hugh would have been comfortable overhearing, as whatever they were feeling was still too new.

Helena was floating. Hugh was a fine dance partner and even though he spun her around as though she was nothing more than a feather, she felt safe in his arms. For the first time, she believed what Charlotte had told her — that all around her would grow quiet and she would know. But surely, she couldn't be falling for Hugh…could she?

Presuming she was suffering from a *tendre*, Helena purposely dampened down her emotions. She didn't want Hugh to think she was just another flighty chit, only interested in a rich husband. The little she knew of him suggested that he was an honourable man. One unlikely to pursue a woman unless he was serious, but despite their somewhat almost kiss and the words that followed, not to mention their earlier conversation, Helena did not know what Hugh thought of her. She had the impression that to him she was a bit like a fractious child, that he suffered her endless stream of questions more with long-suffering patience than of any real interest in why she was asking them, and was being friendly because of Stephen.

They barely knew each other and this, along with society's constraints, meant Helena would never consider discussing her bewilderment with the one person who probably could have set her straight immediately. So, they danced the evening away, chattered with their friends and enjoyed each other's company, parting with no definite arrangements to meet again at all.

As she was undressing for bed, Helena remembered Hugh had not set a date for her to visit the shipyard. Chewing on her lip, she wondered whether it would seem too bold if she sent him a note asking him to confirm when it might be convenient, or whether it would be better for Stephen to arrange it. She crawled into bed, succumbing to sleep almost immediately, tired after the evening's festivities. Her dreams revolved around talking with Hugh while he leaned on a balustrade, his cravat hung loose, his shirt was unbuttoned in the most rakish fashion, and his hand was holding hers.

At the same time, less than two miles away, Hugh recalled, with some frustration, not only had he omitted to propose a suitable day for Helena to take a tour around his new ship, he had also forgotten to ask what she did to cause her such painful headaches. To be fair, he had been utterly distracted by her for the entire evening and in his mind's eye he kept seeing her in his arms. Her sparkling eyes and her glossy hair, her infectious laughter, and her riveting conversation. As he was undressing, he decided to send a note around to her house in which he would list all available dates, and ask whether any might be favourable. Once in bed, he was quickly asleep, falling into dreams of Helena standing close by him on a terrace, her head tilted to one side while they talked about the sea and, oddly, he was holding her hand.

Two days later, while her mother and she were enjoying a rare breakfast together, Helena received a letter. Thanking Hudson who carried it through for her, Helena picked up the missive, turning it over and over trying to guess who sent it.

"Oh, do open it Helena?" urged Lady Winchester, as intrigued as her daughter. Helena chuckled at her mother's expression, breaking the seal, unfolding the heavy sheet, and scanning the words therein, impressed by the precise penmanship. She started to laugh, the contents apparently so funny that she was unable to tell her mother what they were. "Helena, goodness me girl, it cannot be that comical, do curb your silliness." Her mother watched in astonishment as Helena gurgled with mirth. Whatever prompted such jocularity was beyond her.

"Oh, oh, I'm so sorry Mama, this is from Hu...Mr Drummond and I've just sent him the same...they must have crossed, well I never..." By now, Lady Winchester had no idea what her daughter was gabbling about and had to wait until Helena got herself under control to discover the reason. "Tis just that yesterday, I sent Mr Drummond a note asking which dates might be acceptable for me to visit the shipyard..." seeing her mother's face she hastened to add, "...with Stephen and Tabitha, don't fret Mama...and here he is sending me a note with a list of possible dates. It's as though we read each other's minds. Oh, how amusing." Helena took a deep breath and regained her composure, recognising her mother was losing patience with her.

"What on earth do you want to go and see a smelly shipyard for, Helena? Honestly my girl, you never cease to amaze me with your desire to spend time in the most unladylike of environments."

"You know how I love the sea Mama, and to watch those wonderful ships skim over the waves. It reminds me of Papa."

Augusta Trevallier smiled fondly at her daughter. Helena was so like her father and her comments brought his sudden death into sharp focus. Augusta had loved her husband — Maximilian Trevallier — and still felt his loss keenly. His determination not only to educate his children about the diverse world beyond their privileged doorstep, but also to encourage them to ensure they did everything in their power to provide for and protect any who were disadvantaged, had resulted in three intelligent, considerate, and empathetic adults.

It was Helena, however, on her own for much of her day — after Giles had gone off, first to university then to war, and while Charlotte was being fêted during in her first season — who had begged her father to take her with him, either to witness the launch of a ship or, more often than not, just to watch the boats sail up and down the river. She would also accompany him when he went to the hospitals to spend time with injured soldiers or visited the poorhouses to check the inmates were properly cared for. Although she was young, and many would have considered her father foolish for allowing her to attend such places, Helena thrived on it.

She came to understand how hard most people had to work to earn enough coin just to put food on the table; began to grasp the issue of poverty, and gained a deep respect for the injured military men as well as the doctors who treated them. Her father took care that Helena's safety was not compromised, nor did he allow her to be exposed to anything detrimental and never left her alone in a situation where she might be at risk in any way, but through those experiences they developed an unshakeable bond. Maximilian delighted in being able to share some of what was important to him with one of his children. Thus, Helena was probably more sorely affected by his death than her older siblings who had not spent anything like the same amount of time with him.

Despite seemingly enthralled by the glitter and extravagance of the multitude of balls and galas and the never-ending picnics and garden parties, Helena preferred quiet spaces, like the great park on their country estate, or the tranquillity of a walk around a lake, or reading in the cool of a library. That is not to say she didn't enjoy beautiful clothes and new shoes, she did, but more for their own sake than as a device to ensnare a husband. Augusta worried her youngest child cared so little for the social gatherings of the elite or the state of marriage that she would get left behind, and suddenly all the suitable men would be taken.

The attentions by a certain Mr Drummond, surprised Augusta therefore, more so because Helena appeared to have more than a cursory interest in the successful shipping magnate. The dowager had written to Giles hoping to ascertain further information about the gentleman — just in case. Dragging her concentration back to Helena, who was chattering excitedly about going to the docks, Augusta contrived to look fascinated by her daughter's activities, asking pertinent questions here and there regarding said visit.

A couple of hours later, after convincing her mother she would be in no danger at the ship yard — and having replied to Hugh — Helena and Nancy were on their way to Sanctuary House. Helena hadn't been for a few days, being called upon to help Tabitha with her wedding preparations and was looking forward to getting back into her routine. The refuge was a hive of activity when they arrived. Classes were underway, several women were preparing the meals for the day and a gaggle of children were playing in the small garden at one side of the building. Helena flung herself into the business of the day with her usual enthusiasm and time sped by. Sybil was still there, but her injuries were healing nicely and she didn't look quite as thin. While they were having lunch, Helena took the opportunity to ask how she was feeling.

"Much better Miss, thank you kindly. I'll 'atta go back t'Archie soon mind, he needs me to keep 'im sorted." The woman sighed, hesitated, and then seemed of a mind to share her misgivings with Helena. "'Tis not that I don't care abaht 'im me lady, I do, we've known each other since we was kids. 'Tis just while I've been here, it's been such relief not to be constantly worried that 'e'll get into a brawl or worse 'n' then come 'ome and take his frustrations out on me. I want to give 'im, to give us, a better life, but how can I if 'e keeps gettin' drunk?"

Helena had no answers for this. It was a complaint echoed by so many families. She ruminated over whether Hugh might have any openings in his yard. Archie was a behemoth of a man; he might be useful on the docks, especially as Stephen had mentioned something about strange incidents. It could be the making of Sybil's husband. Helena tapped her lip as she pondered this, asking Sybil what her husband's occupation was currently.

"He's a coal whipper Miss, down on the river."

Helena was pleased at this. Archie would be familiar with wharves, docks and shipyards and the inherent hazards associated therewith. She made a mental note to ask Hugh whether he thought Archie might be worth trialling. Plus, he was so huge that anybody considering any form of intimidation or had a mind to cause affray would think twice.

"Sybil, I know of someone who owns a shipyard. I cannot promise anything, but should I ask whether he has a place for Archie, do you think your husband might be persuaded to take a different job?"

Sybil gaped at Helena. "You would do that for me Miss?"

Helena nodded slowly, hoping she wasn't making a grave error. "I think a different working environment, and maybe a job with a little more responsibility might make Archie think twice about risking it all for a few tankards of beer. Please do not mention it to your husband. I will need to make enquiries first, but I will be meeting with the owner of the shipyard in a day or so, after which I will know more." She grasped Sybil's hand as she talked, and Sybil squeezed Helena's slim fingers in gratitude.

"Thank you so much m'lady. I reckon if he's away from that crowd o' scoundrels he might just go back to 'ow 'e used to be. He were such a gent when we was courtin' an' even after we was wed, but lately he's become so bad-tempered." Sybil shook her head, mystified by her husband's change in character.

Helena was no longer surprised at such confidences. Many of the women who came to the refuge had the same lament. Husbands who had lost all self-esteem in the drudgery of everyday life, seemingly selling their souls for what little coin they could get, resentment getting the better of them and their wives, who least deserved such treatment, bore the brunt.

"Leave it with me Sybil, and I will do my best." Helena promised patting Sybil's hand as they carried their platters over to the kitchen and went off to whatever afternoon classes they were involved in. While she was apparently engrossed in teaching a group of women the basics of writing, she was also contemplating whether she could arrange to meet Hugh the next day. The sooner Archie's problem was fixed the better it would be for everybody.

Calling one of the young lads they used as messengers, Helena gave him a note and a coin and asked him to take it as fast as possible to Trentams Shipyard. To be handed to Mr

Hugh Drummond and no one else. The lad, Timmy, scuttled off, his short legs pumping as he ran down the street, proud to be on an errand for her Ladyship. Helen chuckled as she watched him go, turning her attention back to the job at hand.

Two hours later, just as Helena was about to leave, Timmy dashed into the classroom, panting with his exertions, and waving a letter about.

"Miss, miss, the gent gave me this for you." Helena thanked him and tried to press another coin in his grubby hand, but he shook his head. "Nah, Miss, 'im at yard gave me a tip. You keep your'n." He grinned cheekily and bounced off to see whether he could scrounge anything from the kitchens. Helena grinned at his boyish irreverence and sat down to read the note.

Dear Lady Helena,

I would be pleased to discuss your suggestion and will be here at the office tomorrow from ten, if that would be convenient. Stephen is with me at the moment and confirms, should this prove agreeable, he will gladly accompany you. There is no need to reply to this note. If you are able to come, I will see you on the morrow, if not, we will simply arrange a more suitable time.

Warm regards,

Mr Hugh Drummond

Helena read it three times and for no reason she could think of, ran her fingers over the paper, tracing the words. As with the previous missive, his writing caught her eye; Hugh's script was bold and clear, the hand of a decisive person. Unbidden an image of Hugh's hands popped into her head sending heat spiralling through her. Pushing it aside as flummery Helena applied herself to tidying up the classroom, called for Nancy and the two women were soon trundling through the streets of London back to Portman Square.

Chapter Nine

Once home, Helena sent a note to Ashbourne House, advising Stephen she was free to attend the shipyard the next morning, and she would await his attendance any time from nine. Stephen responded confirming their arrangements adding that Tabitha had expressed an interest in joining them. Helena grinned at Stephen's turn of phrase knowing exactly how her friend would have reacted to Stephen's suggestion that she might like to accompany them.

She apprised her mother of her intentions, enjoyed a relaxed evening at home and, after asking to be woken at seven, was in bed quite early. When Stephen arrived just after nine the next morning, Helena felt rather apprehensive. Whilst she knew what she was about to ask of Hugh came from a desire to save Sybil from a lifetime of beatings, she also knew her request might have repercussions. Should Hugh be prepared to take on Archie, and Archie not grasp the import of the gesture, continuing with his self-destructive behaviour, any future requests may not be treated so favourably. Helena did not want one man's belligerence to affect, adversely, Sanctuary House and its generous benefactors.

Out of the blue, Helena remembered Hugh still had no idea she worked there, and speculated as to whether she could explain why she wanted to help Archie without giving herself away. Had anyone asked, Helena would have struggled to explain why she wasn't ready to disclose this part of her life. Perhaps it was because she didn't want Hugh to think her a do-gooder, another superficial young lady of the *ton* playing on the fringes without any real understanding of the plight of those who needed help.

Stephen helped Helena into the coach, where Tabitha was waiting, the two women greeting each other warmly.

"Stephen, does Mr Drummond know I work at Sanctuary House?" Helena broached the question uppermost in her mind, once they had set off.

Stephen shook his head. "He asked me the night you fainted, but I said it was not up to me to enlighten him. I think you should tell him Helena, he is an honourable man, and discreet."

Helena considered this, "I don't think I'm ready to share this part of me, Stephen. Whilst I agree Hu…Mr Drummond is as you say, I like that this part of me is private, that none of our extended circle is aware of what I do, of what both Tabitha and I do."

Tabitha shook her head. "'Tis long since I helped, Helena. I doubt you can say I do anything."

Helena refuted this, "Tabitha, we have both done what we could and although you are unable to visit the refuge as often, you still procure donations of every kind, which is just as, if not more, important."

Tabitha acknowledged her friend's words with such a pretty blush, Stephen pulled her into quick hug, dropping a kiss on her cheek, causing Helena to raise an eyebrow and comment that it was a good job their wedding was just over a month hence. The three friends laughed and started to chatter about weddings and shipyards and soon the coach rolled to a halt in front of a pair of huge gates emblazoned with the name, Trentams. They had arrived.

The heavy gates swung open ponderously and the coach rumbled though, drawing up outside an austere looking brick building, the many windows of which had the shipyard's name etched into the glass. As the coach pulled up at the entrance, Stephen hopped out and assisted the two women down. Helena smoothed her skirts, her hands shaking a little, but whether from nerves or anticipation she couldn't tell. Pausing for a moment to steady herself, she sniffed the air; it was a strange mix of wood, tar, smoke, and river. As she breathed it in, Helena was surprised to discover it wasn't as malodorous as she expected. From beyond the high wall surrounding this part of the yard, wafted the sounds of the docks. Shouts of men and clanking of equipment, the sounds of things being created, constructed, or repaired. The fact that Helena couldn't see what was happening made it all the more exciting.

While she was standing, Hugh appeared at the door to the building. He welcomed them, ushering them upstairs into a spacious and airy office, its large windows spilling light throughout the room. An enormous desk sat under one window, papers spread across it. Several sets of drawers and tall cupboards were placed at regular intervals around the edge of the room, navigational charts and maps decorated the walls. In the middle a few chairs were set around a table on which stood a pot of coffee, four cups and plate of cakes.

"Thank you so much for agreeing to meet with me, Mr Drummond." Helena said as Hugh invited them to sit. "I realise my request may seem" — she wavered, searching for the politest way of phrasing it — "unconventional, but I fear if I do not try to help, the situation may become untenable."

Hugh smiled gently. "Please, let us enjoy our coffee first, and then we can get down to business. After which, if you have a little time perhaps you would like that tour of my yard?" Helena's face lit up at the prospect, and this effectively distracted all four of them as they sipped the aromatic brew and munched on the tasty cakes. Soon enough, however, the reason for Helena's visit could be put off no longer, and she begged Hugh's indulgence while she outlined the problem.

She spoke tentatively at first, unsure of Hugh's reaction but she quickly warmed to her subject, her desire to help Archie clear in her tones. Helena was careful not to mention Sanctuary House despite being aware her reticence mystified Stephen. She would tell Hugh when she deemed it pertinent and not before. Without saying as much, Helena made it sound as though Archie was related to one of the Winchester household staff, and Hugh listened carefully, asking questions, trying to determine whether Archie would be a worthy employee.

"I must be honest, Mr Drummond. Archie, I think possibly because often he feels inadequate, has a tendency to be rather aggressive and when drunk, has used his wife as a punching bag. He also threatened m…" she caught herself just in time, "…our staff for protecting Sybil while she healed. I suspect however, underneath his belligerence he wants life to go back to the way it was, and I think he wants to feel worthy. I believe him to be more intelligent than he will admit, and his attitude could be owing to a lack of any real mental challenge. I also think he would prove an adequate guard here at Trentams, his size alone would be enough to deter any would-be trouble-makers."

As Helena continued, Hugh glanced at Stephen questions in his eyes. His friend shrugged his shoulders and, unwilling to interrupt Helena, adjusted his expression to convey a tacit message back.

"Please trust me when I say I know it is a huge gamble, and if it were not that I judged it vital, not only for Archie but also for Sybil, I would not dream of discussing this with you. I wholly understand should you decide it is too big a risk, but I had to try..." Helena faltered, her words running out and she sat twiddling her fingers together, fearing not only had she overstated her case, but also she had made Archie sound like a dangerous lunatic. The room fell silent; nobody spoke for what seemed an age. Helena was starting to think she had ruined Archie's chance, when finally, Hugh broke the quiet.

"I am prepared to meet with this Archie and take it from there." Helena started to respond, but Hugh raised his hand. "Do not thank me yet. I make no promises and should our meeting prove satisfactory, initially I will only employ him on a trial basis. I will need to see how he interacts with my other employees, and that when he comes to work he is sober. I cannot have drunks working in this yard it is too dangerous."

Helena forced herself to remain calm. "Thank you, Mr Drummond, I am humbled by your compassion. I will ensure that Archie recognises his responsibility to you." Her words were formal in the extreme, but as she was speaking, Helena lifted her head, locked eyes with Hugh and smiled. Hugh felt his heart hiccup and he simply stared at her, momentarily unable to move. He wrenched his gaze away and offered them more coffee, trying to control his wayward thoughts. This woman, how did she do it? Every time they met she insinuated herself deeper and deeper into his heart.

After a second cup of what was most delicious coffee, Hugh suggested a tour of the yard and to view his new schooner. It was a lovely day, a little blustery, but warm. August was usually much hotter than this, but those who lived in the city were thankful the weather gods had taken pity on them, the last several days, warm but not stifling. Also, here on the river's edge the breeze tended to keep the worst of the heat at bay. His three guests followed Hugh as he led them through the office and out into the receiving yard. Stephen, knowing how many things round dockyards might cause a lady to trip, immediately offered Tabitha his arm. Hugh followed suit with Helena and when she hesitated, he winked,

"This way I can prevent you from falling headlong into the river," he said, waiting for the reaction he expected would be forthcoming. Mildly affronted, Helena was about to give Hugh a piece of her mind, when she noticed the twinkle in his eyes. She giggled instead, feeling the tension roll out of her as she hooked her arm though his.

"Thank you, Sir," was all she said, but he was pleased to feel a slight increase in pressure from her fingers as they curled around his sleeve.

Hugh took them through another towering gate into the main shipyard and up a set of steps to a wide, yet surprisingly sturdy, gantry that circled three sides of the enormous dock. There were people everywhere and the noise, muted when they were sitting in the office, was much louder, making it difficult to hear what Hugh was saying, and they had to lean close to catch his words.

"This is my new vessel," he said proudly, pointing to a ship that at first glance looked far too narrow to be suitable for transporting goods, especially when compared with the lumbering East Indiaman, currently undergoing repair, and moored alongside. "It's a topsail schooner and although unable to carry anything like the cargo of the Indiamen, they are a much faster ship, and I think will prove efficient for the trade of lighter goods, those of high value or perishable consignments between here and the east."

Hugh went on to describe the design, which he said had been honed in the American port of Baltimore. Explaining that its hull was sharper and v-shaped and the stern was strongly raked, which apparently produced a streamlined ship that could skim along the waves and sail into shallower waters than could the Indiamen. Moreover, these features along with the two masts — whose sails worked together in a complementary fashion — created a ship that garnered airflow to an optimum degree allowing it to sail closer to the wind. There was talk of foremasts and mainmasts, bowsprits, sails and something about it being gaffe rigged.

By now this was all far too technical for the ladies, but Hugh was so enthusiastic, neither had the heart to tell him they were totally baffled. Still listening, Helena turned to look out over the river and disregarding convention, removed her bonnet — she hated them anyway — lifting her face to the wind, enjoying the draft across her face. Hugh's breath caught in his throat, she was so beautiful. The breeze ruffled her clothes and began to unravel her black silky hair from its neat bun. Her proud bearing reminded him of the delicately carved ship's figureheads — Neptune's wooden angels, and right now a more fitting description he could not imagine, although Helena was anything but wooden.

Thankfully, Stephen was asking plenty of questions, forcing Hugh's attention back to the task at hand. Helena interjected here and there, with queries about how many decks there would be and how the cabins would slot into the framework and where everything was stored and so forth, delighting Hugh with her interest. He pointed out as much as he was able; bearing in mind the ship was only a third complete.

"In a few weeks, we will be able to go inside, but as you can see the decks have not been installed and it is too dangerous, if anyone were to fall, they would likely be killed." From where they stood, Helena peered down into the bowels of the ship, spotting all manner of curious machinery worked by men who appeared no bigger than mice. When she commented on this Stephen suggested that if she thought they seemed small, she should try looking through the hull of an Indiaman with no decks, for men would appear as ants.

The wind had picked up and feeling suddenly vulnerable so high above everything, Helena realised what it must be like for those sailors who manned the rigging, shuddering at the thought of them putting a foot wrong. Hugh, alert to even the subtlest shift in Helena's demeanour, noticed and tactfully suggested they return to the office. His two siblings had intimated they might put in an appearance today, and he hoped to introduce them to his friends. Grateful for his perception, Helena agreed and, gathering up Tabitha and Stephen the four made their way back to the relative peace of the main building.

Chapter Ten

As they entered, two people so like Hugh they had to be related, placed their cups on the table and stood to receive the newcomers.

"Jess, Nick, I'd like to present Lady Helena Trevallier and Lady Tabitha Daubery, Stephen you already know. Lady Helena and Lady Tabitha, my sister Jessica and my brother Nicholas." There was a flurry of curtseys, bows and handshakes, while Hugh stuck his head through a different door, asking whoever was there to bring more coffee. Then everyone found a seat, and after a moment of awkward silence, all started talking at once. The women began a cheerful conversation about their lives and the men talked about ships and trade and the economy of England. Helena kept one ear on this discussion, as she continued to be possessed by the most absurd desire to amass every morsel of information she could about Hugh.

Another hour or so sped by, during which they were provided with a tasty luncheon until Helena, with an eye to the time, guessed they were likely keeping Hugh from important business.

"While I believe I would enjoy sitting here for the rest of the day listening to talk of ships and trade, I fear we are preventing Mr Drummond from attending to his work. Might I suggest we take our leave and continue this fascinating conversation another day?" She smiled as she spoke, softening her deferential tone, her eyes sweeping around the group and coming to rest on Hugh's face, holding his eyes for slightly longer than she should. Despite not wanting to let her — them — go, Hugh did have a lot to do, and inclined his head in acknowledgement of her thoughtfulness. Helena, Stephen, and Tabitha stood, saying how lovely it had been to meet Jessica and Nick and hoped to see each other again soon.

Just as they were about to step outside, Jessica asked whether Helena would be kind enough to spare a moment for a private word. Bemused, Helena nodded, following her to a small anteroom adjacent to the office.

"I do beg your pardon my lady, but Hugh mentioned it was you who suggested I might be interested in working here." Jessica regarded Helena, her expression giving nothing away, and Helena suddenly felt anxious.

"Please Miss Drummond, I did not intend to interfere. Only Hugh was talking about the business, concerned your brother might not be as interested in it as he and I simply wondered whether you might like to help out now and again. I did not expect him to tell you what I said." Helena grasped Jessica's hands in dismay, her voice reflecting her disquiet.

"No, no my lady, I wanted to thank you. I have been desperate to get my hands on Hugh's desk since first he showed me around. He is hopeless at keeping things in order and I didn't know how to tell him that if he wasn't careful, he would find crucial documents mislaid, or worse, lost altogether." The two women stared at each other, then without warning both burst out laughing, their merriment ringing along the quiet hallways.

"Oh my, I am so relieved," giggled Helena. "My mother is constantly telling me to mind my own business yet Hugh, Mr Drummond, sounded so discouraged, I found myself offering an opinion on affairs I know little about. Although, if as I suspect, you are a fastidious person, I imagined you would willingly help out to keep your brother's domain organised — if only to keep his cravat straight!"

"Hahaha, so you've noticed too. I do not understand what is so hard about keeping the dratted thing tidy, but no matter how neatly he ties it, within minutes it's awry." Jessica chortled. "Thank you, my lady, I appreciate you persuading my brother to see I may be of use to him."

"It was my pleasure and do call me Helena. I think we are going to be great friends, and my lady sounds far too impersonal." They strolled out of the room still chuckling, coming to an abrupt halt as they realised the rest of the group were staring at them askance. Hugh raised an eyebrow at his sister, who merely shook her head commenting that she might, if she was feeling benevolent, tell him later. Helena grinned as she thanked Hugh for being so generous with his time, during what was obviously a busy period.

"I'll be speaking to Archie this afternoon; might I bring him to meet you tomorrow? He usually turns up…errr…finishes around four, if that is not too late."

Hugh nodded absently; distracted by Helena's hair, released from its confines by the breeze, was slowly unwinding itself from the intricate style into which it had been twisted. A long black curl fell against her porcelain skin and it was all he could do not to tuck it behind her ear. Jessica observed her brother with interest, determining a few probing questions might be necessary once his guests departed.

Shortly thereafter the three visitors rattled away in their coach, turning to wave as they disappeared through the gate, just as Hugh realised he had, once again, forgotten to ask Helena about her headaches. Dash it all! Frustrated, he kicked the bottom step before trudging back up into his office where several documents awaited his perusal. Nick had gone off to check something, and Jessica was already occupied, working her way through a pile of papers separating those requiring a reply from those to be filed away or destroyed. She glanced up as he came in.

"So, that's Lady Helena Trevallier?" she murmured quietly, scrutinising her brother's face as she spoke. Hugh ran his fingers through his hair and loosened his cravat, the gesture making Jessica grin in recollection of her conversation with Helena.

"Yes, what of it?" Sitting down and pulling the papers towards him.

"Nothing, but I would say she is exceedingly suitable."

Hugh looked at his sister warily. What was she up to now? "Exceedingly suitable for what, or should I not ask?"

"Oh, I think you know and I have no intention of spelling it out for you. Just don't go all…well…Hugh on her."

"Go 'all Hugh' on her! What on earth are you talking about?"

"You know exactly what I'm talking about. Even from so brief a meeting, I believe her to be bright, funny, highly intelligent and — inexplicably, for a lady of her standing — interested in ships, not to mention quite stunningly beautiful. She is precisely the sort of woman who could make you very happy and, if I'm not mistaken, the pair of you are already more than half way in love with each other. Just don't close down and push her away when it's too late."

Hugh gaped at Jessica, his mouth opening and closing but no words were forthcoming. His sister was too perceptive for her own good.

"Keep out of my business," he grumbled, turning to his papers, and was soon absorbed in his work, oblivious to Jessica's meditative looks.

Meanwhile, Helena requested she be dropped off at Sanctuary House, so she could speak with Archie. Every day like clockwork as soon as his working day was over he came, trying to wheedle his way back into Sybil's good books. Stephen was amenable but added that they would come in with her and wait, the alternative being too complicated.

Once at the refuge, Helena hunted out Sybil and apprised her of what transpired at the shipyard. Sybil, excited for this chance, begged to be there when Helena told Archie. Helena thought her presence might smooth over any objection on Archie's part. He could easily assume the offer was charity, especially since Sybil might well be persuaded to return home, should her husband be open to a new challenge. They continued to chatter about it until Archie's less than dulcet tones were heard in the passage.

Opening the door of the classroom in which she and Sybil were sitting, Helena invited Archie to join them. Archie glowered at Helena, whom he considered a meddlesome busybody.

"Archie, I know you are angry with me, but please, might I have a moment of your time?" Taken aback, Archie squinted at Helena suspiciously, a lady never needed to make such a request. He nodded slowly, dropping onto the seat next to his wife. "Thank you. I have something I wish to discuss with you, then I will leave you to talk it over with your wife." Helena took a deep breath and as tactfully as possible told Archie about the job at Trentams, skirting over how she had contrived to arrange it and concentrating on how this could be good for him. Better hours, better conditions, and more pay. Not having to worry about whether there would be any work on a given day; it would be stable, regular employment.

"If you are interested, you would be on a one month trial. Should Mr Drummond consider you suitable, you will become a permanent employee. However, and this is important, should you ever arrive at work drunk you will be let go immediately and without references. Do you understand?" Archie was staring at Helena as though she had just brought him manna from heaven. He shook his head and asked her to repeat it, certain he was hearing things.

Helena explained it all again thoroughly, sitting back when she finished giving him time to digest everything. "Now, I must go as my carriage awaits, so I will let you two talk it over. If you decide to take on this role, I will escort you to the shipyard, at this time tomorrow afternoon. Please ensure you are appropriately dressed. Thank you for listening to me Archie." Helena pressed the man's arm as she spoke and smiled at Sybil, leaving them to debate how this might impact the rest of their lives.

Returning to the main entrance, Helena noticed Stephen and Tabitha were talking with Lady Sophia Beaumont, the patroness of Sanctuary House. Dropping a deep curtsy, Helena greeted her friend, who drew her into a warm embrace before filling Helena in on the latest news about the Elliott family. Apparently, Theo, Sophia's brother in law — who lived near the Winchester's country estate — was spending more than a little time with a lady called Grace Fitzgerald. Sophia had an inkling there was a whisper of scandal attached to the woman but it wouldn't come to her. She trusted Theo's judgement, however and was hoping that they might hear wedding bells soon.

"Benedict is in a bit of a flap about it all, but I'm sure he'll get over it," she said ruefully. Her irascible husband was overly critical of his brother's courtship, and Sophia feared that there might be one or two heated arguments between the brothers before Benedict accepted Theo had a right to choose his own wife. "Oh, and Helena, I will be going to the country within the next week or so. I prefer to be there for my confinement rather than here in the city." Helena nodded her agreement.

"Sanctuary House is running quite smoothly at the moment, we will miss you, but given the chance, I would always choose the countryside over the city." The two ladies shared a look of complete understanding, and Sophia took her leave. Stephen offered her his arm, the two taking care down the steps to the waiting Beaumont carriage.

"Ugh, I can never work out what it is about the country that you enjoy so." Tabitha shuddered. "It's full of buzzing insects and smelly animals and it's too quiet."

"Which is exactly why I prefer it, Tabitha." Helena grinned at her friend's mystified expression. Stephen, hearing this as he bounded back up to the entrance, added he too found the open spaces of rural areas quite attractive and was looking forward to taking Tabitha down to his grandmother's house on the Cornish coast, where he thought they might enjoy a long holiday. Tabitha's jaw dropped when she heard this, and was about to upbraid her betrothed when she noticed his face was the picture of innocence.

"Stephen!" she expostulated. "You wouldn't?" Stephen took Tabitha's hand and lifted it to his lips.

"I would never do anything that might make you unhappy, my darling," he said, "but sometimes 'tis pleasant to be away from the city, away from the heat and the noise and the traffic. My grandmother's home is no dark cottage and she has plenty of staff, so we would not be fending for ourselves. Think of it, to be answerable only to us, with no one else demanding our time. Mayhap you could consider it?" Tabitha rolled this around in her head, the thought of having Stephen all to herself, tantalising. They started to become absorbed in each other, causing Helena to cough, bringing them back to earth.

"So sorry Helena, Stephen seems able to distract me at the most unexpected moments." Tabitha apologised.

"It is of no matter," Helena chuckled, "however, I think we should go. It has been a long day and I expect you two have call on your time this evening."

"Oh, we have a dinner party Stephen," Tabitha cried and Stephen groaned. He loved Tabitha but since their betrothal they had not enjoyed a single evening at home; friends and acquaintances inviting them to a multitude of festivities. It was becoming rather exhausting.

"Must we?" he queried.

Tabitha nodded, "I'm afraid we must, my love but after this we have nothing organised for three nights. Mayhap we should spend a little time together. I'm sure there are things we ought to be planning." She grinned artfully, her eyes telling Stephen exactly what might or, and more likely, might not be achieved regarding supposed plans. His response — a smile that needed no words. By now the three were back in the carriage and trundling towards the fashionable districts of London. They chatted desultorily and were soon in front of the Trevallier residence. Arranging to see each other in a few days, Helena said her goodbyes to her two friends and skipped up the steps into her home.

Chapter Eleven

The next afternoon, Havers came as requested, driving Helena and Nancy to Sanctuary House. Nancy was almost as excited as her mistress, hoping this might be a turning point for Sybil and Archie. They arrived an hour or so after luncheon, well before Archie was expected but Helena sought out Sybil who was quick to confirm Archie and she had decided this opportunity was too good to miss, and he would be ready to attend Trentams as arranged.

On cue, Archie appeared and, Helena was pleased to note, dressed in what was likely his Sunday best. He had managed a quick wash after finishing his shift and his hair was tidy. Helena swallowed a grin at his obvious discomfiture, simply commenting that he looked quite dashing and she could see why Sybil had married him. Archie smiled sheepishly, and Helena led the way to the coach, Archie and Sybil following behind. Nancy opted to remain at Sanctuary House with her friend.

The journey to Trentams did not take long and Helena could see Archie was becoming nervous. Needing to calm him, she leaned over and rested her hand lightly on his knee.

"Archie, there is nothing to fear. Mr Drummond has worked in the yard for many years. He does not expect you to behave like one of the gentry. Just be yourself, well yourself only better." She winked, diffusing the tension and Archie chuckled, relaxing suddenly.

"If I did not think you capable, I would not have suggested it. Remember, this is for you and Sybil," she encouraged him as the coach rolled through the gates. When they came to a halt, Archie jumped down and assisted first Helena then Sybil from the carriage. Helena was most impressed, his actions compounding her opinion that Archie wasn't just brawn.

Hugh greeted them at the main door and, pretending not to notice Helena's drab attire as she introduced everyone, escorted them upstairs to his office, ushering the women inside advising them he would interview Archie in the adjoining room. Jessica happened to be there and, once Helena had repeated her introductions, rang for refreshments. By the time Helena had divested herself of her bonnet and shawl, an aide appeared bearing a tray on which stood three glasses of cool lemonade and a plate of biscuits. While they waited, Jessica and Helena chatted comfortably, including Sybil without seeming to, drawing her out. Helena was concerned Sybil might talk about the refuge, but she didn't mention it, concentrating instead on Archie and the shipyard. Sybil asked Jessica one or two rather shrewd questions about Trentams; apparently needing be certain Archie wasn't going to be dragged into illegal activities.

"Trentams aren't smugglers, Sybil," Helena chided gently, "you need to trust me." Sybil blushed and said it wasn't only smugglers, but press gangs used to prowl the streets, grabbing any male who looked able. "Yes, but that was when we were at war, 'tis no longer necessary and I believe the practice has been abolished. Moreover, Trentams employs all its workers, pays them a good wage and ensures their protection. I expect they, like all shipyards, undergo regular checks by His Majesty's inspectors, so you need not fret." Helena's matter-of-fact statement settled Sybil and by way of distraction, Jessica turned the conversation to the frivolous topic of which local market sold the best variety of ribbons.

It was well over an hour later when Hugh brought Archie back into the main office. Archie looked rather overwhelmed and Helena experienced a twinge of unease, but Hugh looked straight at her, inclining his head ever so slightly, and she breathed easy. It had gone well enough that Archie had been offered a position.

"Thank you for coming Archie, I will see you back here on Monday at eight." Turning to Sybil, he bestowed on her his most charming smile, "Mrs Miller, thank you for accompanying your husband. If you have any questions about his work or my company, please do not hesitate to ask." Sybil almost swooned at such gentlemanly behaviour, bobbing a neat curtsy, and expressing her heartfelt appreciation. "Lady Helena, might I have a moment?" Helena excused herself and followed Hugh into the room where she and Jessica had spoken the previous day.

Without preamble Hugh said, "Lady Helena, thank you for suggesting Archie. While I agree he may suffer from an inability to…err…curb his temper, I also agree it stems from a lack of self-esteem. Hopefully the work he will be expected to undertake here will build that up. Assuredly, his size will prove useful should the need arise." He offered no further clarification, but Helena surmised he was referring to the unexplained accidents within the yard.

"Thank you, Hu…Mr Drummond, I am in your debt." Helena beamed at him, her eyes sparkling in the late afternoon sunlight filtering through the window, and Hugh honestly wondered whether it was possible to drown in someone's gaze.

"If you would agree to another walk in the park, there is no debt."

"Why, Mr Drummond, you do make the most delightful suggestions. When?"

Hugh ran his mind's eye over his appointment book, "Does tomorrow afternoon make me sound too eager?"

"Of course it does, but I accept and am looking forward to it already."

"As am I," he affirmed. Then took her hand, lifting it to his lips and, as he had the afternoon he called on her, kissed her palm. Helena drew a sharp breath riveted by his expression and as his eyes bore into hers, that frisson, the one she felt every time they touched, spun like ringlets through her body.

"Helena…" his mellifluous tones enveloped the word, making her name sound like an endearment. She felt herself lean towards him and for the life of her could not pull away.

"M-Mr Drummond?" she stuttered. Held captive by her gaze, Hugh was battling for control, feeling it slipping from his grasp.

"Please call me Hugh," it was barely a sigh and giving up the fight, he kissed her. Helena — who had received the odd peck on the cheek from her would-be suitors and, of course, the afternoon when Hugh had nearly…almost…not quite, kissed her — was still an innocent with no idea what to do. She stood stock still, trying to master the deluge of sensations flowing through her, which threatened to reduce her to a quivering wreck. Hugh paused and stared down at her, reading the bewilderment in her face. "Forgive me Helena, that was unconscionable, but you bewitch me."

Helena took one step backwards and, pressing two fingers on her lips — lips that were tingling, tilted her head so she could see him properly.

"Do that again," she demanded.

Hugh's jaw dropped, "Huh?"

"Please," she whispered, closing the gap between them, "do that again."

He groaned and recaptured her lips with his. Ignoring all reasonable arguments to the contrary, she simply followed his lead and moved her mouth under his. Hugh gathered her close and she could feel the erratic thud of his heart as he moulded her to his body. Seemingly of their own accord, Helena's arms went around him, and her fingers began to trail up and down his spine, the satin of his waistcoat smooth under her hands. Hugh shuddered and deepened their kiss, one hand splayed across her back, the other cupped her head, fingers entwining in her hair.

For Helena, it was surreal; the world around her stilled and quieted. All she could hear was their echoing heartbeats and all she could feel was Hugh. She never wanted to let him go, his lips were cool and firm, yet their caress warmed her whole body. Even accepting that her behaviour was utterly unacceptable she was powerless to stop. In this moment, with this man, nothing else mattered except how wonderful he made her feel.

A door banged in the depths of the building, shattering the peace and reluctantly, Hugh broke their kiss but didn't let her go. They were both breathing hard and Helena's cheeks were flushed. Hugh stroked a finger along her jawline, his thumb brushing against her bottom lip.

"Helena, daughter of a god, wife of a king and mother of an emperor, your name means light and I fear you have become mine, for unless you are nearby, my life seems dim." Hugh realised he sounded poetic, but he couldn't help it, Helena had brightened his world. He was constantly inventing scenarios in which their paths might cross, hoping against hope that whatever dreary party he attended she might be there too, even if he only managed a brief word or a single dance. He knew he was besotted and he welcomed it.

"I-I...oh, Hugh," she smiled, her smile that seemed just for him, before reaching up to smooth her hand over his cheek. As she held his gaze, savouring his words, something from her father's lessons popped into her head. "Do you know your name comes from *hug*, an element in Old German for heart, mind and spirit?" Hugh shook his head, secretly impressed by her knowledge, "And since you started this, I fear you have become all of mine, for when you are not close I feel only half alive; adrift, like a ship without an anchor."

Hugh could feel her trembling as she shared so intimate a confidence and kissed her cheek, tucking her to him, cradling her head on his shoulder.

As Helena relaxed against him, safe in his arms, all her high ideals about maintaining some form of independence, being allowed an opinion, and not wanting a man to define and control her, fell away and she stopped fighting.

They stood, lost in each other, for what felt like an eon, but was barely five minutes until Hugh relinquished his embrace. "There are people waiting for us," he said softly, "and, much as I would like to stay here like this for the rest of my life, I think we should return to the main office."

Helena nodded slowly and stepped away, that strange hint of melancholy, which always assailed her when she parted from Hugh flickering through her.

"I will see you tomorrow afternoon, my dear."

Helena grinned, a wholly unrestrained gesture that, as far as Hugh was concerned, lit the room.

"I am counting the hours." One more brief brush of her lips, and Hugh opened the door. When Helena walked past him she grasped his hand, stroking his fingers, her touch a promise.

The other three hadn't even noticed their absence, engrossed in conversation about the shipyard. Helena suggested it was time to let these good people continue with what was left of their day. Jessica glanced at the small clock on the shelf behind the desk and noted their day was now over.

"All the more reason for us to go," said Helena bracingly, chivvying her charges towards the door. "I am sure you have plenty to do at the end of each day and we are delaying you. Thank you so much for your time, Mr Drummond, Jessica. I am more grateful than you know." Hugh escorted them down the stairs and out into the late afternoon sunshine, helping both Helena and Sybil into the carriage. Archie hopped up beside Havers, the two men chatting about this and that as the coach rumbled away.

Dropping Archie and Sybil at Sanctuary House and confirming she would be there two days hence, Helena collected Nancy, and the pair were soon tripping up the steps into Winchester House.

Surprisingly, Lady Winchester was home, mother and daughter savouring their evening together over a sumptuous meal and family gossip.

The next afternoon, Hugh arrived promptly at three, suggesting a carriage drive to Hyde Park and maybe a walk. The weather had returned to that typical of August — overly warm, and Helena agreed, commenting a stroll along the Serpentine might be just the thing. They were unfashionably early but for Helena this was preferable. There was less likelihood of gossiping mamas and nosey acquaintances and she hoped they would be able to enjoy their walk uninterrupted, before the hordes descended as the afternoon waned.

Once in the park, Tom — Hugh's driver — positioned the carriage in the shade of a leafy oak and Hugh assisted Helena and Nancy down.

"Nancy, I think you might stay here with Tom, 'tis a warm day and the shade is lovely. I will be in full view of whoever chooses to take their constitutional and do not believe I am in any danger of being compromised."

Nancy thanked her mistress, glad of the chance to have a few moments to herself in the middle of a busy day. Hugh offered Helena his arm and the couple meandered slowly along the footpath, which ran all the way around the Serpentine. Fed by the River Westbourne this body of water, although had the appearance of a river, was in reality a long and winding lake and a popular venue for large celebratory events.

For a little while they walked in silence simply appreciating the tranquillity of the park but soon began to talk and despite an initial hesitancy, it wasn't long before they were engaged in an animated discussion about the recent general election. As expected the Earl of Liverpool had retained his position as Prime Minister but there had been an increase in support for the Whig opposition and many of the *ton* were divided on the issues raised during the election process. Interestingly, Helena and Hugh agreed on most everything although both took great delight in playing devil's advocate, just for the fun of it.

Chapter Twelve

Despite a tendency to gravity, Hugh turned out to be an amusing companion and, after they had exhausted the topic of the election, Helena spent much of their walk almost helpless with laughter at some of the ludicrous tales of misadventures in sailing with which Hugh regaled her. They had been following the path for well over half an hour when Hugh directed Helena down a leafy track leading to the edge of the lake. There were several ducks splashing about, chasing down the multitude of water borne insects that buzzed around the slow-moving waterway. The ground was carpeted with flowers and the dappled light through the trees was magical.

Helena sank to her knees, relishing the coolness of the grass and heady scent of the late blossoms. As ever scorning custom, she removed her bonnet, tossing it carelessly to one side, following it with her gloves and, placing her wrap on the ground, turned so she could recline on her elbows. Hugh leaned against the trunk of a tree, watching her through half-closed eyes, wanting to whisk her into his arms and kiss her until she cried out his name. Unwittingly aiding him in his objective, or making it harder depending on how he looked at it, Helena patted the grass.

"Mr Drum…Hugh, do come and sit here! 'Tis so lovely under the tree, the sun is making all sorts of shadow patterns across the ground, it is as though we are in a fairy dell." Helena bit down on her lip as she said this. *Goodness me,* she scolded herself, *you sound like a child*.

Hugh merely offered one of his rare grins and sauntered over, lowering himself onto the grass and stretching out his legs as he made himself comfortable beside her. Helena, more to distract herself from the devastatingly handsome man next to her than for any other reason, sat up and started to make a daisy chain. Hugh was mesmerised by her fingers as she slotted the stems together, a seemingly soporific process but one which made him acutely aware of her slender hands, and how deftly she used them. They sat like this for several minutes, the silence restful.

"Helena?" Hugh quietly asked. Absorbed in her task, Helena barely glanced at him, about to throw out a casual reply when something in his eyes made her falter.

"Yes." Twisting so she could look him full in the face. "Is something amiss?" curious now. He shook his head.

"I have a mind to kiss you." He heard her indrawn breath, and smiled gently.

"I have a mind to let you," she responded, boldly holding his gaze.

He leaned over and wove an errant lock of hair around his finger. Helena didn't move, willing him to take her in his arms. He noticed her eyes darkening and despite knowing everything about what they were doing placed Helena in an unfair position, he also knew that for him there was no going back.

"You make it extraordinarily difficult for me to follow the rules."

"There are rules?" Her lips curved and she winked at him, reminding him of Jessica when she was up to no good.

"There are," he leaned closer and touched his lips to hers, "but I fear I am going to break all of them."

"Well, I should hate to be the voice of reason." Helena murmured, putting one hand on his chest, fingers curling around the crisp white of his shirt. Hugh drew her close, fitting her against his long frame, scattered light kisses over her face before capturing her mouth, his tongue tasting the honeyed sweetness therein.

Helena followed his lead, her tentative response evoking in Hugh the strangest emotions. He believed Helena to be a woman of great passion and he wanted to be the man to unleash it. The thought of another man touching her, kissing her, loving her was something he did not wish to contemplate. Hugh stilled — loving her? Did he love her? Did he even know what love was? He had spoken of her being his light, was that the same thing? He — who refused to contemplate marriage — knew he never wanted to let her go. She made him feel alive, and losing her would bring him to his knees. Suddenly he realised Helena was speaking and forced himself to concentrate.

"…wrong?"

Dazed, he stared at her, "Sorry, I missed that."

Helena frowned, his abstracted manner bothering her.

"I asked what was the matter. You just stopped and I-I wasn't sure. M-maybe I'm doing it wrong…"

Hugh heard the ambivalence in her tones and hastened to reassure her. "Oh Helena, forgive me. It is not that you are doing anything wrong, it is that your touch, your kiss is likely to be the undoing of me." Hugh trailed his fingers along her cheek, down her neck, stroking over the hollow at the base of her throat, feeling her pulse flutter. Helena shifted in his embrace so that her back was against his chest, wrapping her hands into his and bringing them to rest over her stomach.

"'Tis a wondrous feeling though," she whispered coyly, a pink blush blooming up her cheeks. "Very liberating."

Hugh tightened his arms and dropped a kiss on her hair. "Helena, might I ask you something?"

"Well as you've already kissed me, I cannot see how I could possibly refuse a mere question." She smiled candidly.

"What are you involved with that requires you to dress in such plain attire? Why did I nearly knock you off your feet not far from the Rookeries? And what do you do that causes such dreadful headaches?"

Helena bent her head; she knew she should tell him. He acted honourably over her request to help Archie and if they were going to be seeing each other more than occasionally, she ought to share her secret.

"First of all, that was three questions and before I answer, would you be so kind as to clarify something for me? Well two things actually."

Hugh nodded. Helena scrambled up, the sudden change in position creating an invisible barrier, but one Helena needed, to keep her thoughts in order. As she had previously pointed out, her tongue had a mind of its own when she was close to Hugh, and all her senses seemed to abandon her.

"What is happening here?" She waved her hand between them. "You have kissed me twice now, three times if you count your almost nearly kiss the other day. I do not believe you to be a man who kisses random women for the fun of it, or maybe you do?" She paused, the thought of him kissing another woman rendering her speechless. Shaking her head to clear it of such an offensive image, Helena drew a convulsive breath. "I do not expect you to offer for me or pretend you wish to court me for the sake of those rules you keep talking about. So, what do we…how serious you…to spend more…or perhaps…" she trailed off miserably, realising she had said exactly what she hadn't meant to. What on earth possessed her to allude to marriage? Hugh would likely run for the closest ship and sail off towards the far horizon.

Hugh started to reply but, even though it was she who broached the subject, now Helena couldn't bear to hear what she presumed he might say, so infusing a more business-like tone into her voice, she interrupted.

"…and secondly, please tell me about the problems at the yard. If you are prepared to share that, I will tell you about my days."

While Helena was speaking, several things ran through Hugh's head, the most important being that she didn't expect him to offer marriage. What was that all about? Under ordinary circumstances, kissing a woman the way he kissed Helena was tantamount to a proposal, yet he was coming to realise, Helena was no ordinary woman. He regarded her for long moments wanting to get his own thoughts in order before he spoke.

The possibility of life-long happiness rested in his next words and he had no desire to ruin that chance.

Standing, he walked over to where Helena waited, her stance — she was facing away from him slightly, her body rigid — suggesting she feared his response to her first question. That this so obviously bothered her gave him hope she cared too. Sending up a silent prayer, he reached for her hand, feeling a tremor run though her as his fingers entwined around hers.

"Helena, before we get to the problems at my shipyard there is something you should understand. For much of my life, my father was at sea. His months away from home took a toll on my mother and I promised myself I would never inflict that kind of worry on someone I loved." Helena raised her eyes to his and he read apprehension in their violet depths. She tried to extricate her hand, but he refused to let her go. "Wait, I am not finished. Then I met you and you have turned my life upside down. Your face never leaves my thoughts; you consume my days and steal into my dreams. I find myself accepting invitations to the most unlikely events in the hope you might also attend. I am unable to offer you a title, or vast estates and I know my life is far removed from yours. Neither can I promise you it will be smooth sailing," Helena raised an eyebrow, a slight smile beginning to tug at her mouth, "but I *can* promise I love you with all of my heart. Should you but give me a chance, I will spend the rest of my days demonstrating just how much, and maybe one day you might come to love me too."

By this time, Hugh had taken both of Helena's hands and she was held immobile by the luminous golden warmth of his tawny eyes, reminding her of the setting sun. That mysterious hush, the hush she noticed the previous day, settled around her, and she felt as though she had come home. Squeezing his fingers, she leaned towards him and, without thinking kissed him, butterfly soft.

Corralling her chaotic thoughts and gathering her courage Helena said, "My dear Mr Drummond, while I cannot imagine anything more delightful than surrendering to your, what I imagine would be, fervent attentions," colouring at her own audacity, "I fear such persuasion would be unnecessary." She saw the light in his eyes begin to dim and rushed on, "I am already irrevocably in love with you."

Hugh gaped at her. He knew she was not unmoved by him, but that she returned his feelings was a boon he did not expect to be granted.

"You love me?" Surprise clear in his voice. Helena nodded, demurely. "Seriously? You love me — me the sailor? Me? The man with nothing much to offer, save his heart?" He cupped her face kissing her adorable nose.

"Yes Hugh, I love you. You the sailor, you the man who catches me when I fall, you the man who walks me safely home, you the man who trusts me enough to employ someone of questionable temperament, and you the man who openly offers me his heart knowing I might reject it. I have never been sure about love and I definitely didn't believe there was such a thing as a great love — although both Charlotte and Billie swear it isn't a fanciful notion. Then I met you and it was as though our encounter was pre-determined, that my life had been on a course set to converge with yours at that precise moment. Even when I was certain you disliked me, or at least considered me just another empty-headed debutante on the hunt for a husband, I felt drawn to you. I lose the ability to function coherently when you are close, my thoughts are as though a tempest rages in my head and it is inexplicable. Then yesterday, when you kissed me all became clear. I had been struck by the same aberration that afflicts my sister and sister-in-law, even my ever so sensible brother is an advocate of this state…"

Helena paused and cocked her head, the sun through the leaves glinting on the dark blood-red highlights threaded throughout her raven hair. Hugh thought he had never met anyone quite as beautiful.

"…and I never want this aberration to end." Her voice dropped to a murmur.

Hugh recognised that Helena's admission was as difficult for her, as his had been for him. In this they were alike, two souls confident their lives would follow a defined path to find, in an instant, everything was upended in the most extraordinary manner, yet oddly, one which was dauntingly, breathtakingly, undeniably perfect.

As they stood together, at the end and at the beginning, the world around them melted away leaving them alone with each other. Hugh bent his lips to Helena's and kissed her long and tenderly, his heart exposed, his declaration made and his destiny chosen.

Helena, enveloped in his arms, moulded herself to his muscular frame, her curves fitting into his hollows, her heart forever in his.

Chapter Thirteen

Eventually, aware they could get carried away on a tide of emotion, Hugh lifted his head and stared into Helena's eyes; those remarkable eyes that currently reflected his own passion.

"I think we should get back to the matter in hand, before I give in to things I have only dreamt about and take you here on this bed of grass, although I do believe it would be very much worth the risk." His voice was ragged as he strove to control his need.

Helena's breathing hitched. "While I cannot fault your suggestion, maybe one day soon we could return to the issue of taking me." She blushed at the wanton nature of her words but they were out before she could curb her tongue.

Hugh hugged her close for a brief moment. "I guarantee it." He growled, his breath hot against her ear. She giggled, lightening the tension of the moment and they moved to gather their belongings. Helena tied on her hated bonnet, as Hugh draped the shawl over her shoulders. Making sure each looked the picture of respectability, they strolled back along the path, pleasant conversation gradually distracting them from what they really wanted to do.

"You still wish to know about my days?" Helena queried.

"Most assuredly." He replied, pressing the small hand tucked through his arm.

"I often wear gowns more suited to a factory worker than a lady, because I spend most of my days at Sanctuary House."

Hugh was so shocked he stopped dead in his tracks, almost tripping Helena up.

"You do what?" He said, dumbfounded this delicate creature would even be aware of, never mind consider becoming involved with, such a project. Helena repeated her words, going on to explain what prompted her to take an interest in the refuge and her work with the women there.

Adding that although unusual, sometimes if it had been a long day or — as in the recent case — she had been dealing with a quarrelsome couple, which made her over-tired she was afflicted by headaches, the severity of which he already understood. Hugh listened, amazed at her pluck and astounded by her enthusiasm for her work. "So, am I to assume Archie is not related to one of your staff?" He commented drily, as she wound up. She shook her head, self-consciously.

"No, just one of the men whose wives needed our help." Hugh was starting to look as though he regretted his decision to employ Archie. "I beg you not to retract your offer, Hugh. I believe it will be the making of Archie. Sometimes you just have to trust your instincts and mine tell me this will work out better than any of us could imagine." Words Hugh would recall in the not too distant future. "Now, you promised to tell me about the strange incidents at the shipyard."

Hugh realised Helena was not going to discuss Archie any further so he acquiesced and went on to describe the sporadic incidents that had occurred in the yard during the construction of his new schooner.

"I am at a loss to understand what is going on. Taken separately, each incident would seem inconsequential, easily attributable to a momentary lapse in concentration, or negligence, but together there seems to be a pattern. They only ever happen towards the end of a day, when the men are preparing to leave, so the yard is generally less busy than at, say, mid-afternoon. Nobody ever sees the perpetrators and so far, thankfully no one has been badly hurt. They do seem to be escalating though and I am beginning to wonder if it is not, as Stephen suggested, deliberate sabotage." Hugh's voice dwindled as he ruminated over the matter.

"Surely not, 'tis just a ship. Hugh, you must have a care." Helena's horrified gasp jolted Hugh out of his contemplation.

"Hush love, do not fret. I am always cautious. And while it may be just a ship to you, to other shipping companies it is competition. 'Tis a cutthroat business and out there on the high seas, laws are easily flouted. However, I have not received any odd demands or requests to sell my company, so all I can do is tighten my vigilance and increase the guard. This is where

Archie will be useful, a man of his size will likely be reason enough for would-be saboteurs to think twice before they try anything."

A feeling of foreboding washed over Helena. It never crossed her mind that shipping could be a hazardous occupation; she had only ever witnessed the glamour of the industry. Majestic vessels proudly slicing through the waves, sails caught in the breeze, the open ocean, and the endless skies — to an outsider very romantic, a world for the storytellers. That Hugh could be in any kind of danger scared the life out of her; she had only just found him, it would be too cruel of fate to snatch him away.

Determined not to let him see how his revelations affected her, she clenched her jaw and mentally straightened her shoulders, realising they were almost back at the coach. Nancy and Tom were deep in conversation and did not notice their approach. Helena clutched Hugh's jacket sleeve.

"Grant me a moment longer, Hugh. I am not ready to go back to the real world quite yet."

More than happy to while away several hours, never mind a moment, with Helena, Hugh was about to walk over to a convenient seat, when he glanced down seeing her strained expression. He shepherded her into a shadowed area between two stands of trees, just off the path, out of sight from prying eyes and inveterate gossips. Helena raised her eyebrows at such recklessness but didn't demur. Hugh's arms went around her; the knowledge she was concerned for him inducing a need to protect her so strong, he almost forgot to breathe.

Helena leaned against him, his strong body sheltering her like a port in a storm. He had become her safe harbour, and for brief moment she relished the notion. Another stolen kiss then, mindful of where they were, Hugh guided her out into the sunlight and, this time, over to the nearby bench at one side of the path. Here, they were in full view of everybody so convention — albeit belatedly — was observed, but any conversation would not be overheard.

"Have you considered speaking with Major Withers?" Helena enquired after a few moments, during which she tried, without much success, to regain her composure. "He has loose ties to the Runners and is discreet. Giles engaged him last year when trying to discover Billie's identity, after she turned up on his doorstep, totally drenched and with no memory of who she was or how she got there. Subsequently, the Major was instrumental in bringing the spy, who set fire to her father's house and hunted her, to justice. He is the most amenable gentleman and his wife is a delight."

Hugh, who hid a quick grin at her last comment — as though this made all the difference — knew of Major Withers, for Stephen had also proposed the same course of action. He was coming to appreciate Helena's astute mind. Rather than have a fit of the vapours at the mere mention of treachery, here she was offering practical suggestions.

"I have been pondering this very idea and believe it has merit. In fact, I may call in on my way home. Thank you, my love."

Helena turned to look at him. He was leaning back against the seat, legs stretched out in front of him, eyes half-closed, to outward appearances totally unperturbed by the subject of their discussion, but Helena wasn't fooled. Hugh's hands, resting on his stomach, were tightly clasped and his features tense — not solely because of the current topic, it was also the only way he could keep his hands off Helena.

"I haven't really done anything and am sorry for asking you to tell me, Hugh. 'Tis clear how anxious you are, and this afternoon should have been a time to forget your troubles."

"No, please do not apologise. I did not wish to burden you with my problems, but I admit that telling you has eased my disquiet. Just your presence seems to calm my mind, that you are comfortable discussing this with me is simply a bonus." Hugh assured her. "Moreover, I have had the pleasure of your company for longer than I dared hope, and you are the most exquisite distraction." He smiled then, a slow sweet smile and reached out to squeeze her hand. Helena smiled back and, as ever, Hugh felt himself becoming immersed in the smoky grey of her eyes. "I fear we should not tarry. May I call on you tomorrow?"

Helena started to nod, then stopped. "Oh, I will be at Sanctuary House until around four. If you would like to meet me there, I would be glad of your company and we could ride home together, maybe detouring past Gunter's?" naming the popular tea room in Berkeley Square. "An ice might be just the thing after a busy day." She grinned impishly, tugging a chuckle from his own lips. She was irrepressible.

"That sounds most appealing and so we are agreed. Now come, let me get you home before I kidnap you and carry you away never to be seen again." Helena shivered under his smouldering gaze and wished they were alone, any thoughts of behaving like the lady she was deserting her as all she could think about was his kisses and how they made her feel. Kidnapping sounded a wonderful alternative to her normal life, the image of Hugh throwing her over his shoulder and disappearing into the wilds of the countryside making her gurgle with laughter. The man in question raised an eyebrow and she managed to tell him, his mirth mingling with hers as they walked over to the carriage.

The journey back to Portman Square was uneventful; Hugh did manage to hold Helena's hand all the way, Nancy turning a blind eye. He helped her down from the coach and escorted her to the door, bowing over her hand, sneaking a kiss on her wrist as he did so, his lips lingering a moment longer than necessary.

"I will see you tomorrow, my lady," he murmured and before she could reply, was back in his coach. She watched him go, willing him to turn and wave, which he did, much to her satisfaction. She drifted into her home on a cloud of bliss and calling a hello to whomsoever might be listening, wandered slowly up to her bedchamber, intent on changing for the evening.

The next few weeks flew by, August became September and, to the relief of those living in the confines of the city, the weather cooled considerably. Nature doffed its summer attire, the intense dazzling colours softening to a more mellow hue and, here and there, leaves began to show hints of autumnal shades. Two exciting events occurred in the middle of the month. Stephen and Tabitha were wed, and Giles and Billie came for a short visit. As Stephen's sister, Billie would not have missed such a joyous occasion but it transpired they were also in London to see a specialist, and the Winchester family were elated to hear the couple were expecting their first child, due sometime in February.

Stephen and Tabitha's wedding was a wonderful day. By tradition the ceremony itself was a small affair but the ball afterwards — an unexpected yet glittering event in an otherwise dull calendar — was declared to be the event of the non-Season. Hugh had been invited and, by dint of dancing every set with Helena, made his intentions clear. Billie and Charlotte did spend some time dragging the whole story out of Helena and were gratifyingly thrilled by how the romance was unfolding.

Intriguingly for Helena, during the week of Giles' visit, she met Grace Elliott, the lady whom Lord Beaumont, Sophia's husband, had been so against his brother, Theo, courting. Grace — a reserved and, although oblivious of it, regally beautiful woman — was now married to Theo and the couple were, obviously, deeply in love. Helena found her delightful and could not understand Benedict's attitude. Of late, whenever in company, Helena had become aware of the unconscious intimacy shared by those of her family and friends who had married for love not convenience, noticing their behaviour mirrored that of Hugh and her. It was a discovery that pleased her immensely.

Since their walk along the Serpentine, Helena and Hugh were spending more and more time together and, effortlessly, Hugh became part of her family circle. When Helena was not working at the refuge and Hugh managed to find a few free hours in the middle of a busy week, they enjoyed carriage rides or afternoon constitutionals or picnics with mutual friends. Nobody questioned Hugh's heritage or his status, they just saw he made Helena happy and that was enough for them. The pair talked for hours on all manner of issues, which surprised them both, as conversations between unmarried men and women, tended to be restricted to inconsequential matters. In between secret embraces and stolen kisses, they found themselves sharing their lives, their hopes, and their dreams, and slowly came to know each other.

It was a little over a week after the wedding, when trouble reared its ugly head once again. Helena was at Sanctuary House quite early, and as she thanked Havers mentioned that Mr Drummond had offered to drive her home. Hurrying inside, she pulled on a large apron and entered the kitchens. Not adept at cooking, something she had never been required to learn, Helena was always willing to peel and chop vegetables, wash the dishes and set the long tables.

She found Sybil, already hard at work and asked how everything was going. Archie had settled in well at Trentams, never missing a day's work and, to Sybil's joy, hadn't over-imbibed once since being offered the job. Sybil herself, now living at home again, was a different woman. She was bright and cheerful, gossiping away about how much their lives were beginning to change for the better.

"I just 'ope it all works out for us, m'lady. I still worry 'e might slip up."

Helena patted Sybil's thin arm. "I'm sure it will be fine, Sybil. Soon you might be able to think about planning a brief holiday." Cleverly diverting Sybil from her worry that her husband might ruin his chances, the two were soon chattering animatedly about where to visit.

Chapter Fourteen

Sometime towards the end of that afternoon, Seth Collins arrived as had become his habit, looking for Lynette, his long-suffering wife. Lynette had been staying at Sanctuary House for well over a month, since her release from hospital, following one of Seth's drunken frenzies. Seth — being unable to hold his liquor — took out his perceived woes on anyone who got in his way, which usually meant poor Lynette bore the full force of his ire. Every day, he demanded to see his wife and every day he was refused. Sometimes he accepted this, shambling off, bewailing his fate to all and sundry; sometimes he hung around hoping that if he glimpsed Lynette, he could induce her to go home with him.

This day, he arrived in a drunken mess, his angry mutterings virtually incomprehensible. He staggered into the refuge, threatening the guards, the staff, the Runners, the drivers, even God — whom most were sure wasn't currently on the premises and certainly not responsible for Seth's state of inebriation.

Helena corralled her group to the rear of the building far removed from areas of the refuge open to visitors, encountering two other groups cowering in the corners. Helena was vexed, these women came here to escape this kind of behaviour, and it irked her men like Seth refused to respect the boundaries.

"Come on," she said cheerfully, "no need to worry about Seth, he's all bluster. There are far too many people here ready to sort him out if he oversteps the mark. Let us get on with our day and ignore him." She ushered them into a room and locked the door. Lynette was with them and kept trying to apologise for Seth's behaviour.

"Oh Miss, he's a blighter when he's drunk. There'll be no stopping 'im 'til 'e finds me. Mebbe I should just go talk to 'im." Lynette's lilting cockney accent becoming more pronounced in her anxiety.

"Lynette, you will do no such thing," replied Helena crisply. "Look at what he did to you last time. He's in a fine temper this afternoon and none of us needs to get in his way. Let the guards deal with him. They'll send him away with a flea in his ear soon enough. Once he's slept it off, we might be able to get some sense out of him, but I doubt that will be today."

Lynette looked both terrified and distraught; aware her presence was placing everyone else in danger. Helena was wise to this thinking though and was not about to let Lynette accept responsibility for her husband's actions.

"Don't you dare suggest you should leave. What good is a refuge if someone like Seth can frighten us all into submission? We are here to protect you. If you believe 'tis your fault he behaves this way, he has won. Do not let him guilt you into taking the blame for his loutish behaviour."

Helena's calm tones and cool reasoning did the trick and Lynette was persuaded to stay with her friends. They were in the room where donated garments were unpicked and made ready for alteration, several pieces scattered over the tables. Turning their attention to this task, the women were soon absorbed and began to gossip amongst themselves, the problem with Seth Collins pushed to the back of their minds for the time being.

For the most part Seth, when unable to find his wife, became maudlin and ended up in a huddle on the floor, weeping like a petulant boy. A weak man, any power he had over Lynette was lost when she stood up to him and fled his assaults. Today however, was not one of those days. He ranted and raved and rampaged through Sanctuary House. The guards did what they could, ensuring Seth could not get to parts of the building off limits to the public, or find any of the women, let alone Lynette. Unfortunately, short of getting close enough either to knock him unconscious or restrain him in some way, their hands were tied, as apparently shooting a man, however aggravating — and currently their only other option — was considered discourteous, not to mention potentially fatal. Seth knew this and stayed just out of reach.

All at Sanctuary House were familiar with Seth's outbursts but this one was extreme, and Helena could see how badly it was affecting the women in the room with her. Residual trauma resulting from years of abuse and violence took its toll and many never recovered fully. After nearly an hour with no sign of Seth letting up, Helena had had enough.

"Stay here," she instructed them, "and secure the door behind me. Do not, under any circumstances open it unless it is to one of the guards or me. Do you understand?" she held their eyes, her steady demeanour soothing them and they nodded. "Right, I will be back shortly." With that Helena slipped out of the door and along the strangely quiet corridors. She could hear Seth banging things about and it reminded her of the day Archie had done a similar thing and silently praised all that was holy, she had found him something that made him feel worthwhile again.

Two of the haven's sentinels, Mr Barnes and Mr Thirlwell, were standing guard at the end of the hallway she was walking along, and she came up behind them asking what was happening.

"At the moment, he's in the dining room, my lady. Hopefully he'll get fed up with making such a racket and go home," said Mr Thirlwell, his tones placid presuming this, although not Seth's typical tantrum, would soon be over and peace restored. Helena asked whether they knew the whereabouts of the rest of the staff.

"I last saw Mrs Graves and Mrs Forester upstairs, they were sorting laundry. Mrs Parry was in the front office and Mrs Baker should be just along there," Mr Barnes nodded towards the corridor at the other side of the hallway. Glad they were accounted for; Helena hoped any women not with one of the staff had the sense to keep out of Seth's way.

"Do you think we're safe here, or should I get my group out of the refuge?" Helena asked. Both men shook their heads.

"No, you'll be fine where you are, he'll not get through us and the other lads will have 'im surrounded, waiting for 'im to stop being such a fatwit."

Helena thanked them returning to the room and explaining the situation to those within. One or two, who had call on their time elsewhere, asked whether they might be permitted to leave and, as they were not far from the one of the rear doors to the building, Helena escorted them out.

On her return, she noticed all had gone quiet. Helena breathed a sigh of thankfulness. It seemed as though Seth's temper had blown itself out, and she imagined one of the other guards would come and tell them he had either left, or was prostrated on the floor in a drunken stupor. She was approaching her two sentries to see whether they could resume whatever they had been doing before Seth so rudely interrupted them, when a whiff of something tickled her nostrils. She stopped and sniffed, nothing — whatever it was had gone.

Asking Mr Barnes whether he would go and check, Helena chatted with Mr Thirlwell, catching up on any news about his family. He and his wife had recently become grandparents and he was always happy to talk about Molly, his adorable baby granddaughter. Suddenly she caught the smell again, as did Mr Thirlwell. They looked at each other in shock both speaking at the same time.

"Fire!"

For a split second, Helena froze, she was terrified of fire and this was an old wooden building with meandering corridors and dozens of rooms. The long hot summer meant everything was tinder dry and it wouldn't take much for the whole refuge to go up in flames. Mr Thirlwell took one look at her and calmly suggested she get her group out of the building, adding that he would go and find out exactly what was happening. Helena squeezed his hand gratefully

"Stay safe," she whispered and rushed back to where her group was still gossiping away, assuming that they would be given leave to get back to their regular chores. "Ladies," her brisk tones got their attention quickly. "We are concerned there may be a small fire so, as a precaution, we think it would be best if you were to gather anything you wish to take with you, from this room only, and make your way in an orderly fashion out through the rear door at the end of this corridor." Despite her own fear, Helena's voice was unruffled, diffusing panic before it could take hold. There were anxious mutterings but the women did as she asked them and all were soon out in the laneway.

Helena hustled them around to the front of the building, where they should be safe from any flying debris. Going back in she checked along rooms and hallways, collecting anything she deemed too valuable to leave behind, coming across Mr Barnes and Mr Thirlwell who informed her the fire appeared to have started in one of the classrooms. In their opinion it was probably owing to a candle being knocked over in the breeze, and falling against a curtain. Helena stared at them running this through her mind.

"I do not think we had any lit. Those rooms get the afternoon sun; thus, we have no need of candles. Are you sure the fire started there?" The two men could not be positive, but the smoke was coming from that side of the refuge and it seemed the most logical explanation. The three did not have time to ponder the cause, hurrying through the building and corralling any stragglers. All the staff were outside, most having collected what they could from the rooms they were in, just in case the fire took hold. The guards doing a final inspection to make sure no one remained inside.

Helena went over to where the women were waiting. She and Mrs Forester called out names, needing to be sure that everyone was out, however when she got to Sybil's name there was no reply. She shouted it again, nothing. Helena forced herself not to panic; perhaps Sybil had gone home. Not prepared to assume anything, she asked whether anyone had seen the tiny woman but it seemed no one had, which in itself was unusual. Helena thought back over the afternoon, recalling Sybil mentioning she was going to check the stocks in the large storeroom behind the kitchen. If she had been there when Seth arrived she would probably have stayed where she was.

As Helena was debating what to do, the sound of glass shattering made everyone duck. Huge flames could now be seen leaping through the windows at the right side of the building, licking along the wooden walls, sparks drifting up lazily on the breeze. If this fire wasn't extinguished the whole neighbourhood was at risk. Thankfully the refuge was fire marked and the Fire Brigade had been summoned. In the meantime, the guards organised a bucket line, which although unlikely to put out what was already burning, gave them a slim chance of preventing the fire from spreading until the experts arrived.

Without pausing to think, Helena snatched a blanket from a pile dropped on the steps and dumped it into the horse trough at the side of the building, soaking it thoroughly. Ignoring shouts from guards and staff alike not to do so, she covered herself with the blanket and dashed into the building, keeping low and calling for Sybil. Heading to the kitchens, she kept a cautious eye on her surroundings not wanting to be cut off by the encroaching flames.

The smoke wasn't too thick at this side of the refuge and she made her way to the kitchens quite quickly. To her great relief, she spied Sybil cowering behind the shelves.

"Sybil, please come with me. I do believe it's time we got out of here." Helena declared, in the most practical voice she could muster, skidding to a halt next to the terrified woman. Sybil shook her head.

"I can't Miss, I'm sore afraid o' fire."

"Me too Sybil," Helena said comfortingly. "But if we stay here, I think we may get trapped by the flames and I for one do not want to explain to Archie why we perished in an inferno when you could have escaped with me."

Sybil gaped, a rather wobbly chuckle slipped out as she realised what Helena had said.

"You cannot tell him anything if you're dead," she giggled.

"I would not be surprised if your husband stalked us into the afterlife. Now come on, you are one of the bravest women I have ever met; this fire is a mere trifle. We can do this!"

Sybil took a deep breath and gave Helena a small nod.

Helena glanced around and saw that one of the huge pans on the stove had some water in it. She dragged it off and tipped it over the blanket just to be on the safe side, hoping, the now dripping article, would stay wet long enough to protect them until they were outside.

"Right, now get under this blanket with me, put your arm around my waist and whatever you do, do not let go. Ready?"

Sybil croaked a yes and the two began to make their way to the front of the house.

Chapter Fifteen

As all this was unfolding, Hugh and Archie were in Hugh's carriage, trundling towards Sanctuary House. Hugh, knowing Archie liked to meet his wife at the end of the day and walk her home, had offered him a lift to the refuge and the two were engaged in an interesting debate about the continuing incidents at the shipyard. Archie had taken it upon himself to monitor unexpected visitors or unexplained comings and goings, reporting anything untoward to his boss. Although as yet they hadn't uncovered whoever was masterminding the vandalism, their concerted efforts seemed, finally, to be bringing them closer.

As their coach turned down the long street leading up to Sanctuary House both men saw the flames. Without waiting to be instructed, Tom — Hugh's driver — urged on the horses and they reached the ever-growing crowds in seconds. Jumping down, Hugh elbowed his way to the front, grabbing the arm of one of the guards, who was desperately trying to keep the buckets moving, demanding to know where Lady Helena was. The man shrugged his shoulders and pointed to the group of women standing to one side, their eyes fixed on the blazing building. Hugh pushed through the throng towards them, spotting Mrs Parry with whom he had spoken on several occasions when collecting Helena.

"Mrs Parry, where is Lady Helena?" Hugh had to raise his voice over the roar of the flames. Mrs Parry looked at him then looked back at the building. It took Hugh a moment to grasp what she wouldn't say. "She's in there? My God, woman! Helena is in there? Why? How? Did no one think to stop her?" He stared at the refuge. It would be a miracle for anyone to survive such devastation. The thought of Helena being trapped or hit by a piece of burning debris was too much. He began to run towards the steps leading to the front door.

Inside Sanctuary House, the smoke was much thicker, the narrow corridors acting like chimneys, drawing the fire. Helena was concerned she would get disoriented in the maze of hallways and end up leading the two of them into rather than out of the flames. Sybil was sobbing uncontrollably and by now Helena was virtually carrying her. Then relief, when they reached rooms used as offices — they were almost at the front entrance. Glancing into each one as they passed, checking they were empty, Helena noticed a figure huddled on the floor of the second office. It was Seth Collins. Exhorting Sybil to stand still, Helena dropped to her knees and crawled over to the man, who was rocking on his haunches and singing the most peculiar little ditty.

"Seth," she crooned softly, "Seth, please come with me, I have a nice cup of tea waiting in the other room." He stared at her through crazed eyes. Helena shuddered, terror threatening to overwhelm her.

"My Lynette will be happy now, she always likes to sit by a lovely warm fire." Seth gave a deranged cackle; an eerie sound and Helena realised with a shock, it was he who set the blaze, apparently as a gift for his wife. Clearly, the man had lost his mind. Gathering her rapidly failing courage Helena tried again, stretching out her hand and getting hold of his.

"Come Seth, 'tis time to go. Lynette is waiting for you. It wouldn't do to be late, now would it?" Praying he would do as she bid — they had precious little time left to get out. Seth nodded and stood up. She gripped his hand tightly and coaxed him towards the hallway. All around, pieces of wood were tumbling to the ground shattering on impact and showering them with sparks, as the building started to give way. The heat was intense and the smoke so dense they could barely see. The blanket seemed to have disappeared, so Helena instructed Sybil to hang on to her dress, while she gripped Seth with one hand and pressed the other against the wall following it along the corridor, hoping it would guide them out. As they stumbled forward, Helena kept up steady flow of chatter, determined not to show the others how frightened she was, which had the added bonus of helping her to focus.

She could hear a bell clanging; finally, the Fire Brigade. Too late, she thought, there'll be nothing to save. Suddenly they came to a gap in the wall. Was this the entrance? Or was she taking them deeper into the building? All three were staggering now, heat and smoke making every step a herculean task. Praying she wasn't dragging them to their deaths and with a last-ditch effort, Helena pulled her charges through and, wonder of wonders, they were outside where the air was clean and cool. The enormous crowd fell silent as three blackened and bedraggled creatures appeared in the doorway, silhouetted against a backdrop of orange flame.

Helena didn't notice and she didn't stop, everything in her concentrated on getting Seth and Sybil away from the refuge, out of the path of crumbling walls and burning fragments. She nearly made it but half-way down the steps and just as Hugh reached them, Seth wrenched his hand out of hers and charged back into the building. Helena screamed his name and turned to go after him. Hugh only prevented her by dint of seizing her around the waist at the same time as Archie, flying up the steps after his employer, caught his own wife.

Lifting Helena as though she weighed nothing more than a child, Hugh shot back down the steps, carrying her to where Tom waited, yelling for Archie to follow him. Without relinquishing his hold, Hugh climbed into the coach, nestling Helena against him, while Archie did the same with Sybil. Tom, already in the driver's seat, turned the carriage and set a fast pace to Hugh's town house.

Both women were gasping for air, lungs filled with acrid smoke and Helena was trying to speak. Hugh, seeing what a struggle it was, hushed her, rubbing his hand down her back trying to help her body expel the deadly vapours. It seemed a long half an hour or so before they arrived and Hugh was out of the coach and through the front door almost before Tom had stopped.

Shouting for his staff, Hugh dispatched one for the doctor and one to apprise Lady Winchester what had happened, and to escort her here should she wish to attend. Asking his butler to direct Archie to one of the guest bedchambers, Hugh was about to follow when Jessica darted out of the parlour, coming to find out what all the noise was about.

"Hugh! What on earth…?" Her indignant words trailed off as she took in her brother and his sooty burden. "Hugh?"

"There was a fire. I've sent for Dr Phillips and Helena's mother. We will need a lot of tepid water and plenty of cloths. She is finding it hard to breathe. I'm taking her to the Yellow Room. If you want to help, please go and make sure my instructions are being carried out." He knew his manner was terse, but he didn't care, Helena was his priority now.

He took the stairs two at a time and by the time he strode into the bedchamber, Betty and Emily, two of the maids, arrived with buckets and cloths and two glasses of brandy. He thanked them asking they make sure Archie and Sybil were afforded the same courtesy and to please bring the doctor up as soon as he arrived.

Helena was swimming in and out of consciousness. Her chest hurt and it was so hard to breathe. She was aware of motion and possibly being carried but nothing seemed real. She wondered, idly, whether she was asleep and this was simply a dream. That would explain the extraordinary sensations. Then she remembered the fire and Seth and Sybil. She tried to get up, to speak, but her voice was barely a croak and a large hand pushed her back against soft pillows. That was odd — pillows? She couldn't recall getting home. So maybe the whole thing was a dream. But Hugh was supposed to meet her at Sanctuary House and take her for a drive. She needed to send a note, to tell him she wasn't there.

"Must tell Hugh," she rasped, "not there, here. Oh, where's here?" Everything was blurred, and a deep voice spoke as though from far, far away.

"Rest my love, you are safe."

"Sybil?" she knew Sybil was important in all this.

"Sybil is also safe, you can sleep now." The voice was familiar and he called her his love. Relaxing, she felt a smile twitch at her lips as darkness claimed her.

Over the next few hours, Hugh's home was a flurry of activity. The doctor arrived and examined both women, diagnosing that they were both suffering from smoke inhalation. Understanding this was the most common cause of death in fires, more so than being burned, Hugh feared the worst might yet happen. Dr Phillips was less concerned.

"Neither women have burns to their nose, mouth or face and I see no indication of singed nostril hair and swelling therein, or damage to their airways. While very serious, I think they escaped before the smoke in their lungs reached a fatal level. I suggest a tincture of mulberry leaves, in a cup of warm water and honey; it has proved efficacious in circumstances such as these. As luck would have it, I keep some in my rooms and dropped a vial in my bag, when your man mentioned fire. I will leave it with you." He regarded Hugh fixedly, making sure he understood. Hugh nodded, jotting down in a notebook, everything the doctor said.

"Also, keep the room damp, set a kettle full of water on the fire and keep it boiling. Then all you can do is watch and pray. I believe both Lady Helena and Mrs Miller will survive, but at the slightest hint either seem to be deteriorating do not hesitate to call me." Leaving detailed instructions both on how to blend the tincture and what might indicate a change for the worse, the doctor took his leave.

By this time, Helena's mother had arrived, but as Hugh was still with the doctor and none of the rest of his household had much of an idea what was going on — except there had been a fire — Lady Winchester remained none the wiser. Mrs Drummond ordered hot drinks and a plate of sandwiches, but Helena's mother was too distressed to partake and by the time the doctor came downstairs she was beside herself with worry. Unaware he was addressing a dowager countess, Dr Phillips patted her arm placatingly, and explained his diagnosis.

"Do not fret, dear lady. I am confident both women will be up and about in a few days. Sore throats maybe, but after what Hugh told me, I think they came out of this relatively unscathed." He nodded around the room in a rather abstracted manner and said he would be back on the morrow. Augusta Winchester stared at his retreating back in exasperation, but before she could comment, Hugh appeared at the door.

"Ah, Lady Winchester, permit me to escort you upstairs." Hugh's impassive countenance steadied Augusta and she followed him up to a beautiful room, decorated in shades of yellow and cream. Her daughter, still coated in soot, was fast asleep on the bed, but her breathing sounded erratic and her chest wheezed, as though suffering from a chest infection. Hugh explained what the doctor prescribed, and that one of his staff was blending a tincture as he spoke.

"Thank you, Mr Drummond, I am indebted to you for your quick action. Please, might you tell me what happened?"

"I do not have all the details, my Lady, but as far as I can tell, Sanctuary House caught fire and your daughter went into the building to rescue Sybil, one of the ladies whom she has helped, and a man named Seth. Just as she managed to get them out, Seth ran back into the flames and I have no idea whether he survived, as Archie, that's Sybil's husband, and I grabbed the two women and brought them here. I called the doctor and sent a man to fetch you. That is all I know."

Augusta studied the man sitting across the bed from her while he talked. His face was pale, and she surmised this was more than simple concern for the woman between them. He had been spending many hours with her daughter of late and though Helena had not said anything to her mother, Augusta recognised love when she saw it. What she hadn't been quite so confident of was how this man felt about Helena.

"Are your intentions towards my daughter honourable, Mr Drummond?" she asked gently. Hugh raised his eyes to hers then dropped them back to Helena's face.

"Yes," he replied quietly. Everything Augusta needed to know was in that single word and she nodded.

"Then I imagine you might like to sit with her, while I speak with your mother. If you are agreeable, I believe it would be better to leave Helena under your care, at least for a few days, as I do not think it wise to move her. Also, I imagine she will be concerned about Sybil, whom I understand is in the next room. She will be comforted by the knowledge her friend is close by."

Hugh's expression, full of gratitude for her perception, was thanks enough, but she acknowledged his appreciation with a smile, and left him to his vigil.

Shortly thereafter, Betty brought the tincture, it smelt a little strange but if it helped, Hugh didn't care. Slipping an arm under her shoulders, he lifted Helena's head carefully, managing to get several drops over her lips and the maid informed him that Sybil had also swallowed a small amount. Now all they could do was watch and wait. Lady Winchester returned sometime later, and Hugh went to check on Archie and Sybil.

Sybil was half awake, snuggled into her husband's arms and Archie looked as though he was never letting her go again.

"How do you feel Sybil?" Hugh asked. "Do not try to speak if it hurts your throat, just nod or shake your head." She shook her head. He smiled, "I thought as much. Apparently, this mixture," pointing at the goblet on the little table by the bed, "should help your breathing and your sore throat. You will, of course, stay here until you are given a clean bill of health. Archie may need to pop home for a change of attire, he is far too tall for any of my clothes to fit him, but please do not fret about anything." The ghost of a grin crossed Sybil's face when Hugh said this, Archie being much broader than Hugh, and a good head taller.

Hugh chuckled. "The doctor tells me you breathed in too much smoke, but you should make a full recovery. Now, I am going to organise some dinner for Archie and myself. Are you hungry Mrs Miller?" Sybil shook her head her eyes drooping and before Hugh left the room, she was asleep again. Making sure Sybil was comfortable; Archie followed him to the door.

"Thank you, Sir, you are too kind. I…we are in your debt."

Hugh shook his head. "Just continue as you have been, Archie. Prove to Sybil that you are the man she believes you to be and there is no debt." He grinned and, patting Archie on the shoulder, telling him there would be a tray of food delivered forthwith, went down to the kitchens to check on said dinner.

Chapter Sixteen

Several hours later, during the dark watches of the night, when both women had been cleaned as much as possible without placing them in a bath, when the household had been fed, enjoyed a hot drink and a glass of brandy — purely as a fortifier, of course — and when all was quiet and still, Hugh was dozing in a chair at Helena's bedside. Lady Winchester agreed to this on the proviso either Betty or Emily remained in the room with them. She knew Hugh would do nothing to risk Helena's reputation, she was too unwell for a start, but gossips can be found in the most unexpected places, and this way the dowager countess was protecting all concerned.

Helena stirred and slowly opening her eyes. The room was unfamiliar and there was a hand holding hers. Beyond the foot of the bed, she could make out a fire — strange at this time of year — with something hanging over it that was hissing and bubbling. The air felt a little damp, but it seemed to be easing the tightness in her chest. To her left a young lady, a maid by the style of her dress, sat in a large armchair, sewing something by the light of three candles. She moved her head slightly to the right and felt the hand tighten around hers.

"Helena?" As she focused, a face appeared above hers. A face in which she could see the most beautiful brown eyes, whose tawny flecks glowed in the firelight; a face that seemed too pale, but that could have been the gloom. She squeezed the hand and saw the beginnings of a smile curve the sensual lips. Those lips that she wanted to kiss for the rest of her life.

"Hugh?" her voice sounded scratchy. "Where am I?" Hugh explained she was in his home, and the rest should probably wait until the morning. Suffice it to say she would be staying put for a few days; her mother had visited and would return the next day.

"Now, please would you try to drink some of this?" he held a goblet to her lips and she dutifully swallowed most of the mixture. It slid over her sore throat and although tasted rather peculiar, its cool sweetness soothed her. She was having difficulty breathing and couldn't remember why.

"Breathing hurts," she managed. Even that was an effort.

"It is because of how much smoke got into your lungs. The doctor assures me 'tis but temporary. You should start to feel better soon."

She stared at Hugh as he spoke, trying to remember. Smoke in her lungs? Maybe it was not a dream.

"What happened?" she asked, her mind a blank.

"I think you will have to tell us, but 'tis late, or rather early and I expect you feel wearied. Time enough tomorrow, I will be here."

Helena nodded drowsily. "So nice."

"What is, my love?"

"That you are here." She sighed and shifted onto her side, burrowing under the covers, never letting go of Hugh's hand and just as slumber claimed her she whispered, so quietly, Hugh wasn't sure she had spoken, "I love you."

Since the day in the park, neither had repeated their declarations of affection and, as ever when matters of the heart are at stake, that which should be affirmed as often as the waves come in on the tide is not and what was once assured becomes irresolute. Hugh gazed at Helena, her face smudged from the soot they hadn't been able to rinse away, her hair, some of which was badly scorched and would need to be trimmed, tumbling in black rivulets over the pillow and his heart swelled.

"I love you too, sweetheart. Now rest." The merest hint of a smile teased her lips, but he felt the pressure of her fingers against his and knew she had heard. He settled himself back in the chair, absently rubbing her palm with his thumb and soon they were both fast asleep.

The next morning dawned bright and sunny. Hugh, stiff from sleeping in an armchair, stretched awkwardly and carefully extracted his hand from Helena's, retiring to his own bedchamber to indulge in a long hot bath, before dressing and going in search of breakfast. He wanted to find out what had happened to the refuge, but first he needed to make sure his other guest was being properly attended to.

Checking with his staff in the kitchen, it appeared Sybil had been quite restless during the early part of the night, but eventually settled, both she and Archie managing a few hours of solid sleep. Archie had just left to collect a change of clothes for them both, indicating he would also go to Sanctuary House in order to obtain more detailed information about the fire.

Once that was sorted out, Hugh asked Maggie, his cook, whether she might see her way to preparing some porridge for Helena and Sybil, the softer food being easier to swallow. Maggie was ahead of him, a pan of the milky mixture already underway. He thanked them for everything and asked his housekeeper, Mrs Fletcher, whether she might be able to arrange a bath for both the ladies.

"I know you tried to remove all that grime last evening, but I think they would both feel much better for a proper bath. That soot was everywhere and I know Lady Helena still has a greyish cast to her skin this morning, which I do not believe is wholly attributable to her current state of health. It will also prevent any more residual dust being transferred to the bed linens."

Mrs Fletcher, Emily, and Betty all chimed in to say they would get on to it straight away, then shooed their master off to the dining room where the rest of his family were having breakfast.

As he entered the room, they all looked at him expectantly.

"How are our guests, Hugh?" enquired his mother, as Hugh filled his plate with eggs and toast. He sat down and applied himself to his food for several minutes before answering.

"No worse, is probably the best I can say. Helena awoke in the early hours and I persuaded her to swallow some more of the draught the doctor prescribed, but she was still finding it hard to breathe. She fell asleep again almost immediately, and as far as I am aware did not and has not yet roused. I believe Sybil was much the same. I have asked Maggie to concoct some of her famous porridge, in the hopes both ladies find the milky texture less difficult to cope with." Hugh paused.

"Further, Archie was going to see whether he might glean any information about exactly what did happen last night, if there is anyone at what is left of Sanctuary House to whom he can speak."

Jessica, Nick and Mrs Drummond plied him with more questions, until he threw up his hands in surrender.

"I cannot tell you any more than I already have. I arrived on the scene moments before Helena tumbled out with her charges in tow. We must wait until Archie returns. Nick, please would you manage things down at the yard today?" Raising an eyebrow at his brother who nodded.

"I will go with him, Hugh. I can make sure the paperwork is in order if naught else," observed Jessica.

Smiling, Hugh thanked them both and with one less thing to worry about, felt a little more cheerful than he had less than an hour ago. He finished his food, gulped down a second cup of coffee, and said he was going back to check on Helena.

The three left in the dining room looked at each other but it was Jessica who spoke first.

"So 'tis 'Helena' now, did you notice that?" she said with an arch grin. The other two nodded. "I knew he was in love, the first time we met her. She is exactly right for him and I know they have spent quite a lot of time together recently. Let us just hope he doesn't botch it up."

They all smirked sagely. Hugh had only ever shown more than a passing interest in a couple of young and eminently suitable ladies, but after two or three meetings had turned tail and fled, using long sea voyages as an excuse. Helena it seemed had broken through his carefully erected shield, causing a change in him that none of his family ever expected to witness.

"Well, I for one would be very glad to see him happily wed, and that's all I'll say on the matter." Mrs Drummond said, folding her napkin, and getting up from the table. Smiling at her two younger children, she hurried off to attend to whatever was required. Jessica and Nick followed more slowly. Jessica wanted to see Helena, should Hugh allow it, and Nick went off to the study to collect any papers that might be needed during the day.

Jessica knocked quietly on the door of the Yellow Room and was admitted by Betty, Hugh nowhere to be seen. A bath tub — half full of steaming hot water, scented with a light fragrance, stood in the middle of the room, between the bed and the fire — probably explained his absence. Mrs Fletcher was saying something to Helena who was nodding in agreement, and they both turned as Jessica came over to the bed.

"My lady," Helena frowned, "sorry, Helena, how are you feeling this morning?"

Helena lifted her hand wobbling it, an indication she was not too bad and not too good. Pointing to her throat she croaked, "Too sore."

Jessica grinned, "Do not talk, let me." And proceeded to chatter away about nothing of any consequence until Mrs Fletcher informed her Lady Helena was about to take a bath, and she was sure Miss Drummond had things she ought to be getting on with. Jessica grinned unrepentantly and winked at Helena who smiled back albeit rather wearily. Hopping down from the bed and saying she would be back that afternoon, Jessica shot off with little regard for gentility and, yelling for her brother, the pair hurried off to the shipyard.

Sometime later, after Helena had been soaped and washed and washed again — her skin finally looking more or less as it should — she was back in bed and, reluctantly, submitting to another examination by the doctor. That learned gentleman was pleased with the progress of both women, surmising they were out of danger and it was simply a matter of time.

"I must impress on you though, Lady Helena, once you are up and about, you should not to rush straight into helping at the refuge," Hugh having apprised him of what Helena and Sybil did each day. "You will need to take things steadily for a little while. Promise me?" He pinned Helena with his bright blue eyes until she squirmed uncomfortably and nodded her compliance.

"I promise," she croaked. He smiled and patted her hand

"Just keep drinking that infusion, stay warm and let others coddle you for another day or so, after which you might get up. I have given Mrs Miller the same instructions and advised the household at large I expect you both to do as you are told." He smiled as he said the last part, and left saying he would pop around again in a couple of days. Helena thanked him and before he was out of the room had fallen asleep again.

When Archie returned, he had much to tell, but thought it pertinent to share his news with those affected first. Hugh agreed, suggesting once both ladies were awake, Archie might carry Sybil into Helena's room so they all would hear his update at once. Thus, several hours later the Yellow Room, bathed in soft afternoon sunlight, was the scene of many revelations. Helena insisted Sybil slip into bed with her, so they stayed warm, while Archie and Hugh pulled up two of the large leather chairs and made themselves comfortable.

Chapter Seventeen

Hugh asked Helena whether she had yet remembered any details of the previous afternoon.

She shook her head. "The last thing I recall with any certainty is thinking Sybil must be in the storerooms and that I had to go and make sure. Up until then everything is relatively clear. Seth causing chaos and there seemed to be a small fire, but then it all becomes rather vague." Helena was glad she had some voice, despite it sounding as though she had a mouth full of gravel.

Sybil took Helena's hand, "You saved my life my lady. If you hadn't come to find me, I would likely have burned to death. I still don't know how we got out."

Helena's brow creased as she searched her mind for the events of the previous day, but to no avail, it remained stubbornly locked away. She stared at Sybil in bewilderment.

"I did? But I'm petrified of fire, surely you must have mistaken me for someone else." All three gawked at her, amazed she could not recollect anything of the events. Sybil, speaking slowly her voice husky, took up her part of the tale, explaining she had indeed been in one of the storerooms behind the kitchen when Helena suddenly appeared, begging Sybil to go with her because she didn't want to have to tell Archie why they were dead. Archie and Hugh chuckled at this, while Helena blushed sheepishly.

Sybil went to say they found Seth in one of the offices, Helena persuading him to come with them and by the time they got out, the building was collapsing around them. While Sybil was speaking, images began to form in Helena's head; leaping flames, extreme heat, wood splintering, glass shattering and the most terrifying roar. She could see Seth crouched on the floor, fire all around them and the worry that she was taking them the wrong way; that they would never escape.

"That was me?" she rasped. Now they had started, the images wouldn't stop and memories flooded her brain. "Oh God, what on earth possessed me?" She lifted quivering hands to her head, willing the pictures to cease — the horror engulfing her. She turned to Hugh, dove grey eyes, enormous in her pale face, brimming over with tears she desperately tried to hold back. Her hand fluttered towards him and she shuddered, gulping for air as she tried to steady herself, but her control was slipping out of reach.

Without pausing to consider the consequences, Hugh moved to the bed and sitting on the edge, wrapped his arms around Helena just as her composure abandoned her altogether and a torrent of sobs wracked her body. He began to talk, reminding her that without her quick action, Sybil would almost certainly have perished; that both were safe and soon life would return to normal. Cradling her against his chest, he rocked her as though a child, running calming hands up and down her back. Eventually she regained her equanimity and tried to disentangle herself from him. Hugh ignored her, merely holding her closer, his head resting on the top of hers.

"There are four of us in the room and, while I appreciate my behaviour may be somewhat…unconventional, I believe right now, comforting you is far more important than worrying about whether my actions are appropriate. Archie and Sybil are right here."

Helena gave up fighting and leaned into him. Drawing up the bedclothes, Hugh settled them both back against the pillows, his hand stroking along her arm in a soothing motion, while Archie told them what he gleaned that morning.

"I came back by Sanctuary 'ouse," he began, "'tis a rare mess now. Most of the building is gone, a few rooms is left on t'opposite side to where the fire must 'ave started, but I'm not sure as they'll be able to save anything." He went on to describe the destruction, and it was clear the refuge had probably been damaged beyond repair. All their hard work, everything they had hoped to achieve lost in the blink of an eye, although thankfully, surrounding buildings while scorched in places, had survived relatively intact.

"S-Seth?" queried Helena tremulously. Hugh and Archie looked at each other over the heads of their women, and Hugh nodded imperceptibly.

"It seems he perished in the flames, my lady." Archie admitted quietly. Helena shifted convulsively. Hugh, who continued to stroke her arm, pressed his lips on her hair,

"There was nothing you could have done, sweetheart. Just as Archie and I got to you, he pulled his hand from yours and ran back into the flames. It was a miracle you got out, to try to find him would have meant certain death. It was all I could do to stop you going after him. Please don't ever frighten me like that again. To lose you would…" Hugh stopped speaking abruptly, such declarations were too personal to be shared even in front those whose lives have become bound to yours.

Helena listened as the discussion between Archie and Hugh evolved into whether rebuilding was a possibility, the costs involved and whether the wealthy elite might be persuaded into donating large sums of money, bearing in mind one of their own had risked her life. Lady Beaumont would not be prepared to let all their hard work to go to waste, but her second child was due imminently and it was unlikely she would return to her city residence before Christmas. Helena wanted to be involved in whatever the decision was, and was already ruminating over how to address it.

"Hugh, what will happen to the women who relied on Sanctuary House as a place to stay, away from their husbands or from whatever they had fled?" realising there were at least eight women to whom this applied. Where would they sleep? Where would they find food? Clothing? The thought that any may be forced to return to an abusive situation because there was no alternative, too distressing to contemplate. "Some have been living there for months, even years, they have nowhere else to go. We have to help them." Helena's voice rose, cracking painfully as she tried to make clear her consternation.

"Hush my love, you will make yourself cough and with a throat as sore as yours it would not be pleasant." Hugh sought to calm her. "Leave it with us. Archie and I will find out what steps have been taken to look after those now without a bed. Remember there are other staff whose responsibility it is to provide care for these women; who I am sure will have seen to their needs."

"You are correct. I beg your pardon, I forgot myself. Mama is always telling me it is not my place to interfere." Helena croaked, far too primly in Hugh's opinion — a dangerous sign.

"Sweetheart, I think you should interfere as much as you please, your concern for these women is commendable, but you nearly died last afternoon and I, not to mention the doctor, would like to you rest and let others do the worrying for a little while."

Helena twisted in his arms and stared into his face. She read the anxiety in his eyes and recognised she was being selfish — again. Would she ever learn? Useless tears threatened once more and, even though she recognised that they were borne of fatigue, anguish and — if she was really honest — no small amount of fear for what might have been, didn't mean she wanted them to fall. She scrubbed at her face as Hugh, sensing another downpour was in the offing, rang for a maid and nodded to Archie, who scooped up his wife commenting that Sybil looked sleepy and whisked her back to the adjacent bedroom.

As the door closed, Helena began to weep. Hugh simply turned her in his embrace, cradling her against his chest while she cried it out. It wasn't as violent an outburst as earlier, more a release of emotion, an acceptance of what had happened and a way to begin the healing process.

"S-sorry, I c-can't seem to s-stop crying," she blubbered, trying to take deep breaths, and stem her sobs, something she was struggling to master. "I n-never cry and already t-twice this afternoon, i-it won't do."

Hugh chuckled, he couldn't help it; she looked so woebegone. "Do not be too hard on yourself, love. You have been through a rather distressing time, and I think a few tears are allowed." As he spoke a quiet knock heralded Emily, who brought a bowl of delicious smelling soup, a thick slice of fresh bread and another goblet of the mixture prescribed by Doctor Phillips. "Now see what Maggie has made for you, a good meal will make you feel brighter. You haven't eaten for more than a day."

Helena didn't think she had any appetite, but she tried and after the first mouthful realised she was quite hungry. She ate everything in the bowl and managed most of the bread, softening it by dipping it into the soup. Sipping the tincture, she felt drowsy again and was unable to stop herself sliding down the pillows. Handing Hugh the cup, she started to speak, but whatever she intended to say was lost as slumber claimed her. Hugh stood back, allowing Emily to tuck Helena in and once he saw she was properly settled, left the room.

The next couple of days followed a similar pattern. Both Helena and Sybil slept for much of the time, while their lungs began to purify themselves, expelling the toxic build-up, and their bodies to recover from shock. Helena, especially, was besieged by nightmares, eventually persuaded to take a minute dose of laudanum to give her an undisturbed rest. Although reluctant, as she did not like the after effects of the drug, she was sensible enough to realise that if she didn't sleep, regaining her health would take much longer.

Three days later, both women were informed they might spend some time out of bed and both were more than a little pleased. Lady Winchester had brought over some fresh clothes for her daughter as had Archie for his wife. The clothes Helena and Sybil were wearing the night of the fire had to be thrown away, too singed and coated in soot to be salvaged.

Once ensconced in the elegant yet comfortable parlour, the two women looked at each other, unsure what to say or what to talk about. It was ludicrous; they had known each other for months and had just shared the most upsetting experience, yet normal conversation seemed impossible. Helena could feel her lips twitching and just as Betty came in with hot coffee and a plate of ginger biscuits, the pair burst into gales of laughter, clearing the air and while they sipped the heady brew, fell into lively gossip about how they might help the shelter now.

Not long after, Jessica joined them, the three women becoming fast friends, their chatter turning to Trentams and how Jessica was finding the work there. Jessica loved her days at the shipyard and believed she was quite an asset to her brother, commenting that he even thanked her for making his office look as though it had never been used

"…although I'm not entirely sure it was a compliment," she concluded ruefully.

"I don't think Hugh offers compliments he doesn't mean, so I would accept it at face value and not question his motives." Helena chuckled. "'Tis probably more to do with the fact he no longer has any idea where everything is. Well done Jessica, now he cannot do without you." Jessica beamed at her new friend as Helena wondered whether Hugh had mentioned his concerns about the unexplained incidents to his sister and decided it was best not to say anything — just in case.

Chapter Eighteen

Mrs Drummond came in while the three were chatting, and sat with them for a time, making sure her guests had all they required. Helena wished to acknowledge the care Sybil and she — two people whom, other than Hugh, none in the household knew save a brief encounter at the shipyard — had received.

"Thank you, Mrs Drummond. You, your family, and your staff have been so kind. I am sorry we have inconvenienced you this way; it cannot be easy with three extra people under your feet. Now Sybil and I are both nearly recovered, mayhap we should remove to my home, lifting burden from your household."

Sybil added her appreciation, "Oh yes, Mrs Drummond. 'Tis a blessing to have been nursed so attentively and allowing my Archie to stay too, few in your position would have welcomed the likes of us." Sybil stood and dropped a deep curtsy, Helena registering, not for the first time, Sybil's pretty manners. Hugh's mother eyed both women with a sort of benevolent exasperation.

"Mrs Miller, don't you ever think you are unworthy of notice; this city runs on people like you and Archie, and hopefully one day the gap between rich and poor won't be so unbridgeable. As for being a burden, goodness me girl, you, neither of you is a burden." Mrs Drummond tutted at the notion, pooh-poohing Helena's solicitude. "Until this afternoon, you were confined to your bedchambers and have eaten scarcely a scrap of food, barely enough to keep a bird alive never mind two healthy young ladies." Sybil blushed at being referred to as a lady and unconsciously smoothed her already tidy hair. "I am glad Hugh thought to bring you here and I imagine, if his hours of pacing up and down the hallway are anything to go by, you'll be lucky if he lets you out of his sight ever again..." she paused, then patted Helena's hand

"…but thank you for worrying about it my dear. Many ladies of the *ton* would simply assume it was theirs by right."

Helena smiled shyly and squeezed the hand that still lay on hers, warmed both by Mrs Drummond's innate generosity and the fact she didn't seem unduly perturbed that the first time she met the lady to whom her son seemed more than a little attracted, was under such unusual circumstances.

"Thank you," she whispered. Mrs Drummond regarded Helena with a knowing eye.

"Am I to suppose that this is not some trivial dalliance?" she asked pointedly. Helena flushed to the roots of her hair, stammering what she hoped was a lucid reply.

"I-I hope so. I…he…we haven't…I-I think…I trust…b-but if he…m-maybe I shou…" Helena dried up. So much for lucid! She didn't know what to say to Hugh's mother. Hugh hadn't said he wanted to marry her and she told him she didn't expect him to offer for her. Even though she knew she wanted to spend her life with him, she couldn't assume that's what he desired, although he said he wanted to spend the rest of his days proving to her how much he loved her. Suddenly it all seemed rather muddled. Neither did she feel it was her place to discuss it with his mother. Wasn't that Hugh's job? Helena chewed her bottom lip and fiddled with her fingers, wishing the floor might open up and swallow her.

"Do you love my son, Lady Helena?" Mrs Drummond's question, although not entirely unexpected, caught Helena off guard and her head snapped up. Holding the elder woman's gaze steadily, Helena straightened her back and lifted her chin.

"I do, with all my heart." Spoken with deliberation there was no mistaking the joy in Helena's voice. Dorothea Drummond inclined her head and despite seemingly maintaining her rigid posture, Helena could almost see her relax. At that moment, the door opened to admit the object of their discussion, along with Archie, Nick trailing a few seconds behind, engrossed in a newspaper. Helena blushed again, concerned they might have heard her declaration, but none showed any indication of having done so. Shortly thereafter, Mrs Drummond excused herself, saying dinner would be served early allowing the two semi-invalids to retire, should they choose.

Helena, feeling weary again, was discouraged. Normally the picture of health and, except for her occasional headaches, never sick, so needing to rest after doing nothing more than sit in a chair for a couple of hours was frustrating, making her churlish. Her disgruntled expression did not go unnoticed.

"What's wrong Helena?" queried Hugh as he sat next to her, wishing he could take her hand and entwine his fingers through hers, or more preferably entwine his fingers through her hair and kiss her senseless, but holding hands would do for now.

"I'm tired — again. This fatigue is irksome. I wonder whether I will ever feel well again." Hugh chuckled and she glared at him in indignation "'Tis not amusing."

"My lady, today is the first day you have been allowed out of bed, of course you will feel a trifle seedy. Trust me, over the next few days you will come on apace." Knowing he was right didn't stop her from being grumpy and she groused something incomprehensible. Then her upbringing came to the fore.

"I am so sorry," she said, recognising she was behaving badly. "I am being most impolite to you who least deserve my dissatisfaction. I think mayhap I should rest before dinner." Smiling, although to those watching it seemed artificial, Helena dipped a meagre curtsy and slipped out of the room. Suddenly she felt alone; she wanted her Mama and her own house and her own bed, but then she wouldn't see Hugh every day and that made her heart ache.

Halfway up the stairs, she leaned against the wall, swallowing weak tears. Honestly, she was worse than a waterfall at the moment. Blinking them away, she carried on and just as she reached the top she heard the click of a door closing. With no desire to be seen crying like a baby she quickened her steps and was almost at her bedchamber when a voice spoke from behind her.

"Helena?"

She rested her head on the cool wood panelling of the door.

"Sweetheart, what's wrong, it seems more than simple tiredness that troubles you." His hands swept up her arms as he spun her around to face him. Her head drooped and he stroked a finger along her jaw lifting her chin so she had to look at him. "Come on love, it cannot be that bad." He brushed her lips with his.

"I'm not sure you wish to hear it," she sighed. Hugh stared into her arresting eyes, grey as the dawn's mist and felt his heart lurch.

"Please," his entreaty worked and as she gazed back, she knew she had to be honest. They had shared many intimate moments and she knew she wanted more, much more and, innocent as she was, believed Hugh was equally stirred. Passion and love however are not the same and, from what little she understood of men, they could easily have the first without the second. It wasn't that she didn't think Hugh loved her, but it was whether he loved her enough to consider a life together, or whether what he felt was something that would fade all too quickly, leaving them both adrift in an empty sea.

"Might we talk?" she asked quietly, "Alone?" Hugh raked his eyes over her face, seeing tension lurking there. Wordlessly, he led her along the hallway into a room with huge bay windows, through which poured the hazy golden light from the late afternoon sun. There were four armchairs, a table, and a small piano.

"It's our music room," he said, spreading his hands in explanation. Helena nodded absently; sudden nerves making her stomach feel as though hundreds of ants were marching through it. Hugh perched on one of the chairs, but Helena wandered around the room, lifting the lid of the piano, and touching the ivory keys, smoothing her fingers over the heavy silk of the drapery, and staring with sightless eyes over the neat garden. *Come on Helena*, she instructed herself, *get it over with*. Taking a deep breath, she began to speak.

"I have had many hours to think over the last few days and I must tell you I cannot go on as we are." Startled, Hugh made to get up. "No, stay where you are, please let me say this, 'tis already hard enough, if you come close I will forget everything except how much I l…" she stopped abruptly, tugging on a lock of hair in the manner Hugh had come to realise meant she was agitated. "As I said, I have been thinking. So much thinking, I would be happy if I never had to think again. When I say, I cannot go on as we are, it does not mean my affection towards you has changed. I love you more than anything else in this world and hereby lies my problem."

Helena paused, trying to keep her thoughts in order. "When I was younger, if I couldn't sleep, Papa used to tell me stories from his favourite book or maybe it was a collection of poems, I forget now. I imagine the tome is long lost, but one was about moonlight and the sea — I think this was the poem after which the book was entitled. Anyway, the only part I remember was the last verse." Memories flooded in and Helena could see her father sitting next to her as she recited the lines, her voice wavering slightly as long buried sadness caught her unexpectedly —

> *"Light fades from pink to blue*
> *A grey sea kisses the shore*
> *Chill night stalks the waves*
> *As white horses steal a ride*
> *Silhouetted under a waning moon*
> *Two shadows hand in hand*
> *Two souls forever entwined*
> *Love on a winter's tide."*

Hugh was spellbound, though barely even a stanza, Helena made the fragment sound like a lullaby. He had never heard the words, but they struck a chord with him. He started to understand where Helena was going with her somewhat convoluted confession and he wanted to be the one to ask. Not wishing to interrupt however, he settled back into the chair and waited for the right moment.

Swallowing her grief, Helena composed herself to continue. "This particular verse keeps rolling around my head, two souls forever entwined. I'm not sure what a winter's tide is; maybe there is no such thing, but that's what makes it magical, mysterious and indefinable. My love for you is this way. I am at a loss to explain my depth of feeling but I know it will last forever. I want a lifetime of laughter and shared kisses and promises and secrets. I want to hold your hand until we are old and grey and mayhap have forgotten how and when we fell in we love, but content knowing we did and it is timeless, like the moon and the tide."

She drew a shuddering breath determined to clarify why she had started this, but before she could say anymore, Hugh was on his feet and she was in his arms.

"My darling Helena. For weeks, I have dreamed of saying these same words to you, but held back for fear I was rushing you, or placing too much pressure on you. From the moment we met, you have enchanted me. Your beautiful eyes, your glorious hair and your smile, your smile that captured my soul the first time you bestowed it on me. I tried to fight it; my life, my world is far removed from yours, my status much lower. Further, should I have reason to cross the seas, I may not return." He felt a tremor run through her and kissed her forehead.

"To cause you sorrow would break me, but the more I tried to distance myself, the more of my heart you stole, piece by piece until one day it was wholly yours. Without you being aware you had done so, you claimed me and I knew without any doubt this was as it should be. When they told me you had run into the fire, my heart stopped and I realised if I lost you, my world would become desolate. Nothing is of any importance unless I am able to share it with you." He paused, his own emotions threatening to consume him.

"The day we admitted our feelings, you said you believed our paths were meant to collide, that somewhere, somehow our lives were supposed to weave together. My dearest, I also want to love, laugh, cry, dance, kiss and grow old with you, we are navigating the same timeless course, guided by the moon and the tide. Helena Trevallier, I love you with an abiding love and the thought of not having you by my side until the end of my days is an ordeal I do not wish to contemplate. Will you do me the greatest honour and marry me?"

While Hugh was talking, Helena's jaw had dropped. She knew he cared, but that the strength of his love mirrored her own, stunned her. His words ensnared her; they echoed the poem, soft and seductive yet vital and enduring — like the tide. He wanted to marry her...he actually wanted to marry her.

"Are you sure? It's forever you know," she ventured, her brow creasing as she leaned back, the better to read his face. Hugh smiled and pressed his lips lightly to hers, even so brief a touch enough to send heat coiling through her.

"Which is precisely why I want it," he replied.

Helena read the truth in his eyes and nodded, her own eyes shining, all the love she felt spilling out. "Yes! Yes! Yes!"

Hugh kissed her then, long and tenderly, the passion that never failed to flare circled them, but he held it at bay. Time enough for that, now was for love.

Chapter Nineteen

How long they kissed, Helena would never recall, it felt like an age yet was over too soon. Both were trembling when finally, Hugh broke their embrace.

"We must travel to your brother's estate, so I may ask him for your hand." Helena started to speak but he interrupted her, adding, "I know you are of age, but I would like to give your family the chance to approve our betrothal. I am not a member of the *ton*, only of the merchant class. Your brother may not think me suitable."

"I think my brother will be heartily glad anyone wants to marry me," she said wryly. "He hoped someone would offer for me during the Season. I wasn't interested, however, and so never let it get that far. I imagine he will deem your suit acceptable."

"Well if he doesn't, I might just have to return to that kidnapping option and whisk you away to Gretna Green," Hugh murmured, cupping her face in his hands and kissing her again. Helena giggled and, as Hugh didn't seem inclined to release her lips, surrendered to the remarkable sensations he was inducing. With one hand curved around the back of her neck cradling her head, Hugh let his other hand trail along her body, light fingers ghosting across the creamy skin of her throat, teasing over her shoulder and down her spine.

Under his touch, Helena whimpered softly, her own hands involuntarily tracing the muscles flexing under his waistcoat. Without thinking, she pulled his shirt free, gliding cool fingers across his skin. Hugh groaned and his mouth recaptured hers, their kiss deepening as the passion Hugh had earlier tried so desperately to subdue, returned with a vengeance. His hands rippled over her willowy frame with the delicacy of a violinist mastering his instrument, composing a melody only they heard, its resonance making Helena's body sing. All the while firm lips scattered butterfly kisses down the sensitive skin of her neck to the rise of her breast.

The room receded, and for Helena there was nothing except this man who had turned her world upside down, a world that was currently spinning out of control. Emboldened, she let her hands travel further under his shirt, resting briefly on his chest — loving the erratic beat of his heart — over his stomach, seeking out those muscles that taunted her, then down, daring to brush her fingers over the fall of his trousers, his need for her unmistakable. She knew she should be scandalised by her own brazen behaviour, never mind the liberties she was allowing Hugh, but found she didn't care.

Hugh, almost undone by Helena's gestures — which somehow managed to be tentative and audacious at the same time — felt as though he was drowning in her. Everything about her bewitched him and every time they kissed, he was assaulted by the same tidal wave of sensations that assailed him the first time their lips met.

Restless heat flared between them, making Helena feel curiously weightless. Right at that moment, her legs decided that holding her upright was no longer in their purview and, had Hugh not been holding her tightly, would have crumpled ignominiously to the floor.

"Seems 'tis my lot in life to catch you, my love," he muttered in her ear, his breathing ragged, lifting her against his chest as his lips prevented her huffed response. Helena considered telling him, it was no such thing but realised he was quite correct, and anyway, kissing was far more enjoyable than arguing.

"As long as you do not let me fall," she replied, eventually, when he relinquished her lips the more to explore her neck.

"Never." A single word yet it gave them a lifetime. Sinking into his embrace, Helena simply let go. Hearts thudding, all reason abandoned them and it would have been so easy to succumb to their desires.

A voice in the hallway brought them to their senses. Helena shot over to the window, as Hugh stuffed his shirt untidily into his trousers. By the time Jessica burst through the door, both looked the picture of respectability — if one ignored their flushed faces.

"What on earth are you two doing in here?" she demanded, her glance flicking suspiciously between the two.

"I wished to speak to your brother in private, Jessica. I hope you understand." Helena's tone was courteous but invited no further questioning. "There are matters I needed to discuss regarding the refuge with someone who has a mind for business and I did not feel it appropriate to do so in front of Sybil, 'tis likely too upsetting for her at present."

Jessica nodded slowly, her expression telling them that she did not believe a word of it, but was too polite to say so. "Well, anyway, Mama says dinner will be served in an hour, in case either of you needed to prolong your…err…discussion." Jessica grinned impishly and skipped out, hugging herself with the knowledge that her solemn and, in her opinion, rather staid brother had just been kissing her new friend.

There was silence in the room as the doors closed.

"Oh dear, Jessica knows," said Helena ruefully.

"Is that such a bad thing?" Hugh asked, walking over to where she stood by the window and drawing her against him.

"I was hoping to keep it between us until 'tis official. I like just us knowing, our secret, it makes it all utterly delicious." Helena felt laughter rumble through Hugh's chest.

"You are the delicious one, my love." He bent his head and kissed her gently. "Come, I think we should join the others before our ardour runs away with us." She stared up at him, stroking a hand up his neck and along his jaw as that thought filled her mind. "No! Don't you dare distract me. I'm trying to behave like a gentleman yet you insist on inveigling me. Stop with your sorcery."

Helena smiled and pressed her lips to his. "If you insist, although I do believe we may need to revisit this particular discussion later." With that, she swung away from him and fled to her bedchamber where she spent some time writing to both her mother and her brother while trying, without much success, to calm her fluttering heart.

Two days later, the doctor agreed that both Helena and Sybil had recovered enough to return to their respective homes. Sybil found it especially hard as the contrast between her house and the Drummond residence was as day is to night. She was nothing if not grateful however and, after she had departed, the small gift she left in appreciation for her care, warmed their hearts. Helena's gratitude was also evidenced in the beautiful bouquet of flowers and a letter deliberately left in her room so it would not be found until she had gone; neither woman good at farewells.

Once home, Helena found the time to share a few more details with her mother as to what had transpired between Hugh and her. As Lady Winchester had been expecting such an admission since the night of the fire, she wasn't unduly surprised, but was pleased Hugh intended to visit with her son. That the man who would marry her daughter wished to abide by convention merely increased his stature in her eyes and affirmed his gentility.

Helena begged her mother not to say anything until they had been to see Giles. "'Tis not that I don't want the whole world to know Mama, but we prefer to wait until Giles has given his approval. Hugh is concerned that because he is not a member of the nobility, Giles might refuse his offer. Even though I am old enough to marry without permission we do not wish our betrothal to cause division." Spoiling her nicely rehearsed speech by adding, "Of course I hope Giles realises if he does refuse I will run away and marry Hugh anyway."

As Augusta had already corresponded with her son and knew of his feelings on this matter, she wasn't in the slightest anxious, but knew also that Giles, as Earl and head of the family, wanted to be the one to give his blessing. She kept her peace, merely chuckling at her daughter's effrontery, and turning their conversation to other matters.

Hugh wrote to the Earl of Winchester receiving a warm response, inviting him to Whiteoaks, along with Lady Winchester and Helena at their earliest convenience. Unfortunately, their visit was delayed by a series of regrettable events, which if not for the quick actions of a loyal shipyard employee, might have ended disastrously.

As her life resumed something akin to a normal routine, Helena knew she needed to find something to take the place of her work at the refuge. She had visited the site, appalled at the damage caused by the fire, realising how fortunate she and Sybil were, to escape with their lives. Two thirds of the building had collapsed and the remaining third was so badly scorched that the authorities had deemed it unstable and it was slowly being demolished.

Seth's body had never been found, but it was assumed he perished in the flames. Despite his actions, Helena was still saddened she had not been able to keep hold of his hand, although maybe it was better that Seth died believing he was doing something kind for Lynette rather than face the magistrate, never mind the wrath of the local community.

On a more positive note, the charitable organisation, which originally established Sanctuary House, also owned the building and the land on which it stood. This meant once sufficient funds had been donated, they could rebuild. It would be a lengthy process, and in the meantime, there was what to do about those women suddenly without a home. Lord Beaumont, under strict instructions from his wife, used his influence to arrange for the refuge to be housed temporarily in a disused warehouse. It was far from ideal, but was solid and had a number of small offices, which could be turned into bedrooms.

Less than two miles from what had been Sanctuary House, it was easily accessible to those who required its shelter. Happy to have something practical to occupy her time, Helena, along with the other staff and several of the women, worked long and hard to prepare it for use. Partitions, tables, a space for a kitchen, wash rooms and a laundry were deemed the basic requirements, and for a few days the women weren't sure how they would manage. Then, late one afternoon, Archie appeared with those of his friends whose help he had commandeered. Once they knew what was needed, the men turned up every day armed with all manner of tools, working long into the evenings, glad of the work and the coin they received. After almost three weeks of hard work not to mention a lot of noise, the place was habitable.

Tabitha, back from her honeymoon, launched herself into the project with her usual enthusiasm. Adept at persuading members of the nobility to donate anything from money to clothes to livestock — not that any of the latter were needed — Tabitha soon had many willing benefactors. Especially when she whispered in their ears, confidentially, that Lady Helena Trevallier, one of their own, had risked her life to save not only one of the women under the protection of the haven, but also the man believed to have started the blaze.

Hugh was still contending with problems at Trentams. The incidents had increased in frequency and several men had been injured. Thankfully, not badly, but the fact they had been hurt at all in a shipyard with an unblemished record was of grave concern. Hugh was starting to think there must be someone within his employ who was either precipitating the accidents or admitting into the yard others who were.

He spent many hours talking with Helena about their courtship, suspicious those behind the trouble might use her to coerce him to bow to an as yet unknown petition, and the thought of her being in harm's way was untenable. To that end, although they continued to be seen together in public occasionally, their relationship appeared doomed. Their behaviour excruciatingly polite and to the undiscerning eye, they looked to suffer each other's company with barely concealed distaste.

However, had anyone been able to see through closed doors or into walled gardens or along any of the secluded pathways around Hyde Park, they might have been forgiven for thinking their eyes deceived them.

Helena was inclined to think Hugh was being over cautious. She could not imagine why anyone would go to the extreme of targeting her, or for that matter any of Hugh's family over a ship or two. What Helena had yet to understand was there were many shipyards, and even though Trentams had been operating for years, it was considered comparatively new. The success of Hugh's company meant they had increased their fleet with unusual rapidity and to some of the long-standing shipping lines, Hugh, and his father before him, were upstarts.

It was frustrating though, as despite the number of unexplained mishaps, Hugh still had not received any demands to sell. Thankfully, so far, the injuries had been minor and although the new schooner had sustained some damage it was rectified quickly. He increased the guard, and appointed Archie as head of security; the man demonstrating an uncanny ability to distinguish accident from sabotage, and intruder from legitimate visitor. From his first day, the confidence shown him by Hugh had worked wonders and Archie proved himself to be wholly reliable and trustworthy. Moreover, since Helena had saved Sybil's life, he would do everything in his power to protect her and Hugh.

Following several meetings with Hugh, Lucas Withers took over the investigation, stationing one or two of his men at the yard, who were to report anything at all that seemed out of place. The attacks appeared designed to cause the most damage with minimum organisation and, privately, Withers was worried that whoever was behind the campaign against Trentams might not stop at inconsequential accidents. So far no one had quit the yard, loyal to their employer, but it would not take much for their fealty to be tested beyond its limits.

A couple of men had been caught trying to damage equipment but fear of who sent them, far outweighed their fear of Withers, Hugh, or the magistrate and both had refused to say a word. One of the men was familiar to Hugh who, although unable to place him, mentioned it to Lucas. Tenacious when he had a knotty problem to deal with, Lucas was painstakingly unravelling the threads, the answer tantalisingly close and, if his suspicions proved correct, would shock the Drummonds to their core.

Chapter Twenty

Hugh was right to be concerned, as a certain — for want of better description — gentleman was determined to see Trentams close completely, or at the least sold at a substantial loss to the current owner; his plans already laid. Unbeknownst to Hugh, the yard had been under observation for months and Helena had come to their attention several weeks previously, during a ball where she, unfortunately for her, met Mr Hugh Drummond. The man behind the plot surmised that Drummond cared more for this chit than he led people to believe. Moreover, if his preferred strategy failed, there was always the sister, whom the aforementioned gentleman imagined would scream loudly, should it prove necessary.

It was irritating that the accidents he had engineered had been attributed to negligence but he knew, once lives were threatened, or worse — lost, there was an excellent chance he would be able to step in and take over. After all, what was the death of one giddy young woman who deliberately ignored safety instructions compared with the power and influence he would gain being the owner of a successful trading fleet? He believed nobody would want to do business with Hugh after such an accident, loss of faith providing the perfect opportunity. He would, of course, be appropriately devastated by what happened, his offer to buy the yard precisely timed so as not to seem insensitive. It would be a seamless transition — after all he knew most everyone who worked at Trentams, and they trusted him. Drummond would be none the wiser.

Lord Faversham gripped his glass of whisky, a malevolent smile hovering over his lips as he ruminated over how soon to implement the last and most heinous part of his scheme.

While Lord Faversham was plotting her demise, Helena, blissfully unaware, was making her way home from the temporary refuge. It was fully operational now and all who required its shelter had returned. September had slithered quietly into October, and although the days were still mild the nights were much colder. The trees were beginning to offer a dazzling display of autumnal colour — red, yellow, bronze and purple, as the city began to prepare for the long winter. Many families who left London for country houses to wait out the worst of the heat returned, while others, required to check on their estates, departed.

That evening Helena was attending a birthday ball for the daughter of some earl or other. Such events were few and far between at this time of the year and often more delightful because of it. Everyone who was anyone would be there — if not invited to a ball during the non-Season, it was the equivalent of being shunned. Hugh would be escorting her, affirming he would collect Stephen and Tabitha on the way.

Once home, Helena asked to have a bath drawn and luxuriated in the scented water, letting it wash away the fatigue of the day. Nancy helped her dress, buttoning her into a velvet gown in a shade of dark rust, with matching leather slippers, then fashioned her hair — thankfully not too short, following the scorching it received — into a stylish bun, one or two locks left loose to frame her face. A charcoal grey cloak completed her outfit, and by the time Hugh arrived she was ready.

When Helena walked down the stairs to meet him, Hugh felt his heart pound. It was becoming harder and harder for them to maintain their distance. He wished he had been able to pinpoint who was at the bottom of what was going on, but despite his growing suspicions, the identity of the main offender remained elusive, and he required incontrovertible proof before exposing the perpetrator.

Helena smiled as she reached the bottom step. Hugh bowed over her hand as she dropped a neat curtsy. Pushing back her glove, he kissed her wrist sending a shiver shimmying up her arm.

"I love you," she whispered, holding his gaze.

"I love you more," he said just as quietly. Relishing even so small a contact the couple held hands for the few steps it took until they were at the front door. Then Hugh stood back and let Helena walk to the carriage on her own, for all the world as though they cared nothing for each other. As the carriage rumbled off, Hugh begged the indulgence of the other three sitting with him. Stephen and Tabitha looked confused but Helena less so, such requests now all too familiar.

"Lucas thinks things are coming to a head and it is possible, because so many will be attending this ball, there will be an approach of sorts tonight, maybe even a threat. It will be a crowded affair; small gatherings in dark corners always go unnoticed. I am convinced someone is trying to intimidate me into selling Trentams, although, as you know, I have received no demands. What concerns me is you, Helena. If anyone is watching, we need to make sure they believe we do not care for each other. If you hear anything along those lines tonight, trust that I am only trying to protect you. I love you with all my heart, and once this is over, we can be wed and spend the rest of our lives without worrying about someone trying to hurt you."

Their two friends wore matching expressions of shock, which at any other time would have been funny. Helena had not shared her news with anyone except her mother, and Tabitha especially was astounded.

"I am sorry Tabitha," Helena said contritely. "We wanted to keep it between us until Hugh spoke with Giles. This tonight has forced our hand," turning to Hugh. "My love, I am more frightened for you, I still do not think anyone will bother with me. Since we have been at pains to make it appear as though we are beginning to dislike each other, they would not expect me to be particularly saddened should I overhear a derogatory comment from you. I can, however, pretend to be furious, if you think that might divert them."

Hugh considered this and nodded his agreement. "You will have to leave without me though, and we cannot be seen together until Lucas has found the perpetrators. I am sorry my darling, but it is the only way."

Helena patted his knee. "I think if we have a whole lifetime to look forward to, a few days will be as the blink of an eye."

With complete disregard for etiquette and the couple sitting opposite, Hugh dragged Helena into his arms and kissed her with a passion that threatened to undo her. Tactfully, Stephen and Tabitha looked the other way, apparently engrossed in each other, not that they found that unduly difficult.

As the coach pulled to a halt outside the residence of Lord and Lady Challerford, Hugh released Helena, made sure she was not dishevelled in any way, and calmly climbed down. Helena steeled herself, assuming a façade of bland indifference, while she waited until Stephen had helped Tabitha down, then followed. Hugh offered Helena his arm, which she refused, giving him a haughty glare, ruined when she dropped sly wink. Trying not to grin, he followed her up the steps into the brightly lit house where they promptly separated.

The ball was in full swing; every room blazoned with light from the multitude of candles, while music and laughter filtered through the ballroom and along the hallways, a cheerful accompaniment to the sound of glasses clinking and people gossiping. Helena stood for a moment gathering herself. There were couples everywhere, and it was hard seeing them happily dancing or disappearing into quiet alcoves, when she could not do the same with Hugh. Forcing herself to appear detached, Helena discreetly made a note of who had attended, what they were doing, with whom they spent most time, and whether any of them seemed to be watching her.

Tabitha guided her to a quiet table while Stephen went to fetch them a drink each.

"Right Helena Trevallier, what is going on? You need to tell me." Helena looked at her friend, considering her request. Tabitha reached over the gripped her hand. "Helena, please!"

Helena nodded, "When Stephen joins us, but whatever I tell you must go no further. It is imperative people believe Hugh and I are finished, you will understand why when I explain." Stephen found them shortly thereafter, handing a glass of Negus to both women. Helena took an unladylike gulp of hers; setting the glass down before she was tempted to swallow the lot in one go.

"Remember, no one else must know," she warned them. Stephen raised a questioning eyebrow, prompting Tabitha to whisper in his ear. He offered a humourless smile as he leaned forward, keen to hear the latest developments. Helena went on to disclose what had been happening. Stephen knew much of it having been the one to suggest Withers' involvement in the first place, but that Hugh believed Helena might be at risk was a revelation.

"Does he expect us to sit back and do nothing?" he demanded in fierce undertone.

"No, he expects us to behave as though we are having a marvellous time, and should anyone corner him tonight, we act accordingly. If I overhear something and react with a nicely timed bout of temper, hopefully it will be enough to persuade whoever is coordinating this, we no longer care for each other. That should take some of this pressure off Hugh. If it does happen, I will leave the ball immediately. It would not do to stay after such a demonstration of anger. Problem is, I have no idea who to look for. Stephen, if you see anyone talking to Hugh who we don't really know or who doesn't usually attend these balls, please tell me."

Stephen nodded, "Fret not, Helena. Withers will have everything under control. Now, let me take a brief walk around and I will report back forthwith." Relishing the opportunity to help the friend who had been so solicitous of him last year when others believed him culpable of the fire at Ashbourne House, Stephen strolled off. Chatting to his friends, nodding at acquaintances, he behaved like the cordial gentleman he was. While they waited, Helena and Tabitha gossiped about nothing of any substance, and Helena's calm demeanour masked a woman whose insides felt as though they were in the middle of a boxing match.

Sometime later Stephen reappeared, informing Helena that as far as he could see it was just the usual crowd, no interlopers and, apparently, Hugh was deep in conversation with one of his colleagues. Helena decided it might prove interesting for her to conduct her own survey. A chance to watch how others responded to her being, to all intents and purposes, abandoned by the man who until recently had been so attentive.

She wandered gracefully around the rooms and along the hallways, stopping occasionally to indulge in polite conversation with family friends or to engage in a mild flirtation with one of her erstwhile suitors. She drifted here and there, her gown whispering as she moved, her hair glimmering in the candlelight. Only Tabitha and Stephen saw through the pretence, Tabitha murmuring to her husband she would not be at all surprised if a megrim saw fit to strike Helena down before the end of the evening.

Sometime after midnight, Helena was of the impression Withers had been mistaken. There was no one untoward at this party and the last time she saw Hugh he was discussing politics with Lord Rutland. She wanted to go home, it was becoming too difficult to maintain her poise. Mentioning this to her companions, the three agreed it was time to take their leave. Making their way to the main ballroom, where they expected to find their hosts, Helena was halted in her tracks at the sound of her own name. Putting her fingers to her lips, she walked forward quietly, Stephen and Tabitha close behind. A conversation was going on in an alcove to the left of the hallway. The person who uttered her name spoke in a strident and somewhat acerbic voice, and was not one Helena immediately recognised. Trying to place it, she listened for a few seconds.

"...and I'm sure she would make a most suitable wife, Drummond. What holds you back man?"

There was a bark of mirthless laughter and Hugh replied, "She is naught but a capricious scatter wit, on the hunt for a rich husband, and I have no desire to be leg-shackled by some flighty chit. Moreover, she is the daughter of an earl. Do you imagine her family would allow her to wed someone so far beneath her? No, she was fun for a brief interlude, but she is like all the others, only interested in marriage and a big house and those interminable rounds of parties. That's no life for me."

There was an ugly chuckle as the other man, whom Helena finally recognised as Lord Faversham, suggested they visit brothels and gaming hells as a distraction.

Although Helena knew it a ruse, her heart clenched as she listened to Hugh's words. Maybe marriage wasn't what he wanted; perhaps the difference in their status was insurmountable. Unbidden, a tear ran down her cheek; angrily she brushed it away, just as Stephen leaned towards her

"Do not think that way, Helena. Hugh loves you. He would never have kissed you the way he did in the carriage if he didn't. Hugh does not wear his heart on his sleeve, his emotions have always been far more private than most. Even when his father died, he barely acknowledged it. Trust him Helena."

Helena turned and in the soft light from the candles stared at Stephen, "Truly?' she whispered, needing reassurance.

Stephen nodded, "Without question," he replied, his tones measured and his words ringing with sincerity.

Helena smiled wearily; the headache Tabitha had predicted, beginning to manifest. "I think we'd better get this over with, my head is beginning to ache and I do not wish it to develop into a megrim."

Tabitha risked a glance at Stephen, who squeezed his wife's hand knowingly, as he said, "Come on then, time to pretend you are on stage at Covent Garden."

Helena straightened her shoulders and stepped forward.

Chapter Twenty One

In the alcove, the two men were still talking, although Lord Faversham seemed to be dominating their conversation. Suddenly there was a swish of skirts and Helena appeared in their midst, leaving Stephen and Tabitha loitering in the hall. Hugh was standing at the far side of the recessed room, his face expressionless but Helena noticed the strain in his jaw and how tightly his hands gripped the goblet he was holding. His head shot up at Helena's entrance and, as he took in her pale cheeks and furrowed brow, hoped she wasn't succumbing to another headache.

"So, my dear Mr Drummond," she said, her tones dripping with contempt, "not only do you feel it appropriate to bore me when we are together, you now suppose it acceptable to decry me in front of…" she peered imperiously at the other man, "…Lord Faversham? Shame on you." She moved towards Hugh, positioning herself halfway between the two men in a way that meant Faversham could not see her face. Rapping Hugh's chest with her fan she continued, "I do believe this farce has gone on long enough. I am tired of trying to pretend that there is even one iota of affection left between us." Her glacial tones completely at odds with the warm smile she bestowed on Hugh as she spoke.

Out of Faversham's line of vision, Hugh grasped Helena's hand and rubbed his thumb over her palm as he said sarcastically, "Why, Lady Helena, do forgive me for not prostrating myself at your feet and begging you to reconsider," he paused. "Thank goodness we are not betrothed, just think of the scandal." He stared down at her through hooded eyes, willing her to see how much he loved her. The pressure of his fingers on hers tightening just a fraction and he struggled to sustain his detachment, for in her temper — feigned though it be — Helena was breathtakingly beautiful. Her flashing eyes calling to mind lightning flickering through storm clouds.

"You are nothing but a cad," she spat and, seizing the goblet from Hugh, hurled the contents all over him, sticky red liquid dribbling down his fine clothes. "Why anyone imagines I would settle for some mouldy old shipping magnate when I am courted by nobility is a mystery." Helena concluded derisively. She was mortified by her actions, but she had to make everyone believe it was over. So, she tossed her head, apologised to Lord Faversham for her outburst, remembering to drop a curtsey, and swept out in high dudgeon. "I do beg your pardon my Lord, but some people are simply…" she took a breath and hissed, "…unconscionable."

Lord Faversham was goggling at her, but dodged aside to let her pass.

Helena all but ran to the ballroom, finding their hosts, thanking them for a lovely evening and, after retrieving her cloak was standing on the footpath waiting for the Caswells to join her. She was shaking from the effort of behaving so badly, her headache increasing with every passing second. Stephen and Tabitha appeared moments later, and the three availed themselves of one of the complimentary hackneys laid on by the Challerfords.

"Will you be all right Helena?" asked Tabitha who had taken the seat next to her friend.

"I'll be fine, thank you Tabitha. Hopefully this will be over soon and then Hugh can have his life back. I do believe I will need some of Billie's special infusion tonight though, my head is causing me some discomfort." Helena smiled her gratitude.

"We will call on you tomorrow," Tabitha assured her friend as their carriage pulled up outside Trevallier House. Helena said her goodbyes and Stephen walked the tired woman to her door. Hudson was there to welcome her home, assessing his young mistress immediately, ringing for Nancy and asking her to fetch Helena some of Billie's headache mixture.

Helena's thought processes were becoming disordered, as her brain slowly disconnected itself from the rest of her body. All she wanted was Hugh and, knowing she couldn't have him for a little while at least, proved too much and she burst into tears. After taking a dose of the concoction she hoped would alleviate the pain and before Nancy returned to assist Helena into bed, the young woman had cried herself into an exhausted slumber, tears still wet on her cheeks. Her maid undressed her sleeping mistress, slipping her into a nightrail before finally tucking her under the covers. When she returned to the kitchen where a hot chocolate awaited her, Nancy declared tartly that something was amiss and if Mr Drummond had upset her ladyship she might just give him a piece of her mind.

Hudson did see fit to remark that as they had no idea what was going on, perhaps they should leave well alone, but Nancy was not easily dissuaded. Tapping her nose, she added that something had been going on for a while but she hadn't been able to work it out, and they all knew it was unlike Lady Helena to weep for no reason.

A few days later, as evening fell, there came a knock at the door to the servant's entrance of the Trevallier residence. Robert, one of the footmen, who happened to be sitting nearest, raised his eyebrows at his fellow staff who shrugged their shoulders, not expecting any callers at this hour. Opening the door cautiously, the young man was amazed to see a well-dressed gentleman standing there, his topper low over his brow, hiding his face.

"Yes, sir, how may I help you?" Somewhat pompously asked.

"Robert, may I come in?"

Robert studied the caller, suddenly recognising Mr Drummond, Lady Helena's swain. "Sir, goodness me, sir why are you coming to this door? It ain't right a gentleman such as yourself coming to the tradesmen's entrance."

Hugh smiled grimly, "'Tis the only way nobody will see me, my good man. Is Lady Helena by chance at home?"

Robert nodded enthusiastically, "She is that, sir. You come on in and I'll go and let her know you are here. If you would follow me, I'll take you through to the parlour."

Glancing through the door into the kitchen, Hugh spotted the prepared food on the table, and noticed cook was stirring something, which smelt delicious, Hugh caught Robert's arm, "Wait, is Lady Winchester entertaining?"

"Not at the moment, sir, although there are dinner guests expected later." Robert affirmed.

Hugh considered this then said, "I know this is unusual, but please would you ask whether Lady Helena might consider meeting me here? I think it would be safer."

Momentarily flustered at such a request, Robert stared at Hugh, whose impassive face gave nothing away. "Right you are Mr Drummond, sir, leave it with me." Shaking his head at the vagaries of the gentry, Robert led Hugh into the warm kitchen, offering him a chair.

The rest of the staff gawked at Hugh's arrival, wondering what was going on. Nancy glared at the visitor; her mistress had been quiet and withdrawn since the Challerford ball and Nancy blamed Hugh. He noticed her black look and offered a diffident smile.

"I know Nancy, I know. Believe me, there is more to this than meets the eye and Lady Helena knows the full extent. This is best way I know to protect her." Hugh had no reason to explain himself to a maid, but he was mindful of the loyalty the staff here had for their employers, and part of him wanted to explain what was going on, in case Helena or her family were threatened.

Nancy wasn't prepared to forgive him yet, but before she could say anything there was the sound of running feet and a flurry of silks as Helena blew into the kitchen like a miniature whirlwind, straight into Hugh's arms. Heedless of the stunned faces around them, she lifted her face for his kiss, which he bestowed with devastating efficiency.

"Hugh, Hugh! What is happening? How are you? Did you get the wine of your clothes? I am so sorry I did that, but I thought it very convincing. Already I have heard murmurs of our...err...severed courtship. Please tell me everything. Oh, how I have missed you." Helena gabbled, as Hugh released her lips and held her close for a moment, breathing in her fragrance, which as always tantalised his senses, reminding him of a spring morning.

He grinned at her bright face, wishing he could have her all to himself, mindful for now such luxury was impossible. "I have missed you too. All is quiet at the moment. Withers thinks he has almost uncovered the instigator but wants to check a couple of things before we make our move."

Helena frowned, wondering whether there was any chance that she would suddenly wake up to find this was all a bad dream. Attuned to her, Hugh drew Helena against him once more, oblivious to the expressions of the staff, which ranged from shocked to astute to warmly approving. They were, however, sensitive enough to give the couple as much privacy as was possible in a large and bustling kitchen.

"What of your family?" she asked solicitously. Her loving eyes scanning tired features, seeing the shadows under his eyes, while smoothing cool fingers through his unruly hair.

"They are bemused and, of course, upset but I have simply asked that they trust me. I had to tell my mother something of what is happening, and both Nicholas and Jessica already know. Being at the yard every day I could not shield them and this is our inheritance, they deserve to be kept apprised. Should anything happen to me..." Helena shuddered and Hugh tightened his embrace, "...they will have to assume responsibility for the company thus I could not in all conscience keep them in the dark." Helena nodded in understanding. "Also, I had to persuade Jessica that I hadn't gone 'all Hugh' on you," a mischievous glint in his eye.

"Gone 'all Hugh' on me? What on earth does that mean?" Helena enquired, intrigued enough that Hugh's comment distracted her for a moment. Hugh explained his sister's misgivings, making Helena chuckle, to Hugh's relief. He deplored that because of her association with him, Helena had become entangled in this mess and was glad he could introduce a little humour to their conversation.

For a moment, they stood in silence. Then Helena lifted her head so she could look into his face, committing his features to memory, as though there was the remotest chance she might forget.

"I just want this all to be over," she whispered.

"Me too, my love, me too." He tucked a recalcitrant curl off her face and dropped a kiss on her nose. "I had to make sure you were all right after the ball. I was worried you were getting one of your headaches. This evening is the first chance I have had to get here without the notion I was being followed." Startled, Helena spluttered and words fell from her mouth incoherently, but Hugh pressed a finger to her lips, "Hush, my love, do not take on so. I take the utmost care when I am abroad, and I have Archie."

"Archie is here? He should come and get warm."

Hugh shook his head. "He refused. He is waiting for me in the laneway." They talked in undertones for a little longer neither ready to let the other go. Hugh told Helena what he and Lord Faversham had been discussing the night of the ball. "Seems he has heard rumours that Trentams no longer has the confidence of the traders and unless we can catch the culprits quickly, everything my family has worked for may be lost. In all honesty, I find such innuendo hard to credit, as I have spoken to most of them over the past week or so. However, I am in a fickle business and even the slightest allegation of malfeasance, regardless how baseless the accusations, would be enough for them to take their trade elsewhere."

"Surely none of your customers, or competitors for that matter, would believe you capable of such odious behaviour?" Helena demanded, shocked at the mere idea of Hugh defying the self-imposed conventions exercised by the more discerning shipyards, never mind his own high moral standards. The concept of workers' rights was rather muddied and generally bound up in the principle of *noblesse oblige*, reliant on the honour and decency of an employer. Hugh's father had begun to implement a stringent set of rules safeguarding all who worked for him as well as himself, and it was a tenet Hugh continued. He was not the only business owner by any means, it was becoming less uncommon, especially in fast developing industries, which made the suggestion of impropriety in his yard all the more unimaginable.

"Not so far, love, but you know how gossip works." He was right, once rumours reached the ears of the *ton*, anyone on the wrong end of it was ruined in whatever sphere they moved.

Gentlemen usually fared rather better than ladies, but in matters of business, support from those within the elite was imperative. Hugh grimaced, "Hopefully it won't come to that, but I cannot assume anything." He paused then, "Forgive me sweetheart, but I must go. Even with strict vigilance, to spend any time in proximity to your home may not go unnoticed, and I do not know whom to trust."

He pulled her close for a long, lingering kiss, whispered his love for her, then after thanking the staff for their hospitality — a wicked grin on his face, he was gone.

Chapter Twenty Two

Helena remained motionless for long moments, unsettled by her thoughts, wondering whether there was anything she could do to find out who was causing Hugh so much trouble. Being a member of the *ton* did have its advantages, and now it appeared she and Hugh harboured a dislike for each other she might get people to spill secrets. More than this, something was teasing at the back of her mind, something she couldn't pin it down, to do with the confrontation at the ball and something Hugh just said. She rolled it around for a while, but it refused to take shape. Pushing it aside for now as another thought came to her. She turned to the staff requesting their attention in her innately polite manner.

"If, by chance, anyone attempts to gain information regarding Hugh and myself, please might I request that you simply tell them we are no longer courting? Should any push for more details, say you are unaware and let me know who asked."

Hudson stepped forward, confirming they would be on their guard and not to worry.

Helena smiled gratefully, "Thank you Hudson. I know you are all souls of discretion and hopefully this matter will be resolved soon. 'Tis that we believe someone is trying to destroy Hugh's business, and this is the best way we could think of to thwart them." Sage nods all around and Helena relaxed, beaming her affection for these people who made her life so comfortable. She thanked them for their time and for allowing her a brief moment with Hugh, then disappeared back to the library and her book, feeling much lighter of heart than she had only an hour previously.

More than a week passed with no further word from Hugh and nothing to indicate how the investigation was going.

Owing to the rumours circulating, Helena found it necessary to explain what was going on to her mother. Lady Winchester, although privately horrified her daughter was caught up in such an issue, outwardly remained her imperturbable self, merely suggesting Helena keep her apprised of any new developments.

Helena spent her days as always, mostly at the temporary refuge or calling on friends. Anyone observing her would see only a cheerful young woman seemingly unfettered by any concerns, blithely enjoying her life in a manner customary for one of the *ton*.

The refuge itself was buzzing, even though the cooler days often meant there were fewer women requiring its protection — the change in the weather seemingly had a direct correlation to the tempers of their husband's, or lack thereof — there was always work to do. Many women attended daily simply to better themselves, treating the centre like a school, taking advantage of the many classes offered. Their desire to learn kept Helena busy and for that she was thankful; without this distraction, she would have too much time to think — the last thing she wanted right now. Sybil still came every day and had undertaken a more active role amongst those women staying at the shelter either for a brief respite or to escape an untenable situation. Her own experiences meant she could empathise with them. That this diminutive woman had, with help, reformed and rebuilt the life she and Archie shared, engendered a trust from those who struggled to believe there was any hope.

Meanwhile Hugh and Withers, along with several of Withers' men made the last connection, and although Hugh already had an inkling, to have undeniable proof still stunned him. That the person whom he'd esteemed and respected, who had been a father figure to him and his siblings following the death of their own father, could behave so abominably, beggared belief.

Unfortunately, having proof of intent and being able to bring the earl to justice were two completely different things and as far as the law went, Faversham had not done anything with which they could charge him. Rumour and innuendo were not illegal and, since all the accidents at the yard could be ascribed to negligence on the part of the workers, there was nothing they could attribute directly to the earl. They needed to catch him, or his lackeys in the act, which would likely prove difficult if not impossible.

Withers, used to such frustrations and the epitome of patience, was content to bide his time. By maintaining his vigilance and recognising Faversham believed himself above the law, Withers expected him to slip up — he just hoped this would be sooner rather than later.

Hugh and Archie patrolled the whole yard thoroughly, including all the offices, three times a day. Jessica, Nicholas and Hugh had discussed the situation with every employee from Mr Holland the Master Shipwright down to Joe, the lad who collected all the stray bits of wood and metal, which were stored away on the off chance they could be reused. None of the three Drummonds had reason to suspect any were involved and before this revelation found it inconceivable, a person or persons could access the yard to create mayhem, without inside knowledge of the layout, and the location of specific equipment or material.

Lord Faversham, however, was cognisant with all aspects of Trentams, having seen the preliminary drafts years before and been a regular visitor ever since. It would not be difficult for him to direct his underlings to specific areas, a detail that only added to the evidence against him.

Nonetheless, until Faversham showed his hand, all they could do was wait.

Two more weeks ticked by with paralysing slowness. Helena had received the odd letter from Hugh, delivered to her by Archie when he came to collect Sybil at the refuge. Helena cherished each one, re-reading them so often the paper started to fray from her constant unfolding and refolding. She replied in a similar vein, either sending the letters with Archie or should young Timmy have nothing to do, he was happy to scoot across to the docks for extra coin. It was the closest they came to meeting and despite their enforced separation, Helena savoured the secrecy, endeavouring to couch her letters in terms only Hugh would understand, just in case they were intercepted. She was so successful that sometimes, even Hugh wasn't entirely sure he grasped what she meant, hoping he guessed correctly her gist.

Towards the end of a Thursday afternoon, a little less than a month since the Challerford's ball, Helena was helping a group of women conquer the intricacies of the alphabet and how these letters were joined to make up words. She was often saddened so many people, and women especially, were thought not to require even the most rudimentary knowledge of how to write in their own language. She made their lessons fun and the women were making great strides. A knock at the door disturbed their concentration and Timmy's tow head peeked through, his bright blue eyes and grubby face alight with mischief.

"Yes, young sir. How may we help you this fine afternoon?" enquired Helena, standing so she might drop Timmy a low curtsy, making the lad chortle with mirth.

He removed his cap and described a sweeping bow, his shock of hair nearly brushing the floor, "Why Lady Helena, I am fine. Thank you so much for asking," giggling, "yer an original, m'lady so y'are."

Helena smiled and ruffled his scruffy mop. "Now my lad, what do you need?"

"I was asked to bring this straight to you," Timmy handed over a folded sheet of heavy vellum. Her name was written in a hand she did not recognise, and there was no seal. Helena stared at it trying to work out who, other than Hugh, might send her a letter.

"From whom did you get this Timmy?" She asked, puzzled.

Timmy shrugged his shoulders, "Some gent stopped me just afore I got 'ere." Thumbing in the general direction of the street.

"What did he look like?"

Timmy cocked his head as he tried to remember the man who urged him to take this letter to Lady Helena with all haste.

"Hmmm, 'e were tall, though not as tall as your Mr Drummond. Very smart too, a real natty dresser and 'e carried a cane with one o' them weird shaped shiny 'andles. Oh and 'e used one o' them quizzing glasses while 'e were speaking to me. Didn't think I were that small." Timmy went off into gales of laughter at the recollection of the man peering at him. "Oi told him. Sir, oi said, you should 'ave a care a gent like you down 'ere, there's them'll have yer soon as look at yer. Not all as trustworthy as me..." he puffed out his scrawny chest as he spoke, making Helena press her lips together so as not to laugh. "...and mind, 'e were cross as crabs, when I says as you might not be 'ere today. Said it was vihitaahly himportant you got this letter." Timmy mimicked the cultured tones of whoever had given him the missive sending the rest of the room into peals of mirth. He was a cheeky imp.

Helena grinned at his sauce and opened the letter, reading it twice to make sure she understood.

Dear Lady Helena,

Please, please come to Trentams. Hugh has disappeared and we cannot think to where he might have gone. He had a meeting yesterday in the city after which he did not return to the office and none have seen him since. He did not come home last evening and we are afraid that, with everything else going on, misfortune may have befallen him. I apologise for sending such a letter, but we are at a loss and believe you may be able to offer guidance.

Sincerely,
Miss Jessica Drummond

Helena mused over the contents, the phrasing seemed a trifle peculiar for a young woman with whom she was friends. Moreover, why would Jessica wait so long to contact her or anyone? What about Nicholas? Had he been looking for Hugh? Letting the contents of the letter play around in her head, she came to the conclusion it was not altogether what it appeared to be. Calling Timmy back she asked him whether the gentleman had said he would await a reply.

The lad shook his head, "No m'lady, 'e just stalked off looking vihitaahly himportant, swinging 'is cane like 'e owned the street."

Helena ran her mind over everyone she knew, trying to work out why, if Jessica had sent the letter, a gentleman would be delivering it. There was something odd going on. Recalling Archie was due to collect Sybil shortly, she decided to wait and ask him to go with her.

"Timmy, might I ask you to do me a big favour? 'Twill earn you extra coin." Timmy nodded eagerly. "Wait here please, I will be back momentarily." Helena hurried out of the room and along to the closest office. Sitting at the desk, she penned a brief note to Lucas Withers, apprising him of the letter, adding her own opinion, and that she would go to Trentams with Archie. As she was writing, several things that had been nagging at the edge of her consciousness coalesced and she added an addendum — a name.

Folding it neatly and sealing it closed, she rushed back to the classroom where Timmy was now regaling the women with a set of lurid instructions about how to dodge pickpockets and other vagabonds. He jumped down from the table he'd perched on and tucked the proffered note into his shirt. Helena gave him a handful of coins and told him to take the letter to Lucas Withers in Bow Street, providing the lad with an address.

"Now, are you sure you know where I mean?"

"Yes, m'lady, I knows Mr Wivvers, he's a good 'un. 'E 'elps anyone as needs it, dunnt care wevver they be rich or poor. Dunnt worry, I'll get this to him fast as I can."

"Thank you, Timmy. You are a good lad but please take care it's getting dark, oh and make sure you are not followed."

Timmy chuckled, "Hahaha, there's none can foller me, I knows these streets like the back o' me 'and." And with that he was gone, ramming his cap on his head, sprinting off down the hall and out into the waning afternoon light. Helena went to find Sybil and asked that when Archie arrived, he might find her, as she probably had an extra couple of hours work for him.

Shortly thereafter, Archie stuck his head into the classroom, as Helena was bringing the lesson to a close. He waited patiently until she had answered a few last-minute questions, then came right into the room and leaned against one of the tables.

"What's 'appened my Lady? Sybs said you could 'ave summat extra for me."

"Archie, did anything untoward occur at Trentams today?"

Archie mulled that over, then shook his head. "No m'lady, not even any accidents. 'Twas a normal day. Made good progress so Mr Hugh told me."

"Wait, Hugh was at the yard today?"

Archie looked surprised at her query. "O' course. Lower deck is going in at present and even though the Master has it covered, Mr Hugh likes to be on 'and, just in case." Archie was nothing if not quick on the uptake and he realised there was more to Helena's question than simple interest. "What's going on? If I may be so bold."

"Archie, I received a letter supposedly from Jessica, Miss Drummond, begging me to go to Trentams because Mr Hugh has been missing since yesterday morning."

Archie's jaw dropped, "No, that's not right at all. Miss Drummond wasn't at the office today and Mr Hugh dropped me off along the street not fifteen minutes ago."

Helena needed no more convincing. Whoever was trying to undermine Hugh and his shipyard intended to do something that night, however, she and Archie had the upper hand. The gentleman did not know she suspected trickery; therefore, she might have the element of surprise.

"Archie, I think we must go to Trentams," Archie spluttered his alarm at her suggestion. "I realise I sound addled, but this must end. I am tired of looking over my shoulder, worrying about what might, or might not happen; whether someone is tracking my footsteps and whether I will be able to see Hugh again before I am too old to remember who he is. I have sent Timmy to Lucas Withers informing him of my suspicions. If you and I can sneak into the yard unnoticed, we might be able to prevent serious damage or harm. Are you with me?"

"Well, there is no chance you are going without me m'lady. Mr Hugh would drop me in the Thames if I let any 'arm come to you. Give me ten minutes. I can round up a few o' me mates, for a bit o' back up."

Helena thanked him gratefully, unwilling to admit that despite being incensed, she was also anxious. The fear someone might hurt Hugh circled the periphery of her mind, and any extra support would be most welcome.

Not quite half an hour after Archie arrived in Helena's classroom, a small band of rather unlikely warriors set out along the narrow streets, led by a raven-haired women — who although of average height was dwarfed by her companions — wrapped in a shoddy looking cloak and marching briskly at the front of the group. They were deep in conversation as they hurried towards their destination. Archie had briefed his friends and all were raring for a good brawl. Helena hoped it wouldn't come to that, but she was glad to know they were willing should it prove necessary. She would not want to get on the wrong side of them.

Chapter Twenty Three

Meanwhile across the city, a grubby urchin burst into the spacious lobby of a set of offices adjacent to those of the Bow Street Runners, skidding to a halt at the front desk. A smartly dressed clerk stared, his lips curling in distaste, and was about to kick him out when the lad spoke.

"Begging yer pardon, sir. I 'ave a message for Mr Wivvers. 'Tis from Lady 'Elena Trevallier." Panting his declaration, still trying to catch his breath after running all the way.

"Wait here lad, I will see whether Mr Withers is in." The clerk glanced at the large ledger on his desk, nodded his head and disappeared up the staircase at the far side of the vestibule. Timmy flopped on the bench, glad the space was cool. The day was mild, but his exertions had certainly warmed him thoroughly. Several minutes later the pounding of feet woke him from a pleasant doze and he saw three men thundering back down the same stairs.

"Timmy, is that you?" exclaimed a familiar voice, as Hugh Drummond rounded the desk.

Timmy grinned, "'Ello, Mr Drummond sir. Never 'spected to see you 'ere."

Lucas Withers joined them as the clerk resumed his seat and tried to appear as though he was working and not in the slightest intrigued as to what it was about this lad that had two gentlemen dashing to see why he was here.

Timmy explained his presence and handed the letter to Lucas, who read it quickly before passing it over it to Hugh. Both men looked aghast but, interestingly, not overly surprised. They had accepted long ago, that Lady Helena Trevallier was not one to wait around helplessly until it was too late, rather she hurled herself into situations with scant consideration of the consequences. A quick discussion ensued after which, Hugh ushered Timmy out and into his carriage while Lucas disappeared back up the stairs.

"Right then Timmy, let's go. I am making you my deputy for the time being, do you think you can handle such responsibility?"

Timmy cocked his head, studying Hugh with shrewd eyes, "What would I 'ave to do?"

"Well, when we get to the yard, you must keep watch and warn me of any approach, but you will also have to stay out of sight. It is quite a lot for a youngster such as yourself."

"I can do it, sir," Timmy affirmed, touching his cap "I'm not that young," spoken with all the importance of being ten and two. Hugh chuckled and the two sat back as the carriage rattled through the darkening streets.

Hugh was anxious. What on earth did Helena think she could achieve going to Trentams with only Archie to protect her? Yes, the man was the size of a small building, but he was only one man and, although he knew Helena was adept at many things, fighting off an attacker probably wasn't a skill she had ever learned, nor should she need to. Calling to Tom to go as fast as possible, Hugh tried to repress the dread beginning to grip his heart.

Tom pulled the horses to a halt one street away from Trentams. Hugh did not want to alert any who might be watching, to his presence. Asking his driver to stay with the carriage, Hugh and Timmy hurried quietly along the path and in less than five minutes were at the enormous wooden gates, which stood slightly ajar. They had been waiting only a few minutes when a group of figures loomed up out of the shadows; it was Withers along with a considerable number of his men.

"Someone is in the office," Hugh said in an undertone, pointing out the flickering light moving around an upstairs room. "Jessica and Nichols would be home at this hour. Of late they are easily persuaded that staying after dark is not wise."

Withers nodded and muttered something to three of his men, who slipped through the gates and ran soundlessly across the courtyard to the stairs disappearing into the dusk. Hugh, Timmy, Withers, and the remainder of Withers' men moved stealthily across to the main shipyard. Squinting through the next set of gates, Hugh saw more lights dancing near the dark hull of the schooner.

"Timmy, can you be very brave and wait here for me?" Hugh asked the pale faced youth, whose taste for adventure was beginning to fade as rapidly as the daylight. Timmy nodded. "Good lad, if anyone you do not recognise comes this way, yell your head off, run back to my carriage as fast as you can and stay there with Tom. Have you got that?" Timmy nodded again, not quite trusting himself to speak. "I think Mr Withers may ask you to work for him after this." Hugh suggested, but Timmy whispered that he thought it might be better if he continued to run messages for them women at the refuge as likely they needed a brave lad more than them Runners did.

Hugh grinned, his teeth flashing white in the gloom. "I do believe you are correct Timmy, they'd not want to lose you. Now tuck yourself against this post and remember to keep well hidden." Hugh followed Withers and his men who were already making their way towards the bobbing lights. Voices could be heard, carrying on the still air, but from this distance they could not tell to whom they belonged.

While Timmy was talking to Hugh and Withers in the charming atrium, Helena and her motley crew had already arrived at Trentams and were taking stock of their surroundings. Archie knew the layout of the area intimately, and as they slipped through the main gates he pointed out they had been opened wide enough to allow a person, or people through, but not a carriage. They also noticed the door to the office building was ajar and from within the dockyard itself came sounds, that at any other time would be associated with construction on one or the other of the ships.

"Should there be any men working at this hour Archie?" Helena asked.

Archie shook his head, "No, m'lady, they was all leaving as me and Mr Hugh drove away. Mister Holland doesn't want anyone working too late, the men need good light down in the hull so they can't continue much after three, four at the latest."

Helena nodded, tapping her chin with indecision. It was falling dusk, the daylight nearly gone. "We need to find out how many men are here," she muttered. "I do not want any of your friends to get hurt."

"Don't you worry about us Miss, any skulduggery going on, we'll 'ave 'em afore they know we're coming," one of the men — who she thought might be called Frank — assured her, patting her arm in a comforting manner. Helena wanted to laugh at the sheer absurdity of the situation, but as it was, she merely acknowledged his words politely, adding that they might as well get on with it.

Spreading out over the yard the men, despite their bulk were like wraiths, vanishing as though an illusion, into the building and through into the docks. Helena and Archie followed slowly behind, giving them a chance to locate anyone who should not be there.

As they made their way towards the main building, Helena heard scuffling, the odd grunt, and the thwack of fists against flesh, but preferred not to look too closely. She and Archie climbed the stairs, hesitating outside Hugh's office, listening for any sounds of disturbance. There was nothing, so Archie, motioning for Helena to stand behind him, opened the door, which squeaked as it swung back on its hinges but although the noise was deafening in the quiet, nobody called out or came running.

When Archie motioned it was safe to enter, Helena stepped over the threshold and surveyed the mayhem, clear even in the dim light. Papers were strewn all over the desk and onto the floor, drawers had been pulled open, their contents spilled haphazardly around the room and furniture had been broken. It was chaos. Helena sank to her knees desperately trying to make sense of such wanton destruction, gathering papers into neat piles, accepting she was probably making it worse, but unable to leave it in such a state.

Archie looked around and after making sure no one was hiding in a corner, said he would check the rest of the building. In the darkening room, Helena nodded absently, still deciding where to start tidying up first. As Archie's footsteps died away, she got back on her feet, lit several candles, and began to work from one side of the room, systematically putting paper into piles, pushing drawers back into the correct slots and righting furniture. She had been working for quite some time when she suddenly realised that Archie hadn't returned. Not thinking too much of it, she shouted his name, while continuing with her self-appointed task. A few minutes passed and still no Archie.

"Archie, are you around?" Helena called, forgetting that they were supposed to be as quiet as possible. An odd shuffling caught her attention and, glancing over her shoulder, saw two men half dragging a barely conscious Archie into the room, followed by a tall and exceedingly well-dressed man. It was Timmy's 'gent,' Lord Faversham. Even though she had put the pieces together, Helena gasped in shock — that her supposition was proved correct, appalled her.

"L-Lord Faversham. What, pray tell are you doing?" She stuttered, then paused, and took a calming breath, determined not to let this man fluster her. Archie groaned, a bruise the size of a plate blossoming on his face, his lip bleeding from a nasty cut. "What have you done to Mr Miller?" Sharply asked.

"None of your concern, Lady Helena. Thank you for responding to my letter. I knew your little spat with Drummond was a sham, and if you thought him in danger you would run to his side like a little lamb. Although you did have me fooled for a while," he mused, sounding grudgingly impressed. "I expected you to come alone. What on earth possessed you to involve this wretched excuse of a human being?"

"Who are you to cast aspersions, my lord? You, who had the audacity to cause this mess, who dared to enter this shipyard when you had no authority to do so." She could feel her anger building and knew she needed to rein in her emotions; to lose control would not help. *Remember,* she instructed herself, *you asked Timmy to get Lucas Withers. He should be here soon, and think of Hugh. Just Hugh.* She allowed an image of Hugh's face smiling down at her to fill her mind and an inner strength began to flow through her veins. She would not let this man destroy what Hugh had worked so hard for, if it took her last breath, she would stop his games.

"Why are you doing this?" she demanded, pleased that she sounded exasperated rather than scared. "What has Hugh ever done to you?"

"Nothing really, except take what should be mine." Lord Faversham wandered through the room using his cane to swipe the papers Helena had so neatly stacked, back onto the floor. Idly tipping the furniture back over. "This will make for a lovely fire. One should never leave candles unattended you know."

Helena bit back a moan as panic began to bubble. Not fire, not again. Straightening her shoulders, she asked, in a bid to keep him talking,

"What should have been yours?"

"Why this yard you silly chit."

Helena stared at him in confusion. "What do you mean this yard? How can this be yours? I know you helped finance Trentams when Hugh's father opened it, but Hugh paid it all back. I don't understand." Helena was confounded. Lord Faversham was a wealthy man, his estates were profitable and he owned two horse studs.

"The future is in trade, in shipping, and it was within my grasp. When Arthur Drummond died, he should have bequeathed this yard to me. I had invested in it 'twas my due. What gave him the right to hand it lock, stock and barrel to Hugh; scarcely more than a boy when his father died, with no idea about running a business. I could have guided him, granted him some responsibility. He would have benefited from my knowledge and allowed me to expand the company far more quickly. He is too cautious." The earl railed on, his voice laced with contempt and no small amount of anger. Helena listened carefully, trying to ascertain just how unbalanced Lord Faversham had become.

"Have you considered broaching this subject with him?" she enquired, quite reasonably she thought. "He might be glad to have a partner in the company."

"I don't want a partner. I want it all," he hissed. "I do not share profits."

"How do you intend to persuade him to part with it?" she asked, her interest marginally outweighing her fear.

"Well that is where you come in Lady Helena" he smiled evilly at her, his face in the candlelight taking on a Machiavellian quality.

"Me?" she expostulated. "Why on earth do you imagine I have any sway over him?"

"Because he loves you, my dear and if he thinks you are in danger he will do anything to save you, and if by chance he fails and a terrible accident befalls a young woman — the daughter of a peer no less — in his shipyard, especially after so many other unexplained incidents, his credibility will suffer irreparably. Trentams will lose custom, at which point, I will step in and generously offer to buy the yard, for a vastly reduced sum, of course."

"But if he comes here, surely he will know you are behind this, and expose you for your heinous behaviour whether I am harmed or not." Damping down the alarm now threatening to choke her. *Keep him talking,* she told herself, *the longer he talks the more chance there is that someone will come to your rescue.*

"Oh, I will be long gone before such an act takes place, I do not get my hands dirty."

"Your hands are already dirty, you scoundrel!" yelled Helena, no longer able to stifle her temper. "You think that by harming me you will force Hugh to sell this company? It is in his blood. It is his dream. He will never give it up. Moreover, I told Mr Withers who I suspected was behind the mishaps at the yard. You thought yourself so clever sending me that letter, but I questioned the delivery lad and recognised the description of your fancy cane. I sent a note, naming you. In addition to Archie and myself, we came with several other men who I believe will have subdued your cronies, so you might as well accept defeat. You cannot win." Helena spat the words, her anger obliterating her terror.

"Never!" Faversham bellowed, and hurling himself at Helena, grabbed her by the hair and dragged her towards the corridor. Helena shrieked in pain, kicking out at her captor. As she was hauled through the door, she noticed, out of the corner of her eye that Archie was coming around, and only one of Faversham's henchmen stood guard over him. Fighting with everything she had, Helena clawed and punched at the Earl who barely seemed bothered by her efforts. Wriggling to free herself, she felt a slight loosening of the hand in her hair, but just when she thought she had the chance to escape his clutches, her head exploded in white light, then there was nothing.

Chapter Twenty Four

Her ears were buzzing and it felt as though someone was hammering on her left temple with a sharp instrument. Groaning in pain, Helena twisted around trying to work out what was going on. Her eyelids felt heavy, and the effort to open them was so arduous, she almost did not bother. When she finally did, it was onto a darkness so absolute, she blinked a few times to make sure she was not still asleep, unable to fathom whether this was owing to where she was or just because it was night.

Waiting for her vision to adjust, Helena became aware she was sprawled on her back and her clothing felt wet. That couldn't be right surely? She had been in the office building; it was dry in there. Her thoughts were all tangled, which she assumed was because of the pounding in her skull, but she also realised this wasn't her usual megrim.

Gingerly, she touched the side of her head from where the throbbing seemed to stem, her fingers finding a lump the size of an egg and her hair felt matted and sticky. Absently she wondered whether it was blood but just then — pushing all else aside — memories flooded in. A room in turmoil, screaming at Lord Faversham, Archie lying on the floor, the earl grabbing her hair and dragging her out of the room then nothing; everything after that was a blank.

Forcing her mind back to her current problem and with no idea of where she was or how she came to be there, Helena did register it was probably a good idea to not be there any longer. Plan made, she moved to get up, but everything began to spin and she was hit by a wave of nausea so acute, she could not help but cast up her accounts. Mortified, Helena wiped her mouth with a shaky hand wishing there was some water to rinse away the acid taste, at the same moment as she realised she was standing in a substantial puddle.

"That would be why my dress is damp, and where's my cloak? I'm sure I was wearing a cloak," she muttered, fretfully. Using her hand, she scooped up some of the liquid splashing it onto her face; it smelt peculiar but not fetid, so she risked washing out her mouth with another scoop. It tasted a little brackish and slightly salty, making her think it was probably river water from the Thames, but that still did not explain why she was standing in it.

"Hello" she called. The sound echoed softly. *Oh, this can't be good*, she thought, *where on earth am I?* "HELLOOOO!" She yelled, her cry boomed back making her wince in pain. Stretching out her hand straight in front she moved forward slowly, sliding her feet through the shallow water covering whatever she was standing on. It seemed quite rough and, tentatively, she bent to touch it. It felt like wood. What would have a wet wooden floor? Realisation dawned — a ship!

"Nooooooo," she moaned, "I am on a ship? I will never find my way out in the dark, and be stuck in here 'til day break." Helena wrapped her arms around herself; the chill air, wet feet and damp clothing making her shiver. "Goodness me, if it's not fire it's water." She lamented, then bit down on a giggle, recognising she might be mildly hysterical. "I must stop talking to myself, anyone listening will think me taken by madness." Still gurgling with mirth at her own inanity, she drew a steadying breath and ventured forward again.

Head thumping and badgered by sickness, Helena gritted her teeth and shuffled along ponderously. The darkness was complete and the silence unnerving, although it did indicate she was likely alone. She had not taken many steps when she bumped into something solid. Letting her hands rove across the surface, she guessed this was also wooden, confirming her suspicions. At least now she was at one side of the space and had something to guide her.

Helena made her way cautiously; the water lapping over her feet, her shoes squelching and the ground beneath her swaying, although she didn't know whether that was real or because of the wound. Nausea overtook her again and she vomited, which made her dizzy and she began to fear if she didn't find a way out she might well faint and end up drowning in a puddle.

Unable to tell which section of the boat she was in, or for that matter whose boat and what type it was, Helena had no idea whether there would be any ladders or steps, to offer her escape. How many decks might there be and on which one was she stuck? Scouring her memory, she tried to recall what Hugh had told her. If this was the schooner, she thought he said there would be two main decks and a bilge — which was right at the bottom — then she remembered what Archie had said about the lower deck going in. Was she beneath that deck, in the bilge? Or had she been dumped onto the new deck? On reflection, Helena assumed it must be the bilge, for surely if she were higher up there would be some light from the stars.

Either way there must be an opening of sorts, an egress, otherwise how had she been dumped here in the first place? If she had been dropped onto or through the deck, she would probably already be dead, it being improbable anyone could survive a fall from the main level. She also recalled the lower deck was unfinished and, if this was where she had been left, there was doubtless a large hole she could easily fall through. Dash it all, she really wished she could see. She didn't even know what time it was having no idea how long she laid unconscious.

Determined not to give in to her mounting fear, Helena edged along the side of the ship testing every step before she put her weight down. She hadn't got far when she heard sounds, she stopped, listening intently, but it was just noise and she was unable to discern whether it was people trying to find her or simply voices carried on the night air from other boats sailing up the river. As she continued, she noticed the water, which had been only washing over her feet, was now ankle deep.

"Oh, for goodness sake," she protested in vexed tones as she sloshed along, "this is becoming ridiculous. Now it seems the ship is flooding." Her exasperation spurring her on, Helena lifted her skirts with one hand, keeping the other firmly on the wooden hull of the vessel, and quickened her pace.

In the meantime, the men with Hugh and Withers had dispatched any of the earl's henchmen, missed by Archie's crew, with deadly efficiency. The three who had gone to search the office reported back that there were two men down — none they knew — a lot of damage in the big room upstairs, but no sign of Helena, Archie, or Faversham. As they waited, unsure where to start looking, two brawny fellows approached them.

"Either o' you men Withers?" one asked.

"That would be me," affirmed Lucas, stepping forward.

"Archie went to find her ladyship. He said as how the earl had taken her though int't'main yard. Asked us to let you know. Ned 'ere kept watch, he 'asn't seen the gent come back, but 'tis black as pitch now and there's plenty o' places to hide in that yard."

"Thank you…"

"Frank." Frank supplied.

"…Frank, we are indebted to you all. Right," Lucas called his men over and told them what Frank had said. "It is imperative that we find Lady Helena and Archie. However, it is dark, so be on your guard and take every care, I do not wish any of you to lose your footing, trip or be taken by surprise."

One of Withers' more enterprising men handed out several rush lights, which he had lit from the stub of a candle snatched from the office.

"Let us hope Faversham hasn't slipped through our grasp," brooded Withers. "Although, should that be the case, we have his men, maybe they will give him up for the chance of a lesser sentence."

Hugh nodded, his heart thudding, anxiety for Helena ratcheting through him. By this stage, they had made their way through the gates and were standing between the two ships, the vast bulk of the Indiaman a black shadow in the darkness, while the silhouette of the schooner sitting low in its wet dock, was just visible in the light of a pearly moon beginning its journey across an ebony sky.

"Helena!"

"Archie!"

"Lady Helena!"

"Archie, Archie Miller!"

"Lady 'Elena!" a multitude of voices began to call out for the two still missing, the coarser vocals of the coal tippers, blending with the more erudite tones of Hugh and Withers, to produce a sort of chorus, discordant, yet with a frantic harmony. Not wanting to risk further injury, or worse, the men moved with tortuous slowness towards the edge of the dock, shouting, then waiting to see whether there was any response.

Nothing.

In the bowels of the schooner, Helena could hear the cries getting closer, but although she yelled back no one seemed to hear her and her voice was becoming hoarse. Prudently, she chose to wait until they came nearer, paddling through the ever-deepening water. Suddenly there was a rustling ahead, she stopped and held her breath. *Please do not let this be Faversham.* Her teeth started chattering, more in trepidation than from the cold water, and she clamped her jaw shut.

"Lady 'Elena?" a familiar voice reached her through the pitch-blackness, but in her fright she wasn't prepared to trust her senses. He called her name again. Dared she hope?

"Archie?" she squeaked, willing it to be Sybil's burly husband.

"Aye, 'tis me," replied the voice.

"Prove it." Everything fell silent. Helena was starting to think she would not be comfortable in such quiet surroundings ever again. After long moments —

"You made my wife fink and I told you it weren't good for her."

There was a long pause then Helena started giggling and after several seconds, Archie joined in. The pair moving towards each other laughing as though they had not a care in world.

"My lady, I am so sorry I left you in the office. Sybil will 'ave my guts for this." Archie exclaimed remorsefully.

Helena shook her head then realised Archie couldn't see her. "No, she will not! You were not to know what would happen. The earl is clearly deranged, and you were knocked senseless by at least two of his minions. How did you find me?" she asked curiously.

"I were just comin' round when I saw Faversham draggin' you out o' the office. I tried to get up straight away, but I were terrible woozy so it were a while afore I could stand. Then I 'ad to deal with the cork brained buffoon who was supposed to guard me. He wasn't very good at his job an' will likely 'ave a very bad headache on the morrow. Ha! Serve 'im right." Archie laughed without mirth and on any other occasion Helena might have sympathised with Archie's victim, her own headache almost unbearable — but not tonight.

"Once 'e were no longer a problem, I went through the 'ole building, checking every room, but you weren't to be found. The lads hadn't seen anyone pass 'em, but there's a side gate into the yard so we can keep the main gates shut unless there's deliveries. Stops any Tom, Dick or 'Arry getting in, can't 'ave them what doesn't understand the dangers wandering abaht. Anyhow, I didn't fink they'd take you into the Indiaman — 'tis too big — that left the schooner."

Archie paused. Above them Helena could hear faint shouts, still not near enough to be clearly discerned, and around them the water rose steadily.

"I told Frank and Ned to keep an eye out in case your Mr Withers arrived, then they could tell 'im where I was."

"Archie, you are a remarkably quick thinker. Let us hope they have done precisely that, and even now our rescuers approach. Do you know how we can get out of this ship?"

"There's a ladder, back the way I came. I do not know how they got you down here my lady, 'tis a mystery.

"I am just glad whoever carried me here did not see fit to drop me over the edge. I will follow you Archie, lead on. I am sure we will soon be back in the fresh air." Sounding more positive than she felt, Helena grabbed the back of Archie's shirt and held on for dear life.

Chapter Twenty Five

High above Helena and Archie, their rescuers were closing in. Half of the group had gone to check the Indiaman; despite it being highly unlikely anyone would try to secrete a victim within its hull. For one thing, it was so high, just getting onto the deck would take no small amount of time and for another, they presumed someone must have carried Helena and the risks associated with that would be too great, even for a madman and his lackeys. Still, Withers deemed it important to make sure.

While Withers directed the remainder of his men to check the rest of the dock, Hugh was peering over the hull of the schooner. The cavernous depths were dark as a tomb and, as he worked his way along to where the ladders hung over the side, he shuddered, hoping such a thought wasn't a premonition. No one had seen Lord Faversham, but none were gullible enough to imagine he was no threat. Withers and his men all carried loaded pistols and Hugh had his cane — inside which was a slender rapier — if the war had taught him anything, it was to prepare for the worst.

They reached the ladders, Hugh lifted the torch holding it as far out over the cavity as possible. They could not see anyone but as they waited, from far below an odd sloshing noise could be heard. It was quite rhythmic, like the regular slap of the waves against the dockside when a boat sailed past. Sitting in a wet dock, the schooner was settled low in the water, the dock closed against the tide. There was no sound from the river side of the gates, and the tide wasn't on the turn — it must be from inside the boat itself. How water had got in was a whole other matter, and could not be dealt with tonight.

"Helena!" Hugh roared. The sloshing stopped and he held his breath. Please, let this be her, please. Not usually one to exhort the Almighty, Hugh prayed with everything in him.

"Mr Hugh?" the question wafted up from the abyss, almost inaudible.

"Archie! Yes, we're here. Lady Helena?"

"With me." Faint, but enough to confirm what they wanted to hear. Hugh's relief was so great, his legs buckled, and he grabbed a mooring bollard to stop from making a complete cake of himself. He wanted to go down and help, but Withers held him back.

"Let Joe here go," he advised, indicating a taciturn man standing to one side, his bulk similar to that of Archie. Carrying Helena up, should that prove necessary, would be no hardship for the man. Joe nodded and began climbing down the ladder. He did not take the proffered torch preferring to keep both hands free from encumbrances. He went down steadily, calling a confirmation when he set foot on the lower deck. Taking care to stay at the side, Joe walked carefully along to what eventually would be a hatch down to the bilge. Currently it was a just large hole through which another ladder hung. Kneeling, he stuck his head through the hole and yelled Archie's name. The splashing ceased again as an answering shout came from close by.

"They're here, sir," Joe called up to the men above. "Not be long now and we'll have 'em safe." Joe heard muttering from beneath him. It seemed Lady Helena thought Archie should climb up first whereas Archie insisted it be she.

"M'lady, what sort of man would I be to leave you here while I go up. No. Go on with yer, I need to be 'ere in case you slip. You're soaked through and yer boots is full o' water, wouldn't take much to fall off them rungs.

"B-But." Even though the pain in her head was torture and she was losing the ability to function, Helena tried to argue. After all, Archie had been beaten up and needed treatment, unaware she was probably suffering from a concussion, and her head wound continued to bleed. She was also cold, the water now lapping higher than her knees.

Archie huffed in frustration. "No buts, m'lady, up you go." He swung her around in front of him and hoisted her, so her feet landed several rungs up. He followed straight behind, conscious Helena was fading, and determined to prevent any chance of her plunging back into the murky depths. Not the most sensitive of men, Archie was constantly surprised by Lady Helena's tenacity and her determination not to put herself first. He imagined most gentle born women, would have swooned, expecting to be carried to safety, not this lady. She braced herself and did what she had to, without once complaining. Archie would never tell anyone, but Lady Helena Trevallier had won his devotion for life.

Laboriously, they made their way up the ladder and to Helena, stretching for every rung in the unrelenting darkness, it seemed never-ending. Finally, her head popped up through the hole and Joe lifted her clear. Above her the stars were out in abundance, glittering like a cloak of diamonds in an obsidian sky, it was breathtaking and to Helena one of the most beautiful things she had ever seen.

"Helena!" a voice, hoarse with fear wafted down to her, and she raised her eyes searching for him, but all she could see were shadows.

"Hugh," she sighed. It was barely a whisper yet somehow, he heard and started to breathe again. She was nearly safe and if he had his way, once she set foot on the dockside, he would never let her out of his sight again. He could just make out the ghostly hue of her skin in the obscurity, as Joe helped her along to the next ladder. Archie appeared through the hole, and the three started up the last climb.

Desperately clinging to sanity, all Helena wanted to do was sleep. She had the vaguest recollection of Dr Elliott once telling her that if you banged your head you should not let yourself fall asleep. Unfortunately, she was no longer sure she had any say in the matter, exhaustion stalking her every move. Joe helped her, but other than throwing her over his shoulder — something he was considering — this was the only way for them to get out of the ship.

Helena gathered her strength and forced herself upwards. Her gown kept slapping against her legs like grasping hands trying to drag her back into the black recesses, and the cold seemed to be seeping into her bones. What she would do for a hot bath right now and a warm bed. The mere thought spurred her on and a few minutes later, she reached the top. Willing hands helped her over the side and stood her gently down. Something rough yet dry, like a blanket, was wrapped around her shoulders and a person was talking to her, but she couldn't hear them. Her world was receding into splintering agony, and she felt she ought to tell someone but her mouth wouldn't work.

She turned to thank Joe; words fell from her lips but sounded disjointed to her ears. Joe just smiled and patted her shoulder. Someone came alongside her, drawing her against a warm body before leaning back to check her over. It was Hugh.

"Helena my love," cool lips brushed against her forehead. "Come on sweetheart we must get you home."

She frowned at him seeing his lips moving but she couldn't respond, his words bouncing randomly around her head.

"Helena, can you understand me?" Hugh's question seemed to come from a vast distance.

Withers held the torch closer and there was a muffled gasp when both men saw blood oozing from a gash on the side of her head.

"Pain," was all she could manage as her legs finally gave out, and she began to slither to the ground.

Hugh had her in his arms in an instant, cradling her against him; the beat of his heart — soporific. In the light from the torches, the men began to make their way back along the side of the wet dock towards the main gates. Archie was talking with Frank and Ned, and Withers overhearing their conversation, was suggesting Archie get his bruises checked out, worried some of his ribs had been broken in his earlier scrap with Faversham's ruffians. Even though Withers and his men remained watchful, the mood was more relaxed. They had found Helena alive, and averted further damage to the shipyard and the office. Hopefully luck had turned in their favour.

Not quite yet.

As they neared the end of the dock, a tall figure emerged from the darkness, and Hugh felt something cold and metallic against his cheek.

"Put her down, Drummond or I will kill her." A sibilant hiss instructed him.

Hugh whispered to Helena, that he needed her to stand for just a moment. With a soft mewl, she protested and tried to settle into him but, carefully, Hugh set her on the ground. Helena's legs did buckle then and she crumpled to the floor. Lights flashed in her vision; the nausea she had managed to control, overcame her once again, and she vomited for a third time — all over the earl's trousers. His look of abject disgust would have been funny at any other time but no one was laughing now.

Hugh stepped away from Helena, wanting to put a distance between her and the gun. Withers and his men edged closer to the young woman, as did Archie, everyone in the group determined this madman would not hurt anyone else tonight. Hugh fiddled with his cane, currently hidden from view in the fold of his coat, silently sliding out the rapier and gripping it, ready to thrust at the first opportunity. Faversham aimed the gun at Hugh's chest and as he did so, Withers noticed, with dismay, it was a double-barrelled flintlock. This, along with the volatility of the man wielding the weapon, made for a dangerous mix.

Disoriented, Helena also realised she was no longer in Hugh's arms. Unsure of what was happening, she lifted her head and beheld the horror unfolding in front of her. Would this lunatic ever give up? Accepting her ability to do anything was severely restricted by her injury did not make her any less adamant that Faversham was not going to hurt Hugh. The earl was currently ranting and raving about how the shipyard should be his, but Helena had heard it all before, so she turned warily — mindful that everything was still spinning — and saw a number of men circling closer to Faversham.

Night cloaked the grotesque tableau, faces in the glow from the rush torches were leached of all colour giving the men who moved within the flickering light a macabre aspect. It was like the dance of the dead. Helena took a fortifying breath and pushed herself upright, swaying slightly as she tried to stay balanced.

"Helena, what are you doing? Stay back." Hugh begged in fierce undertones, unwilling to draw Faversham's attention to her. She ignored him and walked unsteadily forward. Summoning the last of her concentration she let her fury fly.

"You snivelling little toad," she snarled at Faversham who twisted to face her, the gun still pointed at Hugh, glaring at this virago who presumed to upbraid him. "You think you can threaten Mr Drummond with my death? You are pathetic and do not deserve to lick the ground he walks on. You will not shoot me or him or anyone, you traitorous coward. You could not fight Hugh, man to man, so you hit me, a mere woman and then leave me for dead in the hold of a ship. Is that any way for a gentleman to behave? What will your family think when they hear of your deeds? For you cannot escape them now. You are surrounded, and will never leave this yard a free man. You odious excuse for a human being, a festering sewer is less rotten than you. I am embarrassed to think you are a member of the nobility. These men who came to save me are more noble than you."

Helena's words sliced through the cool air. Faversham snorted with anger, and actually stamped his foot in rage, like a child in a tantrum. Now he was pointing the pistol at her but, undaunted, she kept walking. Everyone, except Helena seemed transfixed, the final scene of the performance about to play out. Hugh reached to stop her as she passed, but she brushed his hand away, keeping out of his grasp. Glancing at him, Helena shook her head almost imperceptibly, her eyes in the torchlight, dark as a storm swept sky and just as merciless.

Chapter Twenty Six

An icy finger traced its way down Hugh's spine. What was she doing? Without appearing to do so he moved into the shadow and kept pace with Helena, their steps so perfectly timed, Faversham didn't notice. Unobtrusively, Hugh closed the gap. Faversham's attention now riveted on Helena who was in full flow, her furious contempt was stinging, and a lesser man — or one not taken by mania — might have capitulated under the onslaught. Faversham simply curled his lip and laughed; a hollow sound that reverberated off the wooden hulls and came back to them in unearthly echoes.

"My work here is finished. This yard will be flooded before the night is out. 'Tis a shame you did not drown in the schooner my dear; it would have made for an interesting climax. While this yard will not be mine, neither will it be Drummond's. The damage to the dock gates and the hulls of these two vessels is irreparable in the dark and by morning it will be too late." Faversham swung the gun back towards Hugh who, although didn't relish being shot, was relieved the weapon was no long trained on Helena.

Hugh felt his heart sink. What had the man done? He peered at the hulking blackness, trying to ascertain whether the Indiaman was listing, but as far as he could tell, she seemed stable. He knew there was water in the schooner, but it wasn't worth risking any more lives to check it tonight.

"Lives are more important than ships, Faversham. Should my yard flood, I can rebuild. These are only two ships, I have eighteen out at sea and will not risk any lives attempting to fix what you have tried to destroy. A crippled ship is mere wood, metal and cloth, far easier to rebuild than bones, flesh and blood."

"This is why you will never make a profit, you fool," Faversham, jeered derisively, "you care too much for your workers and their conditions. You worry more about them than your assets. What are a few lives here or there compared with the wealth to be made in trade?"

"My workers *are* my assets, your Lordship, without them there are no ships or sails or treasure. You are short sighted indeed if you think you can continue to make a profit without a loyal team of men behind you." Hugh sounded as though he was holding a reasonable discussion in a tavern, rather than trying to distract a madman long enough that others could bring him down before he discharged his weapon.

Meanwhile Helena was inches away from the earl. The hand in which he held the gun was waving around in emphasis as he spoke, and now within easy reach of the young woman. She knew she probably only had one chance to grab it and it was the last thing he would expect. She also realised it was the pain in her head making her braver, or more stupid, than she ever thought possible, and she did not dare to consider how angry Lady Winchester would be when she found out what her daughter had involved herself in. She might well be confined to her bedchamber for life.

It would have to be soon, the pain in her head was distorting her vision, and it would not do to miss.

Hugh suddenly realised her intent and desperately tried to gesture to Withers, hoping he too would understand her purpose. Withers, quick on the uptake, began to drift towards Helena, his approach by necessity agonisingly slow. He was almost there; she was so close that had he stretched out his arm, the tips of his fingers would have touched her hair — when Helena launched herself at Faversham.

Later, when they tried to piece together the night's events, it seemed a multitude of things happened at once. Faversham pulled the trigger but the shot went wide as Helena gripped his arm jerking it skywards, the gun now aimed at the heavens. Several men surged towards the earl as he swung his arm back down in a wide arc catching Helena on the same spot where he hit her earlier. Helena slumped to the ground unconscious. Withers picked her up, found the blanket which had been around her and hurried her away from the melee. Hugh dashed forward, his rapier swinging, the polished metal glinting in the moonlight. As he poised to strike, the earl fired again, skimming the top of Hugh's arm, catapulting the sword out of his grasp. Blood spurted from the wound as the rapier clattered to the ground — but that was Faversham's two shots — they were safe now — it was just matter of time.

Archie, Joe and Frank moved as one, barrelling into Lord Faversham on the dockside.

"You scum! You would hit a woman? One already injured!" roared Archie as he rammed his fists into the earl. "Don't you think you can 'urt 'er yer bastard! The noose is too good for you!"

Faversham hit the ground from the force of the blows, but before Archie could get hold of him, he rolled over, leapt up and ran with surprising alacrity along the yard. The three men followed, gaining quickly as, for all the earl's apparent sprightliness, Archie's thumping had knocked the wind out of the man. Panting hard, Faversham faltered, bending over to try to catch his breath.

Frank reached him first, grabbing the earl's shoulder in his massive fist. Faversham squirmed, trying to free himself, but Frank's grip was like iron.

"You are coming wiv me." He declared loudly yet quite calmly, and started to march the man back towards the gates. In a split second, Faversham ducked away again, leaving Frank, his mouth hanging open in shock, holding naught but a coat, and not even one that would fit him. Archie had had enough, and darted after Faversham between bollards, pallets, and large pieces of random machinery, any one of which would do a person serious harm if they fell over, or into them.

By now Withers, still holding Helena who was rousing, had reached the gate to be joined by Ned and Hugh — whose shoulder was burning like the devil. Another of Withers' men had used his initiative and dashed into the offices, managing to find a couple of cloths he now used to stem the blood seeping from Hugh's wound.

Helena moaned and tried to get down, but Withers told her to stay still.

"No, I'm fine. Walk the carriage to I am able." Her speech was garbled, but oddly the pain in her head had diminished and in her befuddlement she didn't know whether that was good or bad. Determined not to seem so helpless, she wriggled again and, reluctantly, Withers yielded to her persistence, holding her until he was sure she wasn't going to collapse in a heap again. Helena drew herself up and looked for Hugh, her gasp of horror when she saw the blood saturating his shirt propelling him forward until his good arm encircled her. Trembling fingers pushed his coat aside, the light from the torches highlighting a grim spectacle.

"'Tis but a scratch, love. I've suffered worse in battle." He assured her forcing a smile to his lips. "We must get her home, Withers," he begged his friend over her head. "She is ailing badly."

Helena leaned against Hugh, feeling the steady beat of his heart despite his wound, and the strength of his arm around her. "Love you I," she murmured unintelligibly.

"And I you sweetheart," he replied dropping a kiss on her head.

Helena never knew what it was that made her glance across to where Archie and the earl were dodging in and out of the shadows, but as Faversham came within range of the flickering torch light, she noticed a glimmer of something in his hand. Squinting, she tried to make out what he carried, but his erratic movements and the all-encompassing darkness made it impossible. The chase was becoming farcical with neither man gaining on the other. Suddenly, a shaft of moonlight illuminated Faversham's hand and Helena recognised what he held, at the same time as he raised his arm.

"Archie!" she screamed, ignoring a violent jab of pain, "Gun!"

Everything slowed down. Faversham aimed the weapon at Archie who was caught with nowhere to run. Withers darted towards the two men, raising his own gun and firing at the same time as did the earl. Withers' shot reached its mark first, Faversham crumpled, his bullet whizzing past Archie's ear and burying itself into a convenient wooden pallet. Withers and four of his men rushed to the earl but it was too late. Fate was wearied by Faversham's shenanigans and, as a large bloodstain bloomed across his chest, she snatched his life.

Shock paralysed Helena. She struggled to comprehend what she had witnessed, not only in the last few minutes but also the past several hours. Her safe little world seemed far away and after tonight, her appreciation for the tenuous nature of life had increased one hundredfold. Dragging her attention back to their current situation, she recalled Hugh needed help, but moving was too difficult, everything around her was most peculiarly slewed.

"Hugh," she tilted her face to look at him, "shoulder...must blood...clean...doctor..." Helena could hear her words were as scrambled as her brain and, as the last vestiges of sensibility abandoned her, she desperately wanted to convince them she wasn't in her cups. "Not tispy." She felt a laugh rumble through Hugh's chest as, once more, oblivion claimed her.

Withers directed everyone who wasn't injured, up to Hugh's office. He and his men would remain at Trentams throughout the night. For them their work was just beginning. There were reports to write, a magistrate to locate, a family to be informed, and the removal of the body to be organised. Archie wanted to help, but Withers ordered him off the premises suggesting, not ungently, he would be wise to seek medical help immediately or at the very least, rest his bruised and battered body. While everyone did as Withers bid, that gentleman swung the unconscious Helena — who was slumped against Hugh — into his arms ignoring Hugh's protests that he could manage.

"Don't be ridiculous, Drummond! You have a bloodied shoulder, which I imagine is causing a modicum of discomfort, and you have no need to risk further damage while there are plenty of people here to assist you."

Making their way through the huge gates, both men were thankful to see Tom had brought the Drummond carriage into the receiving yard. Once shots were fired, Timmy gave up being brave and hurtled around to where Tom was waiting patiently, gibbering in terror. Hugh's driver, concerned for all involved, brought around the carriage in case it was required in a hurry. Timmy himself had hightailed it home, considering himself safer in the dark streets and alleyways of the Rookeries than among the lunacy of the nobility.

Hugh climbed in, after which Withers and Tom lifted Helena onto the seat at Hugh's uninjured side, allowing him to wrap his arm around her, cradling her comfortably against him. She had not stirred, though as far as Hugh could tell, her heartbeat was steady, as was her breathing. Her wound was no longer bleeding but her head was a dreadful mess, and Hugh guessed she required urgent treatment. Archie, having been instructed to do so by Hugh, climbed in and sat opposite.

"Sybil will be beside herself," commented Hugh, a major understatement bearing in mind it was well over eight hours since Archie and Helena had left the refuge.

Archie grinned wearily. "She knew I were coming here with 'er ladyship, so she'd know as I'd not be 'ome 'til things were sorted." Was his considered response. The two men fell into desultory conversation as Tom turned the carriage and headed the horses for home. Unsure as to whether any in the Winchester residence would still be awake, Hugh dithered about where to take Helena. He was tempted to take her to his house, but Lady Winchester would likely prefer her daughter under her own roof. Calling their destination to Tom, Hugh settled back against the leather seat.

"You should come home with me, Archie," said Hugh. "I would like Phillips to have a look at you, check to make sure you haven't damaged a lung with the beating you took." Archie started to shake his head but Hugh wasn't having any of it. "Now don't be stubborn. I will send someone for Sybil, you saved Helena's life tonight I am in your debt."

Archie shook his head. "Well, sir, you gave me a job, which likely saved my life, so I reckon as we're even." Archie stuck out his hand and Hugh gripped it hard, the two men shaking as another friendship — from the most unlikely quarter — was cemented.

Chapter Twenty Seven

Nearly an hour later, in a quiet street sleeping under a harvest moon, a carriage pulled up in front of an elegant house. Tom hopped down and dropped the steps allowing first Archie, then Hugh to climb down onto the pavement. Trudging tiredly up to the front door, Hugh rapped softly, and was pleased to hear the approach of rapid footsteps. The door swung open and Hudson gaped at the dishevelled men standing on the porch step.

"Good evening Hudson, I do beg your pardon, but there has been an incident."

Hudson, his years in service coming to the fore, took in Hugh's waxy skin and bloodied clothes, as well as Archie's bruised face as though this was an everyday occurrence. He started to offer his assistance, but Hugh interrupted.

"Lady Helena is indisposed, Hudson. I think we need to get her into her own bed and call the family doctor. She has received an injury to her head and spent some time in the bowels of one of my ships."

Hudson's jaw dropped, he simply could not prevent it — this was far removed from anything he ever expected to hear. "Oh my, her Ladyship's not going to be best pleased. Mind, as Lady Helena is not one for living a genteel existence, I doubt she will be overly surprised," was all he said, however, "and I rather think you two might benefit from a doctor's examination yourselves, sir, if you don't mind my saying."

"Maybe Hudson, but I would rather Lady Helena was made comfortable first." Hugh's voice was lacking its usual strength as his own injury continued to smart. The wadding, Withers' man packed against the wound, had staunched the blood but he knew there was a chance the bullet was embedded in the top of his arm, and needed to be excised with all haste. Ignoring it for now, Hugh strode back down the steps to the carriage and with Tom's help managed to lift Helena, who seemed to come to wakefulness. Although her eyelids fluttered they didn't open and Helena simply tucked her head into Hugh's neck. Despite the circumstances, to the man in whose arms she was enfolded, it was as though she'd come home.

Meanwhile, Hudson had rallied the household and when Hugh came inside, directed him to Helena's bedchamber. Edward, one of the footmen, dashed off to get the doctor, while the housekeeper, Mrs Jenkins had gone to wake Lady Winchester. The remaining staff under Nancy's supervision busied themselves getting hot water, bowls, cloths, and a collection of small brown glass bottles, which were placed in a neat cluster on the table near Helena's bed. Hugh tried to lay Helena down, but in her befuddled state she couldn't recall where she was and refused to let him go.

Ignoring the spasm lancing through his shoulder, Hugh sat on a chair near the bed and held her close. He kissed her forehead, and murmured to her, words he hoped would soothe her distress.

"Helena my love, you're safe and at home. You need to let Nancy get you into bed so the doctor can check you over." She muttered something totally incomprehensible and a large tear rolled down one cheek. "Hey sweetheart, 'tis over. You do not have to worry about Faversham any more. You were so brave, not to mention completely and utterly crazy, but thankfully your plan worked."

Helena's eyes did open then and she stared up at him. As misty grey met burnished topaz she tried to understand his words, recalling he had been shot and was bleeding heavily. He needed help! Someone had to help him.

"Shoulder…" her words still jumbled as she panicked, "please to help you…shoulder…gun…wound. Hugh, I thought…" She couldn't finish her sentence and not just because of her dazed state.

"'Twas just a graze, do not fret yourself." He turned as several people came into the room. "Your Mama is here now. I will leave her to look after you."

"No, please don't go, please stay with me." Frantically, she clung to him.

Hugh looked at Lady Winchester who narrowed her eyes at the scene in front of her.

"Mr Drummond, I do believe carrying my daughter into bedchambers is becoming a habit of yours." Augusta Winchester said pointedly, while Hugh grinned sheepishly — her calm acceptance of the two bloodied people in front of her and the third she had just passed in the hall, saying much for her strength of character. After ordering Nancy to light more candles and bring the bowls of water to the side of the bed along with the cloths, Lady Winchester prepared everything the doctor might require, while Hugh tried to persuade Helena that her bed was the best place for her.

"Helena, I am going to lie you on your bed now, please let your Mama look after you." Hugh whispered and was gratified to receive a slight nod. He placed her carefully on the cool sheets, but as his arm slid out from under her she grasped his hand gripping it more tightly than he would have expected given her current state.

"Don't go, please don't go," she reiterated. "Mama," she said, her voice slurring, "please let Hugh stay." Before her mother could answer there was a knock at the door and the doctor, whom Lady Winchester greeted as Dr Irving, was admitted.

"Hugh needs to have his wound checked as do you my girl. Then," she raised her hand as Helena started to splutter, "once everyone has been dealt with, Mr Drummond may come and sit with you, but we must get your injuries examined."

"Promise?" she asked, holding her mother's gaze.

"Promise." her mother affirmed. Helena's lips curved slightly and as the doctor began his examination, she slid back into unconsciousness.

Hugh was escorted downstairs to where Archie was sitting in awkward comfort. Hot drinks, a platter of food and clean shirts had been provided. The two men fell on the food, inhaling everything on the plate and downing the coffee as though parched. Another pile of cloths and more bowls of water had been procured and a few moments later, Robert came in. After advising Archie that one of the grooms had gone to inform Sybil and escort her to Winchester House — should she wish to come — the young footman assisted Hugh out of his coat, removed the ruined shirt and proceeded to clean the blood from the damaged shoulder.

Hugh's pain was dulling to a throbbing burn and the bleeding had stopped. With a level of care unexpected from a footman, Robert peeled away the wad of cloth from the injury and rinsed off most of the congealed blood. He packed a clean pad over the wound, but did not bind it. The doctor would need to remove the bullet and ensure there was no dirt or material wedged where it struck, reducing the risk of infection.

"Thank you, Robert," said Hugh "You have a light touch, I am very grateful."

The young man grinned. "Thank you, Mr Drummond, sir. I used to help on the battlefield," Hugh looked at him sharply, he didn't look old enough to have been a soldier. Robert saw Hugh's expression, and shrugged his shoulders diffidently. "Me Pa was a doctor and me Ma didn't want him over there without us, so we tagged along. I used to help him with the wounded. Just fetching and carrying and the like, but I know how to wash and bandage a wound. Never expected it to come in handy in a place like this mind."

Hugh chuckled wearily. "Well, I for one am grateful. Do you think you might check Archie here? He has had a rough night too."

"Seems to me there's been a rough night had by quite a few of you, if you beg my pardon, sir." Robert noted impassively.

"It has been quite a night Robert and I, for one, never, ever want to experience another like it. I find it remarkable we are all alive save the perpetrator, despite his best efforts." Robert tried not to look inquisitive, but Hugh noticed and, taking pity on him, gave the young man a condensed version of the evening's events. As he finished speaking, the doctor appeared. Hugh asked how Lady Helena fared, while insisting Archie be checked first.

After doing so, the doctor confirmed their suspicions. Archie was suffering from three cracked ribs and severe bruising, which would heal in time, but required rest and no strenuous activity for at least a week, two would be better. Archie balked at that, and received matching frowns from both Hugh and the doctor, his employer asserting that resting was precisely what he would be doing.

Finally, it was Hugh's turn. Dr Irving washed his hands again in a bowl of clean water, to which he added a few drops of vinegar and mint — to help slow the bleeding as well as disinfect.

"Lady Helena sustained a nasty head wound, and may yet develop an infection from being cold and wet for quite a long period of time. What the deuce happened tonight? You two look as though you've been in quite a skirmish." The doctor muttered on about the lunacy of men, until Hugh explained why they were sporting such wounds. Dr Irving was aghast.

"Confound it! I know Lord Faversham. I have treated his children. No, Mr Drummond surely you are mistaken."

"I am sorry to be the bearer of such shocking news, but 'tis all true. He tried to murder Lady Helena and when she managed to escape — with the help of Archie here — he went on another rampage attempting to kill several others. It was only by chance we limited the deaths to his own." Hugh winced as the doctor examined, prodded and poked at his wound.

Dr Irving peered at Hugh over his spectacles. "It appears the bullet has lodged in the flesh at the top of your arm. You are lucky, it just missed the bone." Hugh didn't feel particularly lucky right then. "Hold still, this will likely tickle." Cool metal slid into the wound and there was a stomach churning, squelching noise as the doctor withdrew the bullet. Even knowing it would hurt and clenching his jaw in an attempt to lessen the agony, Hugh blanched and swallowed hard against rising nausea. Probing carefully, until convinced there was no other debris within; the doctor splashed the whole area liberally with a solution of salt, water and more vinegar.

Certain the doctor was jabbing hot pokers into the wound, Hugh was hard pushed to hold onto his senses. Then it was over, fresh wadding was pressed to his shoulder and bound in place. A large glass of whisky was pushed into his trembling hand which he gulped down, the fiery spirit going some way to settling his fraught nerves. He focused on the doctor's voice.

"I will return on the morrow to check you all. This wound especially will need a thorough clean twice a day, until I am sure there is no infection and healing has begun."

Hugh nodded, incapable of speech.

Dr Irving beamed, and thanked Robert for his assistance as the footman showed the doctor out.

Sybil arrived shortly thereafter and clucked over Archie like a mother hen. Grinning at Archie's expression as he tried to assure his wife he was fine, just rather sore, Hugh left them to it, presuming Robert or Hudson would sort them out, and climbed slowly back up the stairs to Helena's room. He knocked quietly and was admitted by Lady Winchester, who brought him up to date in low tones.

"Helena is resting now, although Dr Irving said we ought to rouse her every couple of hours, just to make sure we can. If we cannot, it might be a sign she is deteriorating. He was loath to administer any laudanum to help manage the pain because it might mask other symptoms. She has taken some feverfew and the cloths on her wrists and forehead have been soaked in an infusion of lavender, the fragrance of which, Helena says is invariably soothing."

Lady Winchester paused and studied the face of the man before her. His colour was ghastly. His skin was still slightly clammy from the extraction procedure, and even though he had donned a clean shirt he looked like a wreck.

"If you feel able, pray tell me what happened tonight Mr Drummond," she implored quietly, indicating he should take the chair he vacated earlier. "Helena's mutterings offered no clarity, but I did work out you had been shot, Archie was beaten up by thugs, and Lord Faversham tried to kill various people." Her reserved tones in stark contrast to her words.

Hugh made himself comfortable, currently no easy feat, and corralled his thoughts before telling Helena's mother what had transpired scant hours before. He was careful not to go into too much detail, and was unable to explain how Helena ended up in the bilge of his schooner, but he could provide enough that Lady Winchester was satisfied.

"Until Withers completes his investigation and Lady Helena can fill in the gaps, that is all I have. Please believe me when I say I am horrified, a man such as Faversham thought it appropriate to behave in the manner he did. Thankfully, Lady Helena saw fit to send a note to Withers as well as discuss her intentions with Archie, who was sensible enough to gather several of his friends together before they entered the yard. If not, I believe the outcome would have been far worse. As it is, although Faversham's henchmen were dealt with in a manner suiting their actions, none were killed, neither were any of Withers' men. Archie suffered a serious beating but despite a couple of cracked ribs, he will heal in time. The shot meant for Archie was foiled, and although I could not avoid a bullet it skimmed the top of my arm, missing the bone completely. Doc says it will need some care for the next few days, but he does not foresee any problems."

Hugh spoke with a light-heartedness he was far from feeling and his audience of one was not fooled for a minute.

"Are you sure you would not prefer to rest in one the guest chambers?" Lady Winchester asked solicitously. "You will feel better after a proper sleep."

Hugh shook his head. "Thank you, but if you do not object, I would rather stay here. I promised, and I imagine dawn is about to break. It seems a shame to use a clean and fresh bed for a couple of hours."

Lady Winchester was of the opinion Hugh needed a lot more than just a couple of hours of sleep, but forbore from saying so, merely rested her hand on his good shoulder and told him to call if he needed anything. Hugh nodded absently, his concentration back on Helena. Lady Winchester smiled, a little sadly, knowing soon her daughter would belong to another.

Chapter Twenty Eight

Hugh was correct, it seemed the dawn broke the moment he sat down, although it was a little over an hour later. Helena was fast asleep, but as the light in the room changed, Nancy came over to the bed, so they could try to rouse her. Hugh cupped his hand along her jaw and spoke in undertones, calling her out of her stupor. Helena shifted restlessly, but to their relief came awake. She stared at Hugh, puzzled as to why he was in her room, but too tired to question it.

"Hugh?" she queried drowsily.

"I'm here love, we just needed to make sure you would wake. Go back to sleep now."

"Your shoulder?"

"Is fine."

Helena shuffled up on her pillows and looked down at their linked hands, warmth blossoming through her. They had made it, they were both alive and perhaps now they could have that happily ever after, Billie and Charlotte insisted on waxing so lyrically about.

"You should be in bed, not sitting watching over me. Go and get a proper rest."

"No point now, 'tis morning. I imagine Lucas will want to talk to me as soon as possible, and I will need to apprise my family and my employees about what happened. Hopefully Faversham's threat about sinking both boats was just that, a threat, but if not, there will be much work to do."

"I wish you did not have to go."

Hugh could see Helena was fighting to stay awake. "I doubt you will notice my absence, sweetheart, as I expect you shall sleep for much of today. Later you will need to tell me what happened so I can inform Lucas, then he will have the whole story."

Helena yawned prodigiously, "I always notice your absence Hugh, and I really hope we can ma..." slumber claimed her, right in the middle of a word. Hugh chuckled, working out where he thought she might have been heading with that sentence. He leaned over and pressed his lips butterfly soft against her downy cheek.

"Me too love, me too."

Much later, Hugh was back in Helena's room, reading though some paperwork given to him by Withers. During the day, the doctor returned to re-examine all three of his patients, and Archie had been given permission to return home. This was under the strict condition, from both the doctor and Hugh that he would take two weeks off and that Sybil would send word if she were worried about him. Hugh had also visited his family assuring them, despite rumours to the contrary, he was not dead.

Although apparently engrossed in the documents, his thoughts were on the woman lying so peacefully in the bed. If this last twenty-four hours had taught him anything it was that Helena was more precious to him than everything else in his life, in his world, combined. More than his own family, more than the business, more than his beautiful ships. During their enforced separation, Hugh had begun to mull over the possibility of obtaining a special licence, allowing them to marry as soon as the debacle was over. Following these latest events, however, he rather liked the idea of having the banns read in church, of hearing their names linked together in front of God and man. He wasn't particularly religious, but as many men of the sea will attest, 'tis always useful to have a higher power to pray to when in the middle of a mighty tempest.

As Helena also had a home at Whiteoaks, he wondered whether they could have the banns called there, and marry in the little village church, which he knew she loved, from their many conversations about her life at the country estate. Unbidden, he recalled the first time she mentioned Whiteoaks, how she missed the quietude of the countryside and how she loved to watch the moonrise. While he sat, it came to him that to watch the moonrise with Helena would be just about the most marvellous way to spend every evening for the rest of their lives.

As though aware of his scrutiny, Helena stirred. She rubbed her eyes, blinking a little in the cheerful sunlight filling the room. Nancy had opened the windows, and the sounds of birds wafted through. It was a cold day, autumn was well and truly upon them, but the sun was bright and the air fresh. She turned slowly, realising the hammering in her head had faded to a sluggish thrum. *Oh, thank goodness for that, 'twas enough to drive a person to the madhouse.* Her gaze collided with that of Hugh, who was sitting by her bed. She frowned, had he moved at all? She wriggled, the better to raise herself up on her pillows, and reached for him.

Immediately, Hugh laced his fingers with hers and she pulled him towards her, needing to feel his lips on some part, any part of her. Hugh raised a quizzical eyebrow, but Helena merely smiled and continued to draw him close.

"Kiss me," she pleaded, her eyes — like smoky amethyst — were huge in her pale face and the longer he stared into them the deeper he fell. He could deny her nothing, and even though discretion demanded he do no such thing, he moved to the bed, sat next to her, lifted her into his arms and covered her lips with his.

Helena felt that delicious heat coil through her as they kissed, languorously and tenderly. Hugh's lips were a caress, a promise, a hope and a dream. Everything she ever wanted was right there, in front of her, kissing her as though she was the most loved woman in the history of the world. After several minutes when she imagined a whole orchestra serenaded them, Helena broke their kiss, but did not move out of his embrace. She had a confession to make and even though she hated being in the wrong, knew she had to get it over with or it would haunt her.

"I have something I need to say." Hugh waited. Helena fidgeted a bit, trying to come up with the right words, she huffed a sigh, and Hugh braced himself for a barrage of something. "I am so sorry," was all she managed however, her voice wavering.

Hugh gaped. "What are you sorry for, love?" perplexed.

"For putting everyone in danger. I should never have gone to the yard without trying to find you first and telling you about the letter. I risked so many lives because I was thoughtless and rushed headlong into a situation I had no ability to handle. I know Lord Faversham was doing the wrong thing, but his death is my fault." She went on to explain what had happened the previous afternoon — was it only yesterday? She felt as though she had lived a hundred lifetimes.

The longer she spoke the more appalled Hugh became. Yes, she might have acted without thinking but her motives were laudable and her courage, in an impossible situation, astonishing. He could not think of many women, of any status, who would be able to climb out of a ship's hull and grapple with a gun-wielding madman, all after being bashed unconscious with the carved handle of a cane. During the day, he had spoken with Archie and Lucas, the latter giving him a report on the investigation. Now, with Helena's account, it all fell into place, like finishing one of those children's puzzle toys after finding that one missing piece.

"Hush, sweetheart," he soothed, as Helena became distressed. "It was not your fault. Lucas told me Faversham had been planning your demise for weeks and although, initially, we fooled him with our charade, he decided to continue regardless. According to one of his henchmen, the fact we had seemingly gone our separate ways made it all the more exhilarating for him, because your death after so public a spat would result in greater scandal. He presumed it would cause an irreparable breakdown in the faith my customers have in me and my business, allowing him to sweep in and save the day, buying me out and taking over everything."

"He said he believed Trentams should be his. That your father should have bequeathed to him, the yard in its entirety."

Hugh stared at Helena in shock. "I am dumbfounded by his machinations. I know he helped my father in the beginning, but it was a relatively small investment in comparison with some I have heard about, and definitely not enough to be granted the whole company in a bequest. The man obviously delusional." The pair fell quiet, each lost in contemplation. Helena gave up, it was too hard, too sad and she was still so tired. She leaned into Hugh, her head resting under his chin.

"Do you have to leave again?"

"No, I am under strict instructions to stay here for the rest of the day. Dr Irving will doubtless wish to prod at this wound again — I am sure doctors just like inflicting more pain on their poor unsuspecting patients..." Helena chuckled at this, "...so Lady Winchester suggested I remain here until then at the very least. She has invited me to stay but I'm not sure how good an idea that is."

"Why ever not?" Helena asked, innocently.

Hugh grinned at her expression. "You know precisely why, Lady Helena. Despite my sore shoulder and your sore head, I would find it far too easy to divest you of that very delectable nightgown and play your body until you were crying out my name and begging me to take you."

Helena gulped, his words conjuring up an image she would struggle to forget, heat flaring up her body and making her blush. "I...errr...umm...well..." She shut up; there was no ladylike response to such a statement.

Still grinning and with no obvious remorse, Hugh cupped her hot cheeks and kissed her again, firm lips moving over hers, demanding more. Helena shuddered and skimmed her hands under his shirt. Mindful of his wound, she traced the muscles of his chest feeling them pulse under her touch, making him groan, his heart rate increasing with every passing second.

"Helena this is madness," he gasped as her inquisitive fingers teased under the waistband of his trousers.

She twinkled up at him, "I know, isn't it divine?"

Hugh spluttered with laughter, she really was quite the minx. He dragged his mind away from the delights of her body to the thought, which had been uppermost in his mind while she slept.

"What would you think about asking your brother whether we might marry in the church near Whiteoaks?"

Helena twisted in his arms to gaze up at him. Her bandaged head tilted adorably to one side as a huge grin lit her face. "Could we?" she breathed. "That is the most excellent idea.

You can see my home and we can walk in the park and we can..." before she could finish Hugh interjected

"...watch the moonrise?"

"Yes, oh yes. Oh, Hugh, I did not think it was possible to love you any more than I already do, but this, your suggestion has proved me wrong. How did you know?" She sank against him, cuddling into the crook of his neck, her fingers following the outline of the muscles in his arms through his shirt.

"It came to me while I watched you sleep. I suddenly recalled our first conversation, when you told me how much you loved watching the moonrise at Whiteoaks, and I realised how wonderful it would be to watch it with you. I had already been thinking, rather than apply for a special licence, which I know means we could marry immediately it was issued, I would like to hear our names called in church, to announce our intent to the world, well a congregation at least. Then I wondered whether we might be eligible to marry at Oak Stanton..." he trailed off, unsure whether he sounded overly fanciful.

Apparently not, for Helena leaned close and kissed him. Her lips an invitation and naive to the fact her night gown, which left little to the imagination, was doing all sorts of peculiar things to Hugh's heart rate, she wrapped herself around him. The room faded away and there was only the two of them, lost in each other, hearts and souls as one.

Chapter Twenty Nine

Six weeks later - Whiteoaks, Hampshire

Helena stood on the terrace at Whiteoaks, staring over the frosty gardens and out to the vast expanse of the Great Park beyond. She breathed in the chill air. It was mid-December and, following a milder than usual autumn, the trees were at last almost bare; a few hardy leaves, like flakes of fading jewels, still scattered across the ground. Helena loved this time of year, when everything was grey and silver; foggy mornings, the smell of bonfires and the cold clear nights. Today was her wedding day and she could hardly believe it was here. There had been the odd occasion of late when it seemed highly unlikely.

The past few weeks had been hectic. A dull fortnight of enforced convalescence while her poor head healed proved somewhat frustrating, not only for Helena herself but also for those tending her, for she was inclined to be fractious. After several heated exchanges, with her mother, the doctor, Hugh, Stephen, and Tabitha, she had, eventually and grudgingly, submitted to their instructions, acknowledging it was better to stay put than fall over every time she tried to walk further than her bed chamber.

Once assured of her daughter's recovery, Lady Winchester reduced Helena to tears when the two finally had the opportunity to discuss the incident. She berated Helena for being so impetuous, reminding her that Hugh was a grown man of nearly eight and twenty, and far more able to deal with such problems than a silly girl five years his junior. Helena tried to explain her motives, which her mother scathingly brushed aside, the realisation she could so easily have lost her youngest child, weighing heavily on her mind.

Helena cried herself into another headache and refused to speak to anyone for more than two days, her misery a tangible thing, until Hugh — after being advised by Nancy, who had long forgiven him for upsetting her beloved mistress, whispered that Helena was sending back trays of food untouched — decided enough was enough. Requesting an audience with Lady Winchester, he argued quietly and with the utmost tact, that while Helena acted impulsively, her heart was in the right place, and her quick thinking had averted what could have been a worse disaster. Following a long conversation, Mother and daughter were reconciled, plans for the wedding an effective distraction.

Hugh visited Helena as often as possible, work at Trentams permitting. It was discovered the dock gates were intact and, although both ships had sustained some damage requiring a considerable amount of repair, the breach in their hulls was not as bad as anticipated. Hugh was confident the Indiaman and the schooner would suffer only a slight delay in their schedules, his employees working hard to minimise the loss of trade. His injured shoulder was almost healed. Dr Irving, once satisfied there was no infection, stitched the gash and from then on it improved rapidly.

The couple did spend hours talking about what occurred, but whichever way they looked at it, the outcome remained the same and no amount of 'what ifs' could change it. Helena still had no idea how she got into the bowels of the schooner, and Faversham's men remained tight lipped about the affair, even the threat of hanging did not sway them. Helena claimed she preferred not to know, she had enough painful memories of that night and did not need them adding to.

Although nasty, the blow to Helena's head was more a laceration than deep gash and once the large lump reduced in size, the injury itself began to heal quickly. Mindful of young ladies and their vanity, the doctor had been careful not to cut away too much of her hair. It was already growing back and under Nancy's nimble fingers both the injury and minimal hair loss was cleverly hidden under a variety of inventive styles. Helena endured a few vile headaches in the immediate aftermath, but in light of what had happened this wasn't unexpected. Dr Irving assured her they would decrease as she recuperated, which appeared to be the case. In any event, she was currently under Billie's tender mercies at Whiteoaks and her sister-in-law's knowledge of herbs meant any recurrence was quickly managed.

Once the doctor deemed Helena well enough to get up, she faced the somewhat nerve-wracking matter of being interviewed, first by Lucas Withers, then by a magistrate. It was harrowing, re-living that night, but she had a lot of support. The magistrate did feel moved to contend that a young woman tackling a murderous lunatic, while he brandished a loaded weapon, was foolhardy in the extreme — making the assemblage chuckle and Helena cringe with embarrassment. He tempered this by adding that she acted with remarkable courage, giving the others chance to subdue the man who had schemed to lure her to the shipyard with every intention of killing her. Every scene was etched in her memory and during the first week or so of her recovery — as she had been after the fire — Helena was beset by nightmares, but their frequency seemed to be abating. She had also discovered an aversion to dark spaces; again, something she hoped would fade in time.

Thankfully, her love of the night sky had not been doused, and each evening, since her arrival at the Winchester country estate, five days previously, she snuck away to watch the moonrise. As yet, Hugh had not joined his betrothed in her evening ritual, believing she needed this time on her own, a way to regain her inner calm, and to let the night work its magic.

Hugh and Lady Winchester accompanied Helena to Whiteoaks, the remaining wedding guests arriving in small groups over the last day or so. These included, Stephen and Tabitha, Hugh's family, Lucas Withers with his wife Jemima, and Archie and Sybil. The latter two finding the luxury of Whiteoaks utterly stupefying, but were beginning to relax under the warm hospitality of Billie and Giles who never stood on ceremony and ensured no one felt excluded. A convivial atmosphere enveloped the house, and before long all the guests were enjoying each other's company as though friends for years.

Prior to this, there was the not inconsiderable task of preparing and packing for Helena's temporary remove. Giles offered Helena and Hugh one of the estate houses for their honeymoon, a small manor on the edge of the Great Park, an offer they accepted gladly. A couple of days after her arrival, and although the place was spotless and ready for guests at any moment, Helena, along with Billie, spent several hours making the manor homelier, adding extra comforts and filling the shelves with tasty treats fit for newlyweds. There would be a skeleton staff in attendance but for the most part the couple would be able to enjoy a modicum of privacy. Hugh intended to take his wife to Italy, but not until the spring, sea voyages being too perilus during the winter months. He felt they had both dealt with quite enough danger in recent weeks, and had no desire to tempt fate any further.

At last, it was her day. Helena woke very early and slipped outside before the household started to rouse, enjoying the frozen serenity of the dawn. Wrapped in heavy cloak, she had spent the last hour strolling around the gardens and out into the park, scaring the odd rabbit braving the morning in search of food, and disturbing the birds who had no qualms about squawking their annoyance, all of which she ignored, lost in contemplation.

Eventually she made her way back to the house and was currently leaning against one of the pillars outside the library, delaying, for as long as possible, the moment when she had to turn from the breathtaking landscape and begin her preparations. A sound broke onto her reverie and the door behind her opened. She knew who it was before he reached her side.

"Good morning, Hugh," she murmured, unwilling to shatter the peace.

"Good morning, my love. How long have you been up?" Familiar with her penchant for solitary early morning walks, whatever the weather.

"A little over an hour." She heard a soft chuckle and Hugh's arms came around her, drawing her close. She leaned into him, running her gloved hands over the fine wool of his winter coat.

Slowly he turned her to face him, staring into the fathomless grey of her eyes, calm today as she regarded him steadily, a gentle smile tilting the corners of her mouth. Oh, her smile, it never failed to trip his heart and giving in to his desire to kiss said smile, Hugh curved his hands around her cheeks and bent his lips to hers. Seconds ticked by stretching into minutes and still they kissed, oblivious to everything else around them, and uncaring that Whiteoaks was hosting a number of guests any one of whom might suddenly decide a brisk walk was just the thing before a hearty breakfast.

Reluctantly, Hugh broke their embrace. "I am very much looking forward to be doing that later without worrying that your brother is going to call me out," he muttered on a ragged breath.

Helena giggled. The events at the shipyard and subsequent repercussions prevented Hugh from travelling to Whiteoaks to ask Giles for Helena's hand. The two men, however, had begun a sporadic correspondence, a cordiality growing between them and, in one letter, Giles officially approved Hugh's suit, much to the couple's delight. His blessing leaving them able, at last, to organise their wedding.

When they finally met, Giles and Billie welcomed Hugh with open arms. Two evenings later, over dinner, Helena's brother informed his youngest sister that in his opinion Hugh was eminently suitable and in the next breath advised Hugh that he if ever hurt Helena he was a dead man. Knowing Giles' genial nature, Helena found this hilariously funny, as did Billie who gaped at her husband in astonishment, the pair gleefully chastising him for being so pompous.

Hugh understood Giles' declaration — he too had a sister — the two men discussing the recent events and Helena's part in them at length. Giles, while appalled at the behaviour of Lord Faversham had to admit it wasn't unheard of. Grace, wife of his friend Theo, recently suffered a near deadly assault by a duke who had, previously, also abused her, thus Giles acknowledged such actions were neither defined by nor limited to a person's status within society; it was just that those in the *ton* usually got away with it.

That it was his sister who had borne the brunt of Faversham's deranged obsession was harder for Giles to accept. Organising his day so that he could accompany Helena on walks or the occasional horse ride, Giles persuaded her to open up to him. Unwilling to tell him at first — it was long since Giles and Helena had talked, if ever — eventually she capitulated. Everything that happened over the last few months spilled out, including the fire at Sanctuary House. Giles was astonished at the bravery of his sister, whom he found hard to see as anything other than the guileless child she used to be. During their many conversations, kinship, thought lost was revived, forging a new and deeper bond, to the joy of the rest of their family.

Despite Hugh being a reticent and somewhat grave man, especially with people he didn't know, Giles warmed to him, and the two were becoming good friends. Discovering they had a lot in common, they regaled each other with tales of misdeeds at university, and shared experiences from the battlefields of the Peninsula over cigars and fine whisky. Giles trusted Hugh would care for Helena as though she was the most delicate piece of china, and that was enough for her protective brother.

The nearly wedded couple stood together, enjoying a few more moments to themselves until the sounds of a waking household intervened. They hurried indoors doffing their outer wear before joining the rest of their guests in the dining room, where a sumptuous breakfast awaited.

Helena was stolen away shortly thereafter, with strict instructions from her brother not to be late. She rolled her eyes at Hugh, as Billie, Charlotte, Tabitha, and Jessica dragged her away, all talking at once, and no one listening to anyone else. After luxuriating in a warm bath lightly scented with something Billie had blended specially, Helena began the process of dressing. Hugh had only one request for his bride, that she wear something to match her eyes. The image of her in the stunning gown she wore to Stephen and Tabitha's betrothal never far from his mind.

Thus, Helena's wedding finery was shades of grey and violet, layers of filmy garments that glimmered, their shades dissolving into one another creating another colour entirely, until finally the dress itself, which was the most astonishing hue. Reminiscent of clouds on a winter's evening, whose misty greyness is suddenly warmed just before the setting sun drops below the horizon and the sky morphs from blue to purple, the material was like liquid silk. It flowed around her, forming and reforming when Helena moved, giving the impression she was floating. Her raven hair was coiled and twisted into an elaborate style, entwined with ribbons of silver and violet. By her own choice, Helena wore no facial cosmetics, as she found they made her skin itch, but she was persuaded into a dab of perfume and a little jewellery. Slipping her feet into soft, grey leather shoes, she was ready.

She was trembling now but could not have told anyone whether this was owing to nerves or excitement. Giles met her at the top of the stairs, looking dashing in a dark, charcoal grey jacket and trousers, and white shirt, his waistcoat a deep purple and his cravat silver grey. He paused, suddenly realising his madcap and somewhat unconventional sister had become an elegant and poised young woman. He offered her his arm, which she gripped tightly.

"You look beautiful, Helena," he said. "Papa would be so proud." They shared a long look and Helena found she had to blink rapidly. She absolutely refused to cry today.

"I'm glad I still have you," she whispered.

"Always," he replied. "Are you ready?" he added smiling down at her, still struggling to believe she was old enough to be getting married, ignoring the fact his own wife was a similar age, and they had been married almost a year.

"I do believe I am, your Lordship," she said a wicked grin lighting her face as she dropped a cheeky curtsy, reminding Giles that the irrepressible child hadn't disappeared entirely. He chuckled and squeezed her hand.

"Well, we had best not keep your betrothed waiting." He led her down the stairs and across the hallway, splendidly decorated for the festivities, and out through the main entrance into the cool of the morning. Several carriages were lined up along the driveway, Helena and Giles climbed into theirs and they all rumbled off.

The drive into Oak Stanton did not take long, and when Giles helped Helena down from the carriage it seemed the whole village had come out to wish her well. She felt more tears forming as she thanked them prettily. Such kind people, many of whom had known her since her birth and who cared enough to take time out of their busy days to congratulate her on her marriage.

At the back of the church, Helena stood for a moment or two, gathering herself; then straightened her shoulders and took her brother's arm once more. As they walked slowly down the aisle, she whispered her appreciation to the congregation as she passed, grasping the hand of one or two, making them smile at her complete disregard for the solemnity of their surroundings.

Hugh, tall and handsome, wearing the same dark grey attire as Giles, turned to watch her approach. His face lit up when he saw Helena, his love for her clear in his eyes, and the last of her nerves vanished.

Helena looked radiantly beautiful, her dress the perfect complement to her classical features, and he was mesmerised by the sway of her lissom body as she neared him. He held her gaze all the way until she stood next to him in the chancel, whereupon he took her hand, interlacing their fingers, uncaring whether this was appropriate.

The ceremony was simple and dignified and almost before Helena had time to think about it they were wed.

Chapter Thirty

Helena and Hugh walked out into the churchyard. The early mist had lifted and a pale sun sat low in a yellowish, wintery sky, heralding snow. The villagers were still there, cheering as the happy couple lingered for a few moments chatting with everyone, thanking them for their good wishes. More than one housewife was heard to comment that Mr Hugh Drummond was indeed a most handsome man — next to the earl himself of course. Soon, the wedding party were being assisted into their various carriages before being transported back to Whiteoaks where a feast befitting the occasion was being readied.

The rest of the day flew by in a whirl of joyful merriment, the guests declaring Helena and Hugh were the quintessential couple. Helena was heard to comment she pitied poor Hugh, for his life would never be dull with her around, as her recent escapades attested. Overhearing her, Hugh's wry response had been along the lines of who wants a dull life anyway, when chasing madmen through shipyards and dashing into burning buildings was so much more exciting, making those to whom they were talking chuckle in agreement; Helena's impulsive nature well known.

The couple were barely apart, hands linked, shoulders nearly always touching. If they did happen to separate to chat with friends or family, each always knew where the other was. A gaze drawn, a smile shared, believing their gestures covert, to the unbridled amusement of their guests, who were far more observant than the couple credited.

Later, as the afternoon drew to a close and the guests were retiring for a well-earned rest before the evening entertainment began, Helena and Hugh slipped away quietly. They refused the offer of a carriage and, after shrugging into thick winter coats, enjoyed a brisk walk to the manor, hands entwined, chattering happily about nothing much at all. Darkness was falling, but it wasn't far from the main house and Matthew, one of their appointed staff, was watching out, opening the door to welcome them into a home glowing in the light from a multitude of candles. He took their coats and ushered them into the library, where a huge fire warmed the room. Two large leather chairs fanned the hearth with a small table between, on which stood a decanter of red wine and two crystal glasses, their facets in the flickering light, sending rainbow prisms over the polished surfaces. A platter of food had been placed on the desk behind the chairs, and Matthew asked whether they would like hot drinks.

They both nodded, requesting hot chocolate and Matthew bowed, closing the door as he left them. At last they were alone yet unaccountably, Helena felt self-conscious. She stood in the middle of the room, unsure what to do now. Half of her desperately wanted Hugh to kiss her into insensibility before whisking her off to their bedroom and making love to her, the other half had no idea how any of this worked and didn't want to look like a complete idiot. She twiddled her fingers together, shifting awkwardly from foot to foot. She started to speak, but nothing came out, so she clamped her mouth shut and plopped onto one of the chairs, with none of her customary grace.

Hugh watched all this flit across her eloquent face. Her uncertainty was palpable, and it was so unlike her normal insouciance, his chest tightened, unsure what bothered her. Sitting in the other chair, he poured them both a glass of wine, and handed one to Helena. He noticed her fingers were trembling when she accepted the glass, and he rested his hand over hers. They sipped their drinks, the only sound the crackle of the fire and the soft hiss as moisture from the chimney dripped onto the hot wood. All seemed tranquil, but Helena was still fidgeting, winding the one long black lock of hair, which had detached itself from the ornate style hours before, absently around her finger, the way she did whenever anxious or upset.

"Helena my love, what is it?" he asked quietly.

Helena gulped down the last of her wine, and shook her head as though trying to dismiss troublesome thoughts. "I don't know, I can't explain it. This, you and me — I have wanted this for so long, finally able to..." she couldn't say the words, "...but I have no clue what happens now or what to do, well except for how to kiss and I love it when you kiss me," she added ingenuously, twisting in the chair to face him, her eyes doubtful. He smiled encouragingly and squeezed her hand, knowing there was more. "I-I am afraid I will d-disappoint you." She stammered her apprehension.

Hugh's jaw dropped, "How on earth could you disappoint me?" he asked, searching her face trying to read her mind.

Helena shrugged, "Well, because you are a worldly sailor and you have probably had a mistress or two. You men always seem to know about...errr...hmmm..." — modesty still held her back, so she plumped for — "...this."

Hugh started to laugh, he couldn't help it; she looked so serious. "You make me sound like a profligate rake," he chortled, her affronted expression adding to his mirth. "Oh, my love, if you want the truth I have never taken a mistress and while I cannot say that I have never before lain with a woman, it has never been with love and 'twas years ago, when I was in the army and life seemed fleeting. Since then and until I met you I have had no desire to bed a woman simply to..." — he paused trying to think of a less stark way of phrasing it — "...quench my thirst. So maybe we could learn to make love together." He stared into her eyes and Helena swallowed hard, his admission humbling her.

She nodded, a tentative smile curving her lips. "I cannot think of anything more wonderful," she whispered.

Hugh stood and, still holding her hand, pulled her up from the chair. Bowing politely before stroking a finger along her jaw and kissing the tip of her nose, he murmured, "Mrs Drummond, I must advise I am finding it very difficult to keep my hands off you. Your body bewitches me, your eyes enthral me and your smile touches my soul. I would very much like to escort you upstairs where I can demonstrate just how much I love you."

Helena, amused at such formality, replied, "Why Mr Drummond, you do say the most outrageous things. I admit, however, that your touch thrills me, your eyes captivate me and your smile warms me all the way to my toes. In light of this, I do believe I am disposed to grant you your wish." Finishing on a dainty curtsy.

Grinning, Hugh encircled her in his arms, his lips grazing hers. She moved against him, but just as their embrace deepened, a quiet knock disturbed them and they shot apart, expressions reminiscent of naughty children, as Matthew came in with their hot drinks.

Trying to maintain her equilibrium, Helena thanked him, albeit in a rather wobbly voice, assuring the young man he might retire, for there was nothing else they required. Bowing, Matthew retreated, leaving the couple standing feet apart and somewhat flustered. Hugh caught Helena's eye, his own twinkling and his lips twitching. She started to speak, hiccuped and stopped, feeling mirth building at the sheer incongruity of the scene. As their eyes met they burst out laughing, merriment echoing around the room and lingering while they sipped the rich brew. Each held by the other's gaze, they became aware a heat was building, one which had nothing to do with the drinks. As hilarity died away an urgency overtook them, and their cups clattered to the tray, hot chocolate forgotten.

Hugh reached for Helena's hand. "I love you, Mrs Drummond. Shall we?" She nodded and he leaned down for a quick kiss, which ended up being rather longer, until Hugh broke away, "Not here," huskily, "I want to take my time and be somewhere a little more private."

Helena coloured alluringly, anticipation fluttering through her, as he put his arm around her and led her up to their bedchamber. Nancy had been in. The bedding was turned down, the fire lit and several candelabra were dotted about the room shedding a soft glow. Hugh closed the door and turned the key.

"I do not want to be disturbed until we choose to be," he growled at Helena's raised eyebrow, making her giggle at his fierce expression. In front of the fire, Hugh drew Helena to him, sliding one hand around the back of her head, entwining his fingers through her glossy hair and kissing her gently. Moulding her svelte frame to his much larger one, Helena delighted that they seemed to fit together just so.

Trying not to let her nerves overtake her, Helena followed her instinct, trailing her hands under Hugh's waistcoat, feeling the warmth from his skin through the fine cotton of his shirt. With his free hand, Hugh stroked up and down her spine, finding and slowly undoing all the tiny buttons on her glorious gown. Helena shivered a little as the last button fell to his demands and her dress slithered to the floor in a swish of silk, the intimacy of the sound heightening Helena's senses and sending her heart rate through the ceiling.

Never breaking his kiss, Hugh made short work of her exquisitely delicate under clothes, each layer falling in filmy iridescence at her feet until, and almost without her realising it had happened, Helena was naked.

"Oh, my love, you are so beautiful," Hugh breathed, his heart thudding as he raked his eyes over her alabaster skin, the fever in his expression making her cheeks rosy. He lifted her chin with one finger, brushing his lips over hers, "I adore that you blush, but you have no need to, 'tis only me."

Helena whispered softly, "'Tis never *only* with you." Feeling her nerves evaporating as she gazed into his eyes, the firelight catching the tawny flecks within giving them a mysterious quality. A mystery, Helena perceived, she was about to unravel.

Capturing her lips again, Hugh's mouth moved lazily over hers, his tongue tasting her - wine and chocolate — a heady combination. A wandering hand came to rest momentarily on her slender waist, fingers splaying over her back before slowly teasing along her cool skin, sending thousands of infinitesimal vibrations right through her, while heat blossomed in her centre, rippling outwards along her veins. His skilful touch elicited a soft cry from Helena, her own fingers faltering as she felt the insistent throb of desire.

"Hugh," she whimpered. Her husband slowed his pilgrimage and lifted his head.

"Mmmmm?" His gaze still on her lips.

"If this is going to work, I daresay you should have fewer clothes on," she groused, throatily.

Laughter rumbled through Hugh's chest. "It would be quicker if you were to help." Hugh invited, his eyes darkening to the colour of aged whisky.

"Well, I suppose it would be only fair to return the favour" a saucy grin on her face. Another muffled laugh immediately stifled when Helena stretched up, her body gliding against his, doing neither of them any good at all. Deft fingers untied his cravat, which had been askew almost the whole day — honestly the man simply could not keep one affixed; an endearing quirk and Helena loved that it was peculiar to him. Once removed, she folded the slightly crumpled article neatly, placing it on the little table and turned to unbutton his waistcoat. Taking her time, she heard his breath hitch as she slid the rich brocade from his shoulders, dropping it over the back of a chair. Then she stood, hands on hips and demanded he take off his shirt,

"You are far too tall for me to manage that," she explained meditatively, little realising how enchanting she looked. Her black hair was barely contained within its elaborate style, errant locks falling over her shoulder, ebony against ivory. Hugh shrugged out of his shirt, which joined the waistcoat as Helena began to work at the buttons on the fall of his trousers, her actions doing nothing to slow Hugh's rapid heartbeat.

"Love," he groaned. Fingers paused. "Maybe I should do this. Your touch is…errr…undermining the last of my willpower." Helena stared, baffled. Hugh leaned forward and murmured in her ear. She flushed bright red, at once both embarrassed and aroused.

"R-really?" she stuttered. Hugh nodded as his shoes, stockings and trousers joined the growing pile of discarded clothes he nodded and stood, but when he made to enfold her back into his embrace, Helena held him at arm's length. She was speechless.

"Oh my," she sighed. Pressing her fingers to her lips and tilting her head, she studied his physique, which reminded her of the Greek statuary in the British Museum. A smattering of russet brown hair covered his upper torso, which was toned and defined, the muscles in his arms flexing as he reached for her. She shook her head. "Not yet." Her eyes admired how his strong chest tapered to a trim waist, then ventured further down to where his need for her was evident. Oddly, the sight engendered a visceral reaction in Helena, a responding spark glowing in her core.

"Helena." She heard Hugh groan her name and a quiver ran through her. Helena raised her eyes back to his. Everything stilled as that indefinable hush descended on her again, and for a moment everything was held in thrall. Then Hugh smiled, his heart in his eyes, and the spark burst into flame.

"Play me," she entreated, unconsciously echoing his words following the night at Trentams. Requiring no second bidding, he closed the gap and took her in his arms, kissing her until she questioned whether massed choirs lifting their voices in song, had suddenly blinked into existence around them. Still kissing her, Hugh carefully removed all the pins from her hair letting the shimmering tresses tumble over her shoulders, burying one hand in its luxurious length, while the other roamed over her body. Helena's head fell back and she felt her knees give way, but Hugh caught her, carrying her to the bed and laying her on the crisp white sheets, joining her to continue his voyage of discovery.

A tender hand journeyed down her neck to the swell of her breasts, brushing his fingers over the dusky peaks before palming first one then the other — giving each just enough attention that she began to writhe under him, her body undulating in a bid to get closer — before following his hand with his mouth, tongue circling, teeth nipping gently, wresting low throated moans from Helena. His ceaseless fingers sought out her most sensitive parts until she was sure she would faint from the maelstrom of emotions roiling through her, arching into him, craving his touch, desperate for an as yet unknown relief, but he refused to assuage her, continuing to take her higher and higher.

Meanwhile, and although still not sure what to do, Helena's fingers were weaving their own sorcery; learning, stroking, caressing and swirling over Hugh's heated skin. Cool fingers read the taut planes of his stomach and the curve of his waist, smoothing over his powerful thighs. Reaching down to curl intuitively around the rigid muscle pulsing between them, squeezing and massaging, her occasional hesitation engendering a primal response from Hugh.

His heart was thundering like a horse at full gallop and he knew he wouldn't be able to hold back much longer, his hunger for her becoming all consuming. The same surge of emotions that had nearly brought him to his knees the first time he brushed his lips to hers slammed into him now, like the west wind filling an empty sail.

"Helena, my love" — she looked up at him, grey eyes dark with passion — "Helena I need to take you, and although I will do my best not to hurt you I cannot promise I will succeed." She stared, confusion clouding her gaze. Hugh, in as few words as possible — bearing in mind his control was rapidly slipping from his grasp — explained why. Her eyes widened and involuntarily she glanced between them. Even though Charlotte and Billie had spent an hilarious hour or so trying to teach her about this precise moment, Helena hadn't been paying proper attention, thinking they were being facetious. She groaned inwardly, wishing she had listened.

Hugh, worried she wasn't ready, waited, searching her face.

"Sweetheart, do you want me to stop?" his voice riven with desire, willing her to say no. Her eyes flew back to his as mutely she shook her head. Exhaling a ragged breath, Hugh resumed his caress, stroking and fondling, drawing Helena closer to the edge of the precipice, until she begging for the release only he could give. Not until he was sure she was ready did he claim her as slowly as he was able, letting her body adjust to him gradually.

Helena gasped on a sharp stab of pain, immediately forgotten as the fire that had been burning steadily, blazed into an inferno. Coherent thought had, quite unreasonably, abandoned her, so Helena simply gave herself over to the turbulence raging through her. Without conscious awareness, she hooked her legs around Hugh's drawing him further into her heat as they began to move to a rhythm that seemed as natural as breathing. Quite sure she was becoming molten, Helena contemplated, absently, whether two people could actually fuse together, for she would not have been at all surprised had she merged into Hugh.

Just as she started to drift away on a cloud of euphoria, a whole new raft of sensations bubbled through her, and the most incredible feeling began to simmer, flooding through her until all she knew was desire and colour and light. Crying out Hugh's name, frissons of ecstasy crashed over her like a tidal wave and the world around her erupted, shattering into a million pieces.

She came back to earth, shuddering in the aftermath, to find herself resting in Hugh's arms and he was kissing her tenderly. She whimpered and wriggled closer, the need to be touching every part of him, irresistible.

"I'm sorry I hurt you, love. Are you all right?" he asked, solicitously. Helena kissed his jawline.

"I am the most all right I have ever been" — not altogether intelligibly, drawing a soft laugh from Hugh — "that was quite the most remarkable feeling, utterly stupendous and I trust you will want to do it a *lot*," she added, emphasising the last word.

Hugh smiled, curling a finger around one of her tousled locks, "I am yours to command my love." He intoned gravely, inclining his head.

Helena gurgled with laughter. "Oh good, I command you to do that again immediately."

Hugh chuckled. "You might need to give me a minute, sweetheart," Helena smiled and in the dying candlelight it pierced his heart. Needing to tell her again, he muttered, "My darling, I don't think you realise how much I love you."

"Oh, I think I do," she murmured, sliding her body sinuously over his, making him catch his breath and wrenching a guttural sound from his throat.

"Urrghhh…" She ignored that, kissing him everywhere her lips could reach, intent on driving him as mad as he had driven her. "H-Helena!" he gasped, trying to reach for her but she slithered away, her mouth doing things to him, he had never believed possible. Just when he thought he might actually die from a kiss, she paused and lifting herself up reclaimed his mouth, her lips telling him more than words ever could.

Hugh, miraculously no longer needing a minute, turned her in his embrace and proceeded to make slow and tender yet exquisitely passionate love to his wife several more times that incredible night, until just as dawn broke and almost satiated, they fell asleep in each other's arms.

Epilogue

Four nights later after a pleasant if not rather boisterous evening with their families — who were all still basking in the hospitality provided by Billie and Giles — Hugh and Helena were walking back to the manor house. It was a glorious night, clear skies liberally besprinkled with stars twinkling down on a snow-covered landscape, which glistened as though a reflection of the heavens. Little puffs of white surrounded the couple as they were talking and laughing, hurrying in the frigid air.

Tonight, was the first time they had ventured beyond the confines of their haven, relishing the privacy it offered. Although each already knew much about the other, they enjoyed being able to talk without the usual time constraints, such as the shipyard, or the refuge or others demanding their attention or pretty much anything else. Not being answerable to anyone else was liberating and something they hoped to maintain once they left this idyll for their normal everyday lives.

Reaching the front door, opened for them by the ever-vigilant Matthew, Helena hesitated. Hugh looked down at her vivid face and instinctively knew what she was going to say.

"You want to stargaze?" he asked, smiling as she nodded enthusiastically.

"'Tis the first clear night since our wedding and I would like you to share it with me," she replied, shyly.

"Maybe we should get a blanket first and sit on the terrace in the back garden," he suggested, as Matthew ushered them into the warm hall. Hugh turned to the footman requesting two heavy blankets and two cups of hot chocolate. By now, quite used to the unusual requests of these newlyweds, Matthew grinned and went off to do their bidding and a short time later with one blanket underneath them on the bench acting as a cushion, the second snugly wrapped around them both, they were sipping rich hot chocolate and admiring the legion of stars. Soon they were competing to see who could find the different constellations first, Helena laughing helplessly as she tried to beat Hugh, who won every time.

"You're a sailor, 'tis only to be expected. However, I confess I would be most reluctant to travel with a captain who was unable to distinguish Perseus from Orion." Helena chortled gleefully, as Hugh tried to persuade her that they were the same constellation. "They are quite dissimilar. 'Tis like saying that Canis Major and Ursa Major are the same because they both have 'major' in the title. For a start one is a dog and the other a bear. You must think me a simpleton to believe such silliness," she said, rocking with mirth.

Hugh chuckled and said that it had been worth the try to witness her indignation, which earned him a jab to his arm. Leaning back against the seat, they finished their hot drinks in comfortable silence, Helena resting her head on Hugh's shoulder elated that she could do so whenever she chose without anyone questioning her actions.

"I love that we can do this," she sighed. "To be able to sit together, or hold hands or kiss or even hug — and in public should we feel inclined, is quite the most marvellous feeling. 'Tis a shame we must go back to London and our busy schedules, this has been a boon I have appreciated greatly." Unconsciously she burrowed in until Hugh lifted his arm around her, tucking her against his side.

"I wholeheartedly agree, my love," he murmured into her hair, kissing the raven locks that glimmered in the moonlight. "We have several days left, let us not think on returning until we must. I can think of so many things I'd rather be doing than worrying about city life."

"Hmmm…like what?" Helena's question was drowsy, the warmth of her husband's body, the blanket and the hot chocolate making her sleepy.

"Well, like this for instance," kissing the top of her head, "and this," lifting her chin and kissing her nose, "and most especially this," slanting his lips over hers. The spark ignited, banishing sleep and Helena twisted in Hugh's arms as familiar longing swept through her. Squirming until she was facing him, she wriggled onto his lap, running her fingers through his hair and brought his mouth back to hers. Hugh shifted the blanket so it covered her shoulders, undoing her coat, his hands roaming under layers of frothy material, seeking out her silky skin. Helena shuddered as his inquisitive fingers slid up her leg, reaching all the way to her stomach, before returning to where the fire burned the hottest, his quest relentless.

"Should…staff…dare…risk?" The hypnotic dance inflicted by Hugh's fingers prevented Helena from articulating her concerns about what she guessed they were about to do, then all doubt fled as he found her centre. "Oh God, H-Hugh, please…" she fumbled with the fall of his trousers, "h-help…need…argghhh…." Losing all dexterity not to mention control, Helena struggled to undo the buttons, but finally managed. Uncaring that it was the middle of winter, that they were outside, that the temperature had plummeted to well below zero or that any moment one of their staff might come upon them, Hugh made intoxicatingly fervent love to his wife under an inky sky in the ethereal light of a pearly moon and her glittering guardians.

Much later, after Hugh had taken his wife upstairs to continue their tantalising exploration of each other, they were curled up together in the cosy bedroom. Heart still pounding and breathing a long way from steady, Hugh reached across to the small table next to their bed and withdrew a slim and neatly wrapped package from under a pile of papers, handing it to Helena. She opened it to find a book and in the candlelight, peered at the title — 'Love on a Winter's Tide.' Running her fingers over the gilt words, tracing them with her finger, she gazed at Hugh, stunned.

Hugh smiled, almost shyly, and said. "On the day I proposed, you told me of a book from which your father read to you. The verse you remembered touched my heart, for it seemed to bind my life to yours. Odd really as neither of us could have known our paths would lead us to each other. You believed the book lost and you sounded desolate that this link to your father and a life less complicated was no more. Since then I have been searching for the volume through every avenue available to me and, eventually, with the help of willing friends, I found a copy. I asked an acquaintance to add something special and it was delivered to Whiteoaks today. I know 'tis not the one your father had, but mayhap it will relieve your sorrow and also remind you of the day you shared it with me, which remains one of the happiest of my life."

Tears formed in Helena's eyes, luminous in the soft light. Gripping his hand, she turned to the flyleaf on which he had inscribed in his distinctive hand, *To Helena, light of my life, love of my heart and treasure of my soul, may this always bring you solace. Forever entwined, Hugh.* Underneath two H's had been woven together in the same gilt as the lettering on the cover — presumably the 'something special' to which Hugh referred, although to Helena, his words were special enough.

"H-Hugh" — try as she might, Helena couldn't stop those pesky tears from spilling over — "th-this is the m-most precious g-gift I h-have ever received, well, s-save you." She stumbled over the words, her body quivering as she fought to suppress her sobs. "Oh, no, I haven't anything f-for you." Hugh enclosed her in his arms, cradling her until she started to regain her composure.

"I don't need or want a gift my love, I have you," Hugh murmured kissing her gently, which, of course, set her off again. "Sweetheart, I didn't intend to make you weep," contritely.

Helena made a determined effort and, equanimity restored, shook her head. "These are not sad tears Hugh, these are tears of love and joy and happiness." Hugh raised an extremely sceptical eyebrow and she tried to explain. "'Tis just sometimes a wonderful moment catches the heart unawares and it seems the sentiment is so intense the only release is through tears. Like mothers at the first sight of their new born." Suddenly remembering Charlotte's reaction when baby Noah made his appearance. She bit her lip, "although I don't suppose you have ever witnessed that." She added, colouring prettily.

"No, but should we ever be blessed with children of our own, I imagine that you will not be the only one in tears." Hugh countered, a picture of them with children popping into his mind making his heart swell. Helena smiled her breathtaking smile and as the last candle flickered out, she illustrated to her adoring husband, just how much his gift meant.

A year later - south coast of England

A couple walked along a windswept beach, night had fallen but they didn't seem to notice. The day had been — surprisingly for this time of year — sunny and clear, although cold, and they had spent hours exploring the delights of the Dorset shoreline, astonished at the beauty of the surrounding area as well as the numerous fossils, which could be found right underfoot. They were halfway through a fortnight's holiday and, while seemingly an odd time of the year to do so, their reasons were twofold. Trentams' new schooner the *Lady Helena* and second vessel of its type in the company's fleet — Hugh Drummond refused to consider naming his first schooner after his wife, it being associated with painful memories — was undergoing its final sea trials. This stretch of coastline was perilous to shipping and Hugh had decided to see for himself, how well the schooner handled the treacherous currents. It was also the ideal excuse for Helena to join him, the pair savouring their well-earned rest in Weymouth a most attractive little town.

It had been a hectic year. Returning to London after their wedding, Helena and Hugh were both immediately absorbed into their busy routines. The refurbishment of the two damaged ships had been nearing completion, but on top of this there was the construction of three new ones, the rebuilding of Sanctuary House as well as the excitement of finding and furnishing their own home. Although the Drummond residence was sizeable enough to accommodate the newlyweds, Hugh had no wish to begin married life sharing a home with the rest of his family, a sentiment Helena shared. After several weeks of fruitless searching they had finally come across a beautiful town house situated mid-way between their two families. Although less grand than some, it was elegant. The rooms were nicely proportioned with an airy aspect making the whole house seem much larger than it was, and it came with a small garden and carriage house.

One of Helena's greatest concerns was how she would cope when Hugh had to go to sea. Her anxiety however proved unwarranted, as there had been a fortuitous development. Hugh's brother, who up until now had shown only reluctant interest in Trentams, had undertaken many of Hugh's business obligations in the aftermath of Faversham's attack, and again after Helena and Hugh's marriage. This had been a blessing in disguise for, unexpectedly, Nicholas realised he was fascinated by all things shipping and had, during Hugh's absence, begged Mr Holland to help him understand the finer points of the company.

Thus, when Hugh returned to the yard after his honeymoon, Nicholas asked to be allowed to oversee the sea trials for all new vessels, and accompany those voyages normally requiring Hugh's supervision. This freed up Hugh to concentrate on managing the business, for although his staff was eminently competent, it fell to him to ensure Trentams' continued success. It was an arrangement that pleased everyone, especially Helena and, truth be told, Hugh did not relish the thought of being away from his wife unless there was no alternative.

Three weeks previously, Hugh arrived home after a long day. Greeting Helena with his customary and satisfyingly passionate embrace, Hugh asked how she fared as, recently, she had been laid low with a number of inexplicable and debilitating headaches. Helena informed him, in her most casual tones, that following a visit from Dr Irving, it seemed she was expecting their first child. So nonchalantly did she impart this life-altering news that he was halfway up the stairs to change for dinner before he grasped the import of her words. Racing back into the parlour he found Helena sitting on the window ledge, a mischievous grin curving her kissable lips. After asking her to confirm he had indeed heard what he thought he heard, Hugh swung Helena into his arms and proceeded to demonstrate, in a deliriously gratifying manner, just how elated he was.

This short break therefore was partly to ensure Helena, who found herself inordinately tired of late — although everyone assured her this was normal — reaped the benefits of two weeks with no responsibilities, lots of fresh air and plenty of rest.

After yet another delicious meal at their hotel, Helena asked whether Hugh fancied a stroll along the beach. She found it relaxing to take an evening constitutional, and it was an excellent excuse to indulge in one of her favourite pastimes — stargazing. They were muffled into heavy winter cloaks and Hugh had his arm around his wife, holding her close. Even though it was dark, there was enough light from the moon to guide their way and they didn't intend to go far. Stopping occasionally to stare out over the vast expanse of water and watch the waves roll in, listening to the rhythmic swoosh as they crashed onto the shingle.

All was peaceful.

Across a sky as black as onyx, a crescent moon was following its ceaseless odyssey, surrounded by a myriad of stars lighting the way. Unable to help herself, Helena angled her head to gaze up at the celestial illuminations. Hugh steadied her so she didn't topple over backwards, and she leaned against him, relishing the warmth of his body. After several moments, she turned in his arms and stretching up on her toes, brushed her lips to his, murmuring softly,

"'Tis a waning moon."

Hugh glanced down, smiling at the reference, and bent to kiss her, the couple quickly becoming immersed in each other. The glowing spark, as ever, starting to kindle.

"Mayhap we should return to our lodgings," Hugh growled hoarsely, "before I lose my senses and take you here on this isolated beach."

Helena giggled at the image his words invoked but agreed, in a voice slightly higher than normal, that his suggestion had merit; grabbing his hand and setting a fine pace back towards the small town.

"Helena," laughter laced Hugh's tones as he pulled her back to him, slowing her steps, "Helena, we do not need to rush, we have all night and all day tomorrow and then the next day, should we choose."

Helena inhaled sharply, as she read his expression which could only be described as sizzling — igniting deep within, her own passion.

"Today, tomorrow, the rest of our lives, such love, magical, mysterious and indefinable," she murmured, so quietly her words were almost lost on the breeze. Hugh drew her against him for another heartfelt kiss, then they turned and strolled back along the water's edge, silhouetted under a waning moon, two shadows hand in hand, two souls forever entwined — love on a winter's tide.

Thank you for purchasing this book, I do hope you enjoyed it. If you have a moment to write a quick review on Amazon I would be most grateful.

The synopses for my other books follow.

I hope we meet again soon,

Rosie

You can find me on,

Facebook:
https://www.facebook.com/RosieChapelTheAuthor/
Twitter: @RosieChapel2015
Website: www.rosiechapel.com
Goodreads:
https://www.goodreads.com/author/show/14759605.Rosie_Chapel

Once Upon An Earl
A Regency Romance
Linen and Lace - Book One

When Fate saw fit to intervene in the life of Giles Trevallier, the very respectable Earl of Winchester, by dropping a female — soaked to the skin and with no memory of who she is or how she came to be there — literally at his feet, no one could have predicted the outcome.

The woman eventually recalls that her name is Willow and as Giles begins discreet enquiries, he is shocked to discover that she is rumoured to be responsible for a fire that destroyed her family home, killing her father.

While trying to unravel the mystery surrounding her, Giles realises that he is falling hopelessly in love with Willow, who unbeknownst to him is fighting similar emotions; and as with anything involving the heart, a thoughtless word or gesture has a tendency to thwart even Fate's best-laid plans.

Faced with misunderstandings, whispers of scandal, secret documents and foreign agents, their chance at a happy ever after seems elusive, but fairy tales often happen when least expected, and love — however inconvenient — usually finds a way to conquer all.

To Unlock Her Heart

A Regency Romance
Linen and Lace - Book Two

After being caught in a scandal with a duke, Grace Aldeburgh has
been shunned by everyone ~ family, friends and Society. To shield
herself from the trauma she was subjected to, Grace buried her heart
away, so deeply that she wasn't sure it could ever be found.

Two years later, with little hope of ever being free of the stigma,
relief seems at hand in the guise of a bequest from her Great Aunt.
Grace has inherited a house in a tiny village, far from prying eyes and
malicious gossips. Once there, she meets Theo Elliott, the village
doctor and what begins as a tentative friendship, blossoms into
something more enduring. Fearing further censure, Grace knows she
must tell Theo her secret, but the doctor is no fair-weather suitor and
has already resolved to be the man to unlock her heart.

Just as happiness appears to be within her grasp, her erstwhile
tormentor once again stalks Grace. After a failed kidnap attempt, the
duke's quest culminates in an acrimonious confrontation with Grace
and suddenly the reason for his venal pursuit of her becomes
agonisingly clear.

A Love Unquenchable
A Regency Romance
Linen and Lace - Book Four

Jessica Drummond, a bright and cheerful young woman, rarely gives romance, let alone love, a thought. Long hours working in her brother's shipping office affords little chance of her ever meeting an eligible bachelor.

Duncan Barrington, veteran of the Napoleonic Wars, believes himself wounded in both body and soul. He has no intention of inflicting his demons on anyone, certainly not a beautiful and, in his opinion, irresponsible city lady.

One cold and snowy morning, the plight of a bedraggled puppy throws Jessica and Duncan together and, as a spark of something indefinable yet wholly unquenchable begins to burn, it is unclear who rescued whom.

A Hidden Rose

A Regency Romance
Linen and Lace - Book Five

After witnessing his mother's grief at the loss of his father, Nick Drummond resolved never to cause someone he loved such distress. Even the happiness of his siblings would not sway him – until he met Rose.

Rose Archer was almost content assisting her doctor father in a tiny fishing village in the north of Yorkshire. To experience the world beyond, a tantalising dream – until she met Nick.

Unexpectedly, the impossible becomes possible, and the renounced – desired above all things, but the shipwreck that brought them together, may yet tear them apart. Will Nick learn to trust his heart, or will his love for Rose remain forever hidden?

His Fiery Hoyden
A Regency Novella

Please inform your master, Sasha is perfectly happy here with me and there is more chance of hell freezing over, than of my brother dancing attendance on his Grace."

A plea for help ignored. A child left to bring up her baby brother. Livvy has no respect for the nobility; they let her down when she most needed them. Why should she accede to their demands now?

Philip, Lord Harrington, is stunned to discover the young heir to the dukedom lives a stone's throw away in a ramshackle cottage, and resolves to restore the child to his birthright.

They meet in a clash of wills, but just when it seems Livvy might surrender, the victory Philip desires, may not taste all that sweet.

The Pomegranate Tree
Hannah's Heirloom - Book One

Hoping to trace the origins of an ancient ruby clasp, a gift from her long dead grandmother, Hannah Wilson travels to the fortress of Masada with her best friend, Max. Strange dreams concerning a rebel ambush begin to haunt Hannah and following a tragic accident, she slips into the world of Ancient Masada.

A woman out of time, Hannah must rely on her instincts and her knowledge of what will befall this citadel to survive. Will she escape, or is she doomed to die along with hundreds of others as Masada falls – and what does any of this have to do with an ancient ruby clasp?

Echoes of Stone and Fire
Hannah's Heirloom - Book Two

Pompeii - a vibrant city lost in time following the AD79 eruption of Vesuvius. Now rediscovered, archaeologists yearn for an opportunity to uncover the town's past. Some things however, are best left alone - revealing the secrets hidden beneath the stones could prove perilous. Hannah and Max are brought to Pompeii by a surprise invitation to join an excavation team who are trying to uncover the city's long history.

After entering an excavated house that bears a Hebrew inscription, Hannah's two worlds collide and she falls back through time to ancient Pompeii. A place where her ancestor is a physician to gladiators engaged in mortal combat, where riotous mobs run amok and where a ghost from the past returns to haunt her.

Will Hannah and her loved ones manage to escape the devastation she knows is coming, before the town is engulfed in volcanic ash? Will she ever find her way back to Max the love of her life, waiting not so patiently millennia away? Or will echoes be all that remain?

Embers of Destiny
Hannah's Heirloom - Book Three

AD80 - Hannah and Maxentius must embark on a new journey to Northern Britannia. This harsh frontier is far from the comforts of Rome and danger lurks where least expected; a garrison of soldiers, some unhappy with their isolated posting; local tribes, outwardly accepting of their Roman occupier, but who may still resent the seizure of their lands.

Millennia away, Hannah Vallier finds a familiar item while working in a museum near Hadrian's Wall. It is the pomegranate; carved by Maxentius on Masada. Before Hannah can discuss it with Max, disaster strikes! Believing her husband has been killed, Hannah retreats into the past, her soul melding with that of her ancestor, but with little idea of what they could face. Is the risk from the conquered tribes, or much closer to home?

As rebellion threatens to shatter a fragile peace, Hannah's heart whispers that just maybe Max isn't dead and that he is calling her home. Can she trust her heart or will she remain caught out of time, her destiny floating away like embers on a breeze?

Etched in Starlight
Hannah's Heirloom - Prequel

Maxentius - a Roman soldier fresh from the battlefields of
Armenia, arrives to take command of the military outpost of Masada,
Herod's isolated citadel in the Judaean desert. A seemingly mundane
posting after years of warfare, Maxentius finds it more challenging to
maintain a focused garrison than to face the wrath of the Parthians
across a disputed frontier.

Hannah - a young Hebrew physician spends her days dealing with
injuries from street brawls, deprivation, disease and loss. As her
beloved Jerusalem plunges into chaos; her brother — who belongs to
a band of rebels determined to drive out their Roman occupiers —
tells her of their plans to storm a desert fortress and steal the weapons
stored there, persuading his reluctant sister to go with him.

Masada - following the ambush, Hannah finds and treats three
badly wounded Roman soldiers. In the aftermath and against
impossible odds, Hannah and Maxentius realise that they are more
than healer and captive, their fate already etched in starlight.

Prelude to Fate

For Lucia, staring into the jaws of an horrific death, escape seems impossible.

Rufius Atellus, a veteran Roman soldier, is appalled when he recognises one of the victims about to be executed. Surely this is a ghastly mistake?

A ferocious she-wolf, anticipating a tasty meal, suddenly finds herself under a human's control.

In an unexpected twist, and as danger threatens, the lives of all three become inextricably entwined. Was it chance brought them together in that theatre of bloodshed, or simply a prelude to fate?

Of Ruins and Romance

While escorting a group of tourists around the ancient Roman port of Ostia, Kassandra Winters bumps into someone she first met in less than auspicious circumstances two years previously. The encounter leads to a job offer - to be the assistant guide for a three-week tour of ancient sites in and around Rome. Unable to resist such an opportunity, Kassie agrees.

Kassie has intrigued Gabriel St Germain since he accidentally knocked her flying outside her university professor's office. Her face haunts his dreams, yet he never expected to see her again. So, he is surprised when she appears, as though destined to do so, in the middle of a ruin, and he concocts a plan to win her heart.

Gabriel's old-fashioned courtship touches something deep inside Kassie and, although struggling to believe someone as handsome as Gabriel could possibly be interested in her, she soon realises she has fallen irrevocably in love with him. However, just as Kassie shares everything of herself with Gabriel, her world comes crashing down. Can their romance survive or will it fall in ruins, like the relics of antiquity that brought them together.

All At Once It's You

When Alex arrives in the small village of Rosedale Abbey, to take up a position as a research assistant for a renowned archaeologist, the last thing she is looking for, or expects to find, is love.

Jake was perfectly happy with the status quo. When it came to relationships, he didn't do committed or long term. He called the shots, and if his current flame didn't like it, she knew what to do. A philosophy, which served him well - until he met Alex.

Romance blooms, but even as the untamed wilderness of the North Yorkshire moors weaves its spell, a long buried secret might yet jeopardise their happily ever after.